SHATTERED Dreams

CHRISTINA SOL

Shattered Dreams

By: Christina Sol

Published by: Sol Media LLC

Cover Design: LJ Anderson, Mayhem Cover Creations

Proofreader: Judy's Proofreading

Paperback ISBN: 979-8-9898861-1-1

❀ Created with Vellum

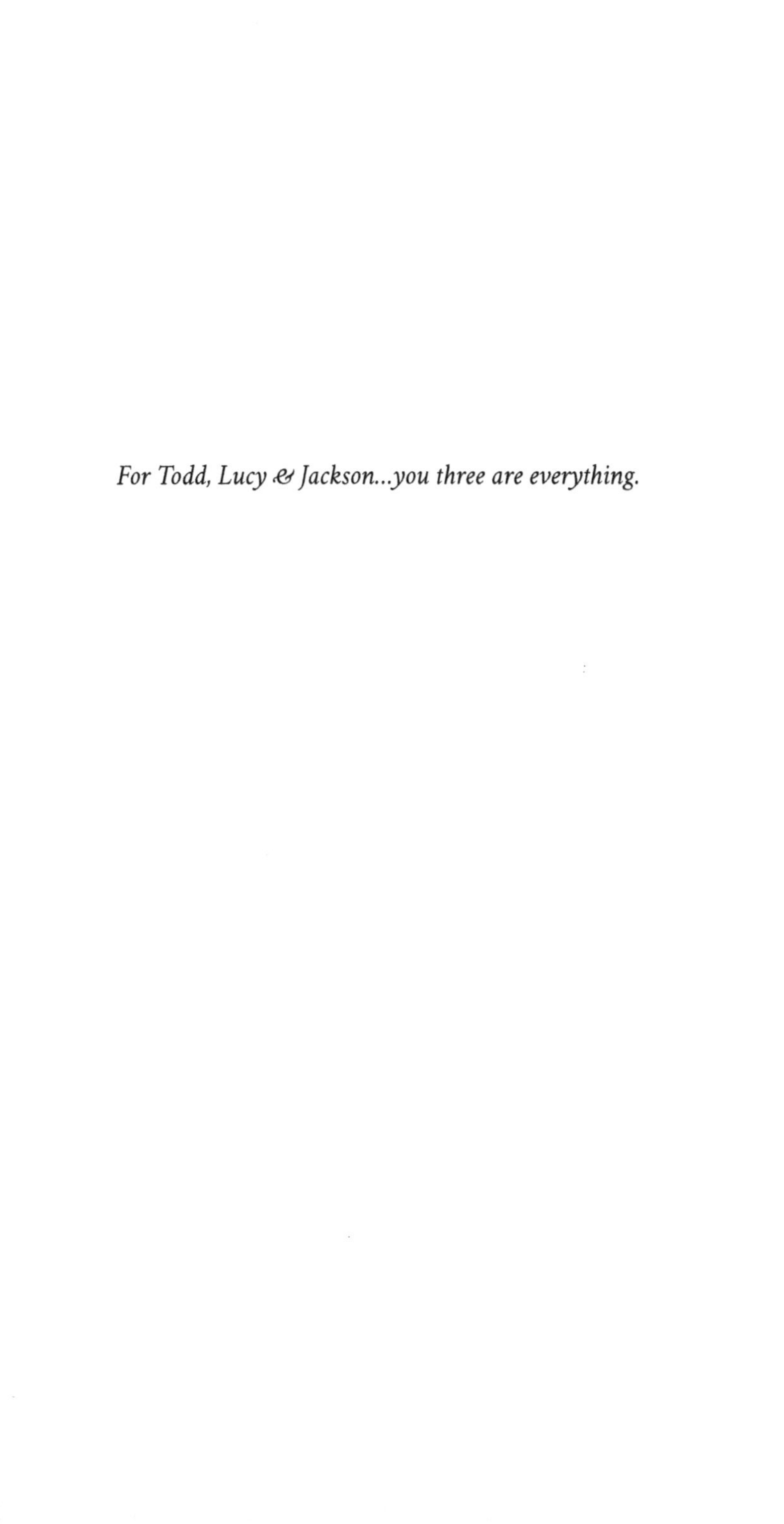

For Todd, Lucy & Jackson...you three are everything.

CHAPTER ONE

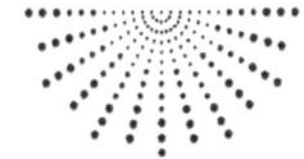

Poppy Walker let out her breath in a whoosh. She'd expected to feel relief, peace, closure . . . something, *anything* along those lines. Instead, the paper in her hand shook, and she swallowed past the lump in her throat. The words on the letter blurred, and she blinked back tears.

She was officially divorced.

There was no relief. No peace. No closure. Only immense sadness and a weariness that took her breath away, that had her wanting to wave the proverbial white flag. She'd been taken for a fool. And for so long. Too long. But that had been her own fault.

The last year had been the longest of her life. And considering that she'd gotten unexpectedly pregnant with twins when she was only sixteen—and subsequently kicked out of her childhood home—that said a lot.

The bells on the front door chimed. She stuffed the letter from her lawyer back into its envelope, tucked it into the cabinet beneath the counter, and shoved the weariness down. She didn't have time for it.

Pasting a smile on her face, she called out to the group of

middle-aged tourists—three women and two men—who'd entered her shop. "Welcome to Rainy Day Boutique. If there's anything I can help you with, just let me know." She bit down a chuckle at the resigned looks on the men's faces. Gesturing to the back of the store, she said, "We also have a seating area with self-serve coffee and tea."

They perked up.

"You're a lifesaver," one man said with a grateful smile.

The other laughed and tipped his baseball hat to her. "Who'd have thought such a little town would have so many stores?"

"Well," Poppy said in a conspiratorial whisper, "if you end up at Hudson Island Antiques, make sure you go to the very back right corner. Mr. Wayland has a couple recliners, a couch, and a sixty-inch flat-screen hiding back there."

The men each barked out a laugh.

"Will do, miss. Will do."

Poppy watched as they made their way to her seating area, and she tried to imagine what visitors saw when they entered her store.

Aside from her two sons, Rainy Day Boutique was her pride and joy. It rivaled any big-city shop, featuring an eclectic selection that catered to tourists and local residents alike: high-end Hudson Island souvenirs and logo wear; jewelry, pottery, home décor, and leatherwork from local artists; resort-style clothing and—as her sons called it— fancy, frou-frou bath stuff; and a small section for children's clothes, linens, and toys.

A woman placed numerous items on the counter, pulling Poppy from her musings. "I hope you know, this place is lovely."

Poppy smiled, and happiness bloomed in her chest. Hearing that never got old. Ever. "Oh, thank you. That's kind of you to say. I'm Poppy, the owner." She extended her hand to the woman, who looked like an M.M.LaFleur model.

"I'm Yvette." The woman shook her hand and nodded at the other two women in her group. "We have friends who were here last weekend and just raved about your store. They said that you had the most lovely items. And wouldn't you know it?" Smiling brightly, she waved at what she'd placed on the counter. "They were right. Now, can I leave these here while I pick up a few more things?"

"Of course," Poppy said with a grin. The businesswoman in her was thrilled for what looked to be an amazing sale, but knowing the group was a referral made her extra happy. Word of mouth was absolute gold, and with the way things had been going these last few months, she needed the reassurance that she could keep her boutique operating.

Twenty minutes later, with more customers coming and going, she rang up the ladies and gave them her favorite dining recommendations within Hudson Island's three-block downtown: Ray's Diner for stick-to-your-bones meals with portions large enough to share, Monty's Tavern for great cocktails and gastropub fare, and Comfort Food for delicious treats and coffee.

Poppy was a regular at both Ray's and Monty's. While she enjoyed the delicacies and ambiance at Comfort Food, she didn't venture in often. She was friendly with the café's owner, Roxie Jameson, but after everything that had happened over the last few months, it was . . . awkward for her to be around the other woman. But that was on Poppy. Completely. Which made her feel a bit guilty. So, she always went out of her way to promote and recommend Comfort Food, which had just celebrated its grand reopening the week prior after a devastating fire.

She stole a glance at the cabinet beneath the counter, thinking of the letter hidden away there, and stifled a wince.

As the group made their way out of her store, one of the men shot Poppy a wink and called out, "You know, after we get food, we should check out that Hudson Island Antiques place. I hear it's got stuff you ladies might like."

Poppy chuckled as she rounded the counter to reorganize a display of Hudson Island–embossed wineglasses. The door chimed again, and her gaze went to the front of her shop.

She froze.

Eli, her newly minted ex-husband, stormed toward her, waving a stack of papers in his hand. He stopped an arm's length away. "What the hell is this, Poppy?"

She blinked. Twice. Then ground her molars together. He had to be joking. "It's your official notice to vacate."

"What the fuck, Poppy?" His face turned an unnatural shade of red.

She'd seen him act like this countless times. Before, she'd worried he'd give himself a heart attack. Now? She mentally shrugged. *Meh.*

He took a menacing step closer and shoved the papers in her face. "What. The. Fuck?"

The front door bells chimed as she swatted Eli's hand away. She stepped backward and scanned the shop. Her heart stopped when her gaze locked on a pair of dark-brown eyes that were narrowed and angry. Taking in the man they belonged to, she sighed with part relief, part embarrassment.

Great. Cade de la Rosa. Local business owner and resident celebrity athlete. Not only was the man the epitome of tall, dark, and handsome, but by all accounts, he was a genuinely good guy, too.

On one hand, Poppy was grateful for his presence. She knew Eli would never get too aggressive with a witness nearby, let alone that witness being Cade, an internationally renowned former mixed martial arts champion. On the other hand, it was *Cade de la Rosa*. Having him observe this situation with her ex was beyond mortifying.

Bringing her attention back to Eli, she strove for calm. Unfortunately, her racing heart didn't get the memo. "You agreed to this. That"—she pointed at the papers clutched in his hand—"is just a formality."

"That's a load of crap. I *never* agreed to move out of my office!"

Her lips pursed, and she took in a breath. *Calm, dammit. Stay calm.* "When you signed the divorce papers, that was part of the terms you agreed to."

"You're a fucking liar, Poppy," he hissed. "You can't kick me out of my own goddamn building!"

Oh. My. God. Was he always this delusional?

"Eli." Anger and a whole lot of frustration began to chip away at her calm. The bells chimed again, but she didn't dare take her attention away from her ex. "You and I both know— as do our lawyers—that this building is in *my* name. It was in *my* name before we got married. Your name was never added. Therefore, you weren't entitled to any of it in the divorce. And *you* signed the papers agreeing to move your business out."

"Bullshit! Like always, you don't know what the hell you're talking—"

"Is there a problem here?" a low voice interrupted.

Poppy prayed that voice didn't belong to whom she suspected it did. Peeking over her shoulder, she cringed. Fantastic. Sheriff Quinn O'Conner. Behind him stood Cade, arms crossed over his massive chest, a scowl painted on his usually happy face. Just fantastic.

"I'll ask again," Quinn said, glancing between her and Eli. "Is there a problem?"

"Last I checked, Sheriff," Eli said with a sneer, "this is private property and none of your business."

The muscle in Quinn's jaw pulsed, and Poppy braced herself. Holy crap, had Eli always been this big of an ass?

You know the answer to that.

"Well, Eli," Quinn replied, "when I get a call about a disturbance, about someone harassing a local business-woman, then private property or not, it becomes my business."

She stole a glance at Cade. Considering he was the only other person in her shop, it didn't take a rocket scientist to figure out who had called the sheriff. And seeing as there was now a crowd—well, five people made up a crowd on Hudson Island—peering through her front window, it was time to end this ridiculousness.

"Eli was just leaving," Poppy said, making sure to put extra steel in her voice. Steel that she didn't feel. But with the sheriff and Cade within arm's distance, she managed to straighten her spine and square her shoulders. He couldn't hurt her here. "Eli, if you have an issue with the divorce terms that you not only agreed to, but that have been final-ized by the courts—like moving out of *my* building—then you can take that up with your lawyer."

Eli's eyes narrowed and that unnatural shade of red returned. But fuck him.

She looked at Quinn. "Could you please escort him out, Sheriff?"

"Of course, Poppy." Quinn nodded at her, and his eyes softened. "If you need anything, you call us, okay?"

"Thanks, Quinn," she said as her grumbling ex-husband stalked outside.

Only when the front door closed behind them, and when the group gathered around her front window waved to her and continued down the street, did she let out a breath. She was shocked the ass hadn't knocked anything over on his way out. He was a petty jerk like that.

"I'm sorry if I overstepped by calling Quinn."

The deep baritone had her jumping. With a hand over her heart, she turned. How had she forgotten Cade was still here? No clue.

"No, it's fine. I appreciate the help." A slight tremor shook her hands. She clenched her fists and hid them in the pockets of her dress. "Thank you."

"You're welcome. If I'm being honest, though, it was self-preservation that made me call Quinn." He chuckled, but there was zero humor in his eyes. When she frowned in confusion, he shrugged. "Men who bully women are scum. The way he was talking to you? Hovering over you and trying to intimidate you? I didn't trust myself to not deck the guy."

She tilted her head. "How's that self-preservation?"

He tucked his hands into his jeans pockets and rocked back on his heels. "I have extensive martial arts training. I'm not allowed to punch people."

"Why not?" She wasn't going to lie. The idea of Cade punching Eli was oddly satisfying. She wasn't a violent person, so that said a lot.

"It's that whole assault-with-a-deadly-weapon thing." He held his fists up, then tucked them back into his pockets, flashing her a lopsided grin. "Makes it a little problematic for me."

"Oh yeah. Wow. Okay. I can see how that would be an issue." She nodded and couldn't help but return his grin. "That was a smart move on your part, too. Because Eli? He'd totally press charges. Probably try to sue you and get a piece of your gym or something. I'm sure it's not a shocker that he's a vulture like that."

The front door chimed and a small group of customers entered. She called out a welcome, then turned back to Cade. For a split second, she could only stare. As business owners on Hudson Island, they knew each other. While they also had a number of friends in common, this was probably the longest conversation they'd ever had. She took a weekly cardio kickboxing class at his gym that he occasionally led, but it wasn't like they had time for personal conversations or anything. The class was tough, and frankly, it took all her concentration and effort to not fall over and die. But talking to him was nice. Cade seemed really . . . nice.

Oh good freaking god. Nice? Really?

She cleared her throat. "Thank you again for the save, Cade."

"You're welcome, Poppy." Glancing around the shop, he shifted on his feet. The man was adorable. That is, if a six-one guy who was basically muscles on top of muscles could be considered adorable.

"Is there something I can help you find?" she asked.

"Yeah, actually. I'm looking for a gift. You know my brother and his wife, right?"

She nodded, though she didn't know Dante and Rebecca well.

"They're having another baby soon—"

"Congratulations, Uncle," she interrupted with a clap of her hands and a smile. Babies were the best.

"Thanks," he said, and Poppy swore his eyes were twinkling. "I'm excited for them. So yeah, Rebecca is having a, uh, sprinkle." With a furrowed brow, he opened his mouth, then shut it. Then opened it again. "I have no idea what that means, but I mentioned it to Roxie, who's apparently catering the deal, and she sent me here." He held his hands out and grimaced. "So . . . I take it this sprinkle thing isn't actually cupcake related?"

Poppy laughed. Yup, adorable. "Follow me, Mr. De la Rosa."

CHAPTER TWO

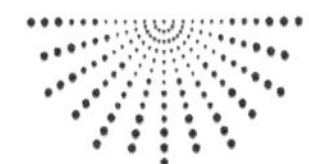

With the decorative bag from Rainy Day Boutique clutched in his hand, Cade pushed open the front door of Ray's Diner. He waved to the owners, Ray and Martha, who stood behind the counter, then scanned the customers who were already seated. Spotting his friend in a booth, he made his way to the far side of the restaurant.

"What's up, man?" he said, sliding onto the opposite bench.

Matt Alvarez gave him a chin lift, then nodded at the bag Cade set beside him. "Didn't think high-end resort wear was your style."

"Funny," Cade said, reaching for a menu. "Dante and Rebecca are expecting their second, so they're having a party." He glanced up. "Did you know that they call baby showers 'sprinkles' for the second kid?"

"Why?" His buddy's face scrunched in bewilderment, reflecting exactly how Cade felt.

"Poppy explained it, but . . ." He shrugged. "I wasn't invited to the first baby shower—it was a women-only thing

—so I'm not really sure why I'm invited to this one. But apparently I have to bring a present."

"At least the food at those things is usually good, so that's a plus."

"True." Cade studied the menu, though he wasn't sure why he bothered. There were only three things he ever ordered at Ray's: fried chicken and mashed potatoes, a bacon double cheeseburger, or biscuits and gravy. He was sure all the other stuff was good, but why mess with perfection? "You know Poppy, right? Rainy Day Boutique?"

Matt nodded. "We've met in passing. She's Four's cousin, right?"

"Yeah." He pursed his lips. "You know, I don't think they're actually blood related, but yeah. They're basically cousins. Anyway, have you met her husband? Wait, I take that back. They got divorced recently. So her ex. Eli. Have you met him?"

Matt's brow crinkled in thought. "Real estate guy? Douchebag blowhard?"

He smirked. "That's the one. When I went to her shop, he was shoving papers in her face. Literally. In her fucking face. And then bitched at her about their divorce."

"I've heard the fucker's slime," Matt growled. "You should give him a free pass to the gym and then have all the guys wail on his sorry ass."

Cade chuckled. He and his brother were the owners of De La Rosa Gym, so he certainly had the power to do so. "Now that, my friend, is not a bad idea. Not a bad idea at all."

A young woman wearing a bubblegum-pink 1950s diner uniform approached their table. Her long nearly black hair had streaks of pink, teal, and purple, and it was pulled back in a claw-looking thing. She placed two glasses of water on their table.

"Hey there," she greeted with a pleasant smile. "How are you guys today?"

"Good," Cade said as Matt grunted his reply. He glanced at his friend and saw Matt staring down at the menu like it was his job. "How have you been, Scarlet?"

"All is well, thank you."

"How's Daisy?"

The young woman's smile grew, and her eyes softened at the mention of her daughter. "She's good. Growing like a little weed."

"Dante mentioned that Daisy is all that little Rocco can talk about these days." His sister-in-law, Rebecca, ran a small home-based day care. Of the five children she cared for, Daisy was the oldest at four. According to his two-year-old nephew, Rocco, Daisy had hung the moon. And the stars. And everything in between.

"That's so sweet." Scarlet laughed. "It's funny because Daisy's so stinking shy with everyone. Other kids, adults—it doesn't matter. She barely makes eye contact with anyone. But Rocco?" A look of wonder crossed her pixie-like face, and she shook her head. "They're like soul siblings, I tell ya. It's the cutest thing."

Cade started to agree, but then Matt coughed. Loudly.

"Sorry," Matt mumbled, taking a sip of water.

"Are you okay?" Scarlet asked, turning her attention to Matt.

He nodded without looking up from his menu, and his naturally tan face flushed.

Cade's eyebrows rose in surprise. He'd never seen the man turn red. The sight was almost alarming.

A few awkward seconds ticked by before Scarlet cleared her throat. "Well, if you're ready, what can I get you guys?"

"I'll have a bacon double cheeseburger with cheddar," Cade said. "Side salad with balsamic instead of fries."

As Matt grumbled out his order, Cade caught Scarlet's perplexed gaze and shrugged, mouthing, *I don't know.* She returned the shrug and gave him a wink before leaving.

Silence descended on their table. Cade used the quiet moment to take in the man seated across from him.

Matt had moved to Hudson Island to recover from a gunshot wound just over a year ago. Or maybe to hide out, given his personal life had imploded around the same time. He was a detective with the Seattle Police Department, but he'd been out on medical leave since the shooting, despite having been cleared to return after six months.

Matt hadn't confided his reasons for extending his time away from the force, and Cade hadn't pushed. All he knew was that his buddy, who'd once been laid-back and happy, was now a fucking growly-ass beast. Most people tended to tiptoe around the guy—Matt was, after all, six-four and looked like The Rock's younger brother—but not Cade. They'd been friends forever.

"So, Alvarez, care to explain what the fuck that was?"

Matt's gaze shot up to meet his. "What?"

He rolled his eyes. "What do you mean 'what'?"

"I don't know what the fuck you're talking about."

"Oh, *now* you're okay speaking full sentences?"

"Whatever, man." Matt sipped his water. "I still don't know what you're talking about."

Cade leaned back in the booth and studied his friend. Matt tended to be quiet. A man of few words. But the way he'd just treated Scarlet? *That* had been borderline rude. Cade knew his friend was struggling, but fuck.

"Bro," he said, dropping his voice low. "You can growl and grumble at the dudes in the gym. That's fine. In fact, they expect that shit from you. But you can't be an asshole to Scarlet. She's, like, the nicest fucking person."

"I wasn't."

Cade shot him a glare.

Matt glared back. "Fine. I didn't mean to be. I'll apologize when she brings out the food. Satisfied?"

Concerned, more like it. But he knew Matt kept things close to the vest. "You doing okay, man?"

"Yes, Mom, I'm fine." Matt scrubbed his hands over his face and sighed. "My captain called this morning."

Cade's eyes widened. "How much longer do you have on your leave?"

"A month."

He waited for more.

Nothing.

Holy shit, he loved the guy like a brother, but it was like pulling teeth with him. "So, when are you heading back?"

"I don't know yet." A shadow crossed Matt's face. "I'm still sorting through some . . . bureaucratic bullshit and all that."

The concern in Cade's gut grew. "Well, if there's anything I can help with, you let me know. Okay, man?"

Matt's chin lifted. "Thanks. I appreciate—"

His friend's words came to an abrupt halt as Scarlet arrived with a tray full of food.

"Hey, guys," she said, placing their plates on the table. "Martha put a rush on your order. She said that she didn't— and I quote—'want you boys to starve.'"

The scent of bacon filled Cade's nose and made his mouth water. "Thanks, Scar."

"Hey, uh, Scarlet, um . . ." Matt stammered.

Cade's jaw dropped open. Because Matt Alvarez did *not* stammer. Ever. But having to apologize to Scarlet? Apparently, that was enough to turn the man into a chastised child who'd been called into the principal's office. The twelve-year-old in Cade desperately wanted to laugh. Instead, he shut his trap and took a giant bite of his burger. He was a damn good friend like that.

"I, uh," Matt continued, "I'm sorry I was rude to you earlier. I didn't mean to be. It's just a . . . bad day, you know? I apologize."

Scarlet blinked a couple of times before a blush stole across her cheeks. "Oh, you're fine, Matt. No worries at all." She cleared her throat and looked between them. "Let me know if there's anything else I can get you guys."

They waited to resume their conversation until she'd walked away.

"Happy?" Matt asked, taking a bite of fried chicken.

"Hey, someone's gotta look out for you, dude." Cade wiped his mouth with his napkin. "Speaking of, I was at Comfort Food earlier this morning and overheard some juicy info from the gossip train. Be forewarned, brother. You and Four are in the matchmaking mamas' crosshairs."

"The fuck?"

He laughed at the look of pure horror on Matt's face. "Yup. Something about the cure to both your growliness being a lady . . . or man. They were very clear that the genders of your soulmates are up to you guys." He shrugged. "When I left, they had a list of women and men they thought might be good matches for you and Four."

"Oh Jesus," Matt groaned.

"Look at it this way, the gossip train ladies definitely consider you a local now. You should be honored."

Matt shook his head. "Why the hell aren't they making a list for you? You're sure as fuck single and basically a local son."

That he was. On both counts.

"I'm not growly enough, and I—unlike you—am nice. Besides, most of them are in my cardio kickboxing class. I'm sure the last thing they want to do is piss off their instructor." Matt shot him a get-real look, and he laughed. "I'm serious. Those ladies know I'm not a pushover. They can get away with a lot of shit with the other teachers, but not when I'm in charge. If they gossip too much in class, I make them do wall sits."

Matt's eyes widened. "Are you serious? You make women in their *sixties* do wall sits as punishment?"

"They're there to work out." Cade shrugged and took another bite of his burger. "They can gossip later. But if they insist on gossiping during class time, then they can gossip while doing wall sits."

"Holy fuck, dude. And you call *me* rude?"

"It's not rude, brother. It's discipline. It keeps the class focused, and the side benefit is they aren't making fucking lists of possible significant others for me."

"Shit. You got me on that one." Matt chomped on a fry.

They ate in companionable silence for a few minutes.

"Holy shit," Matt said, pushing away his nearly empty plate. "Congrats, by the way, on the big win."

Cade smiled and pride surged through him.

He and Dante ran De La Rosa Gym, and they had two locations—their original gym in Seattle and their newer facility on Hudson Island. They also had another business partnership that focused specifically on law enforcement and private security training.

Dante spent the majority of his time at their Seattle gym, which focused more on classes, from entry level to elite. Cade's baby was the Hudson Island gym. While they did offer a number of public classes, their main focus was on fighter coaching and training. Individual fight camps, specialized retreats, all that good stuff. Their twenty-five-thousand-square-foot training facility was top tier and one of the most sought-after in the world. He was the gym's head MMA coach and, again, one of the best in the world. It wasn't bragging; it was just a simple fact.

The weekend before, one of his top fighters, Jason

Rokovich, had won the UFC light heavyweight title. It had been a hard-fought, five-round battle. Cade had led Jason through a twelve-week training camp for the fight, so he'd been confident that the young man was prepared for his first title shot.

The heart-bursting elation he'd felt watching Jason put it all out there and finish victorious had been amazing. It was one of the reasons he loved coaching so much. He'd experienced that kind of elation as a fighter but experiencing it as a coach was a different thing entirely. There was a little extra oomph to the joy. He imagined it was akin to how parents felt watching their kids succeed.

"Thanks, man. It was a fantastic fight. Jason was phenomenal. Vegas is always electric on fight night, but that was something else entirely—"

"Cade de la Rosa?"

Cade leaned back and glanced at the stranger now standing beside their table. Wearing an untucked blue polo shirt and jeans, the man looked to be in his early thirties. Slight beer belly, thinning brown hair, and no muscle definition in his arms. Nondescript to a T. "Yes. Can I help you?"

"These are for you. Have a good day." The man placed papers on the table, then walked away.

Worry knotted Cade's stomach as he picked up the papers. Two pages stapled together. He quickly scanned the top page. It was a court document listing him as the defendant. The name of the plaintiff was familiar, but for the life of him, he couldn't picture their face. He frowned, trying to remember.

And then his brain caught up to what was happening. His breath left in a soundless whoosh.

"Holy fuck. I'm being sued."

CHAPTER THREE

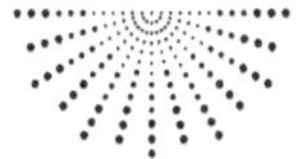

"Have a good night, Serena," Poppy called out as her employee waved goodbye. "See you tomorrow."

When the front door closed, she made her way over and locked it, then turned off the lighted Open sign. Her stomach growled, reminding her she hadn't eaten since breakfast. But truly, the thought of food made her want to puke. She went to the cabinet below the checkout counter and gathered her purse, then reached for the letter from her lawyer. For a moment, her hand hovered over it, and the sour ball in her stomach rolled. Then she stuffed it inside her bag and straightened.

After doing a final sweep of the counter area and double-checking that the back door was locked, she let herself out the front and headed for her car. Halfway there, her footsteps stilled, and she sighed. The very last thing she wanted to do was go home. To an empty, quiet house.

God, she missed her boys. Carter and Dylan were loud and loving and constantly in motion. If one wasn't talking her ear off, then the other was "creating" something that would undoubtedly be loud or messy or both. Whenever she thought back to the twins' younger years, she wasn't sure how they'd all survived. Their entire situation was the perfect example of "ignorance is bliss." But they'd made it. Somehow.

And now her babies were freshmen at the University of Washington. Both lived on campus—together, which soothed her mama-heart—and both had received full-ride academic scholarships. *Proud* did not begin to describe how she felt about them. Though a selfish part of her would give anything to have them home, causing mischief and mayhem.

Poppy let out another sigh and turned in the opposite direction from where her car was parked. She wasn't sure she could handle being alone right now. Crossing the street, she made her way to Monty's Tavern. Pushing the pub's heavy wood door open, a smile tipped her lips; the charming old-world nautical theme never failed to lift her spirits.

With a wave to the hostess, she made her way to the bar and took a seat. Seeing Four was busy behind the counter, she picked up the cocktail menu. She deserved a drink after the day she'd had. The customers had all been wonderful, and her employees were great . . . but that confrontation with Eli had left her rattled. Even now, she couldn't shake the worry and dread.

Her phone buzzed, and when she brought up her group chat with the boys, tears sprung to her eyes.

CARTER

Hey mom! Thinking of you.

DYLAN

Hey mom! We'll be home this weekend. Want to go to dinner at Uncle Four's on Friday?

CARTER

Do you think Uncle Four will let us go with him to his jiu-jitsu class on Saturday?

DYLAN

We can also go with you to your cardio
kickboxing class too. And FYI, we don't have
to be back until Monday night.

Wiping away a tear, she responded.

That all sounds great. I'm at the shop until
five on Friday. Serena's closing, so come
over when you get off the ferry and we'll hit
up Four's.

DYLAN

Great. See you then. Love you!

CARTER

Love you, mom!

Love you guys. So much!

"I miss you," she murmured.

"Rough Monday, cuz?" Montgomery Dumas IV—or Four as he'd been called since forever—placed a coaster down in front of her and topped it with a glass of ice water. Standing at just over six feet tall, he had tousled black hair—rockstar hair, as her boys often teased—indigo eyes, and a perpetual five-o'clock shadow. By all accounts other than hers, the man was smoking hot.

She and Four didn't share a drop of blood, but they were family in all the ways that mattered. They even introduced each other as cousins, though they were truly more like siblings. From the moment they'd met nearly nineteen years earlier—when she'd been sixteen, pregnant, and homeless— to when she'd moved to Hudson Island eleven years ago, and to this very day, the guy had been like an older brother. He'd not only had her back, but he'd provided a shoulder to cry on numerous times.

"Oh, it was beyond rough, Four. Trust me." Some of the

tension in her shoulders lessened, and she heaved out a breath. She'd made the right call coming here tonight.

"Nice hair, by the way," he said, examining her. Like she was a bug in a petri dish.

"Thanks." Self-conscious, she ran a hand over her long hair that, for once, she'd styled in loose beachy waves.

Over the weekend, she'd gone to the spa at Pacific View Resort with the intention of relaxing with a massage and facial. The drama of her divorce had been wearing on her, and she'd wanted to treat herself for once. And she had. Hours later, she'd left the spa utterly calm from said massage and facial, along with a fresh mani and pedi. On top of all that, she'd had some blondish highlights added to her brown hair. Were they too much? Too obvious? Too trying-too-hard?

She peeked up at Four. "Divorce hair is totally cliché, right?"

He shrugged. "Pretty sure it's divorce bangs that are cliché."

Poppy choked on the sip of water she was taking and stared at her pseudo-brother in bafflement. The man was a perpetual bachelor. A certified manwhore. Thankfully—because god knew Hudson was a gossipy little island—he steered clear of the local ladies. Though for some mind-boggling reason, that just added to his supposedly broody mystique.

"How do *you* know that?" she asked.

Four smirked. "I've dated one or two freshly divorced ladies in my time."

Her eyes rolled. Well, *that* made perfect sense. Still, she pursed her lips as her unruly emotions bubbled to the surface. These last few weeks had been . . . a lot.

"Seriously, Poppy. Everything okay?"

"Oh, you know. The boys." She pointed at her phone with a watery laugh and brushed away a renegade tear.

"This one's on me." He tossed another coaster down and placed her usual in front of her, a gin and soda with extra muddled limes. "Now, tell me what else is going on. I know you miss the boys, but this?" He drew an air circle around her face with his finger. "This is more than just missing the boys. What's up?"

She took a long sip of her drink. The tart, herby flavor soothed her nerves, and she leaned back on the barstool. "I got the official letter today. The divorce finalized."

Four's expression hardened. "Well then, congratu-fuck-ing-lations."

She released an awkward chuckle. "Thanks . . . I think."

"There's no 'I think' about it, Pop. You're a million times better off without that asshole. The *boys* are a million times better off without that asshole."

"I know." She sighed. And she did know. But that didn't make it suck any less. That didn't make it hurt any less.

He gave her a stern look. "Poppy."

"I *do* know. I swear. It's just . . . I don't know. I didn't think it would feel like this."

Eli wasn't all bad. At least, he hadn't been at first. He'd gotten worse the longer they'd stayed together, berating her in ways she'd never thought she would allow. He'd made her feel like absolute shit about herself. Yet she'd kept up appearances for years. *Years.* Until everything had come crashing down.

So, yes, she knew she was better off without him in her life. She really did. Through therapy and conversations with her boys, she'd become very familiar with the word *gaslighting* over the last year. But she still felt like a failure.

"Poppy, honey, look at me."

She didn't want to because Four knew her so well. Too

well. He could read her like a damn book. From the very beginning, she'd never been able to hide anything from him. The man truly was annoying like that. But he was also persistent and wouldn't let up until he made his point. So, she met his indigo gaze and braced. For better or worse, tough love had always been Four's thing. At least with her and the boys.

"You've spent the last eight years married to a piece of shit. I'm sure the asshole had his moments, but as a whole, he treated you like garbage. He treated the boys . . . well, he basically ignored them unless it was convenient for him."

She cringed at the truth in his words. Eli had never been mean to the boys. He'd even had moments when he'd been an attentive and doting stepfather. But those moments had generally come when he'd known he would get something out of the deal, like the bolstering of his public image. The rest of the time, he'd been indifferent. He'd paid for whatever lessons or activities the boys had needed and called it done. He'd gone to their baseball and football games but spent the entire time mingling with the other parents.

Eli had reserved the mean for her. Especially recently. From the weeks leading up to Thanksgiving to now, the past four months had been . . . a lot.

"Look, Pop, whatever bad things you're thinking about yourself, stop it. You've come a long-ass way. You've raised two amazing young men who are off at college but still remember to text their mama. You run a successful shop in town and own a damn building."

She chewed her lip. "Yeah, but I didn't really earn either, did I?"

Rainy Day Boutique, and the building that housed it, had been transferred to Poppy's name a decade ago by her honorary aunt Mirabelle, who was also Four's blood-related aunt. To this day, she was still shocked by the gift. Both had been in Aunt Mirabelle's family since the 1960s, and Poppy was beyond honored and thankful to continue the store's legacy. Even if she'd done nothing to deserve it.

"Bullshit. So you had some help along the way. So what? After what your asshole family put you through—when you were just a damn kid yourself—don't you think you deserve a break? Besides, your blood, sweat, and tears matter. You worked your ass off and earned every bit of that building." He gestured around them. "Do you think less of me because I inherited this place from my family?"

"You know I don't."

"So why do you think less of yourself because Aunt Mirabelle gave you your building?"

She glared at him and let out a small huff. "Aren't you supposed to be all grumpy and shit?"

"Yeah, but not with you, lucky duck." He winked. "My point is, you've come a long way. There's a lot you should be proud of. *And* you're only thirty-four."

"Thirty-*five*," she groaned. Thirteen days earlier, on Valentine's Day, she'd had a quiet birthday celebration in her flannel pj's, on her couch, with popcorn and *Stranger Things*.

"Whatever, old lady," he teased. "You're finally free, Pop. Get out there. Date. Spend a Friday night out instead of doing inventory."

Her laugh was borderline hysterical. "You're kidding, right?"

"You'll find out there are a lot better dudes out there than Eli fucking Walker."

"I'm sure there are, Four, but I'm not exactly dating material."

His scowl was immediate. "What the fuck's that supposed to mean?"

She suppressed an eye roll. Barely. "As you so eloquently put it, I'm old."

And plain. She was five-three with boring brown hair and

boring hazel eyes and a blah figure. There wasn't anything special about her. However, she knew better than to say that in front of Four. He was her biggest cheerleader and tended to get annoyed when she spoke honestly about her looks.

He pulled a ticket from the point-of-sale machine. "Please. I'm forty-two, and even I date."

She scoffed. "Date? Really?"

"Yes, Pop. There's usually a meal or an outing beforehand. So I do technically date."

She shuddered, took a large gulp of water, then made the time-out signal with her hands. "Nope. Yuck."

"If I can get out and date, then so can you," he said with a laugh.

"I have twin boys who're turning nineteen. *Nineteen*, Four."

"Aaand?" He sugared the rim of a martini glass.

"Aaand I've dated two guys in my entire life. The boys' dad and Eli. I think it's safe to say that dating isn't exactly my thing."

"Well, fuck, cuz. When you put it like that . . ." Grinning, he placed a lemon drop on the service rail at the end of the bar.

"My divorce literally just finalized. Give me a week or twenty before you foist dating on me? Oh, and speaking of Fridays, the boys are coming home this weekend. They want to have dinner here if you're free. They're also hoping to tag along with you to the gym on Saturday. Apparently, they started taking classes at the De la Rosa brothers' Seattle gym. That work for you?"

"Of course." He held up a finger, then stepped away to help a couple of customers. When he returned, he said, "I heard through the gossip train that Eli was being a dick at your shop this morning. I assume he was responsible for your whole 'rough day' thing?"

See? Small-town gossip. Her stomach twisted at the thought of everyone talking about her. "He was being his usual charming self. It was no big deal."

Four's eyebrow arched. "That's not what I heard."

She arched an eyebrow back at him.

"I heard Quinn got called in."

She sucked down the rest of her drink and sighed. "Yeah."

"Eli's always up to something. I don't trust that fucker. You need to watch your back." He nodded to her empty glass. "Another?"

"Please."

"Single or double?"

Poppy hesitated for a split second. "Single. I have to drive." If she didn't, it would be a double tall gin kind of night.

"Food?" he asked, refilling her water.

She glanced at the menu. "Cup of soup?"

He stared at her.

"What?" Her brow furrowed. "Your chef's *zuppa toscana* is amazing."

Grumbling, he entered her order onto the point-of-sale screen. "Be right back."

A few minutes later, Four placed a plate in front of her. It held a cup of soup and three chicken parm sliders.

She frowned. "Four, I didn't order—"

"If you want another drink, you have to eat the sliders."

Her eyes narrowed.

"You're a lightweight, Pop. Besides, you've dropped, what, fifteen pounds since all the shit with Eli went down? Not to be nitpicky or anything, but that's fifteen pounds you can't really afford to lose."

Damn Four and his stupid perceptiveness. Giving him her best death glare, she picked up a slider and took a huge bite. Juvenile? Absolutely. Did she care? Not one bit.

"Satisfied?" she mumbled around her food. The crispy chicken and spicy-sweet red sauce were a flavor explosion. The smooth mozzarella and salty parmesan? Warm-your-soul goodness. Damn. It was hard to be irritated when the food he'd forced on her was so sublime.

He chuckled as he finished making her drink. Swiping her empty, he placed the fresh cocktail on the coaster. "I'm serious, Pop. You need to be careful with Eli. Where's he staying?"

"He's still at the rental," she said, grimacing.

Eli had grown up on Hudson, and though his parents had moved south years ago, they'd kept their waterfront home as a vacation rental. Eli managed it on their behalf. Resentfully. He blamed Poppy and the boys for his parents not outright giving him the property when they'd moved. His parents had never approved of her, and he refused to let her forget it.

When they'd separated three months ago, Eli had moved into the rental with the permission of his parents. They'd given him a generous timeline for how long he could stay there, but he'd hated having any timeline at all.

Then when Eli had proceeded to make one god-awful decision after another, and it had epically blown up in his face, his parents had shrunk that timeline. Poppy was pretty sure he had to find another place to live in the next couple of weeks.

Of course, his current housing woes were all *her* fault, too.

"Chin up, Pop," Four said, pulling her from her musings. "You're officially divorced. That's a positive step. All the shit of the past few months is behind you now. It's only up from here."

She cringed. "Jeez, Four. Don't go jinxing it for me!"

Because one thing she'd learned over the years? Just when

you thought things couldn't get worse, they did. They really, really did.

CHAPTER FOUR

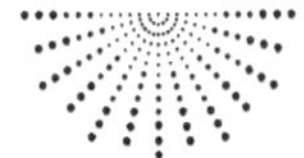

Rainy Day Boutique's bell chimed, and Poppy spun to face the entrance, ready to greet her first customer of the day. Instead, the welcoming words died on her lips.

Eli. Again. Shit.

Gone was yesterday's bluster, replaced by the smarmy-ass grin she hated. Now that they were divorced, she didn't have to hold back her irritation, so she crossed her arms over her chest and frowned.

Damn. It was depressing to think she'd had to hold anything back when she'd been married. She really was better off without the jackass. She should have left him years ago.

"What is it now, Eli?"

"What?" The mock-innocent expression he donned grated on her last nerve. It was only ten in the damn morning—way too early for his nonsense. Correction: too early for *him*.

She waved her hand toward his face. "You have that look. What are you up to?"

He laughed. The sound was arrogant and patronizing. "Oh, you think you know me so well, don't you?"

Poppy did know him well. Too well, in fact. And that obnoxious gleam in his eyes? Yeah, the bastard was up to something. She arched an eyebrow, refusing to be baited.

"Fine." He shrugged. "I have news about the house."

She held completely still. There was no way in hell she would let him see the dread now turning her stomach.

"As you're so fond of saying, Poppy, per our divorce agreement . . ." His laugh wasn't the only thing that came off arrogant and patronizing. His tone did, too. And his dramatic pause. ". . . I agreed to allow you to stay in the house until we found a buyer. Then even though the house is mine, I graciously agreed to split the proceeds fifty-fifty."

She fought to keep her expression neutral. Steady. Because, for once, Eli spoke the truth. The house *was* his. He hadn't been obligated to give her any part of the house sale proceeds. However, it wasn't him being gracious. It had been a flat-out PR move on his part. And she was certain there was a catch . . .

"Well," he continued, that annoying grin growing on his face, "I found a cash buyer. The sale closes and they take possession on Monday, so you need to move out this weekend."

She blinked. Twice. There's no way she'd heard that right.

"It's a Seattle buyer who's agreed to take it as is. They waived inspection."

Holy shit. What? "Without even seeing it?"

Eli shrugged. "It was a good opportunity. They jumped on it."

Her eyes narrowed. "What exactly did you sell it for?"

He said a price that was easily hundreds of thousands of dollars less than what the house was worth. Her jaw dropped. He had to be joking. Housing prices in the Pacific

Northwest were astronomical, especially on Hudson Island. Most of the people who lived here full-time had owned their property for generations.

"Eli, why the hell would you sell the house for such a low price?"

"I don't know what you mean. It was a great offer."

Bullshit. He'd done it to fuck her over. Classic freaking Eli.

"Let me get this straight. You decided to list the house at a fire-sale price just to stick it to me." She laughed, but there was zero humor in it. "God, you're so stupid. You're so petty that you thought it would be a good idea to forgo at least *three hundred thousand dollars*—minimum!—to what? Make me homeless? Make me scramble for a place to live? Make me beg you to take me back?"

His weaselly eyes twinkled, and Poppy knew she'd guessed right. She shook her head and scoffed. "You really are an idiot, Eli. None of those scenarios are happening. Ever. Yes, moving this weekend will be an inconvenience. But guess what? I have a place to stay. Rent-free, in fact." She pointed up. "Or did you forget once again that I own this entire building, including the vacant apartment upstairs?"

Eli's mouth gaped, and angry red splotches dotted his cheeks.

She strolled past him to greet two customers who'd just walked in. "Mrs. Abbot, Mrs. Yoshida, how are you this morning?"

Eli huffed, then stalked toward the front door, knocking into her shoulder. He grumbled curses as he yanked the door open and tried to slam it shut behind him. She smirked when the door's soft-close hinges thwarted his plan.

Poppy chuckled and brought her focus back to the ladies in front of her. The Hudson Island locals were somewhere in their sixties and had been best friends for decades. While they were two of the gossip train's leaders, they were also two of the kindest and funniest women she had ever met. Over the last few months, they'd deftly steered the gossip away from her and her twins. For that, she would forever be indebted to them.

"Sorry about that, ladies."

"No worries at all, dear," Mrs. Abbot said, patting her on the shoulder.

Mrs. Yoshida nodded at the now-closed door. "That one's always been a questionable egg, even when he was growing up."

"I'll say." Mrs. Abbot's nose scrunched. "No surprise, though. It's a whole apple-falling-from-the-tree situation. That entire family is . . ."

"Exactly. They say the right things, but there's something just a little off." Mrs. Yoshida waved a dismissive hand. "No matter. You and those handsome sons of yours are better off."

A smile lifted Poppy's lips. That's right, dammit. She *was* better off.

"Thank you. That means a lot." It really did. She knew she shouldn't look to others to validate her decisions, but it was hard not to. Baby steps, right? Clapping her hands together, she said, "Now, ladies, what can I help you find?"

Mrs. Yoshida glanced around the store. "Well, we're shopping for little prizes."

"Our knitting group is having a contest, and we're in charge of the prizes," Mrs. Abbot clarified with a sweet smile.

A sweet smile that Poppy knew was full of shit. Oh, these ladies . . .

Biting the inside of her cheek, Poppy pressed for more details. "What type of contest is it, exactly?"

"A shot contest," Mrs. Yoshida said simply.

"But not *gross* shots, of course." Mrs. Abbot's eyes

sparkled with excitement. "It's to see who can create the best shot in our craft circle. Every shot will be judged on taste, color, and potency. Each category will have a winner. Then we'll have one overall winner."

Mrs. Yoshida nodded in agreement. "There are extra points, of course, for creativity. If you can light it on fire, if you can add whipped cream, if it can go on the shot ski . . . That kind of thing."

Poppy's wide eyes darted between the women. Fire? Whipped cream? Shot ski? After taking in their matching sweet smiles, she burst into laughter. "Oh my god, ladies! I knew I loved you two before, but now? I'm obsessed with you both!" She wiped away tears. "Follow me, girls. I think I have some gift options that may work for your crazy crew."

Thirty minutes later, Poppy waved Mrs. Abbot and Mrs. Yoshida goodbye as they merrily left her shop, each toting a bag of insulated wine tumblers decorated with witty, alcohol-related sayings. When they disappeared from view, she ran to the back and grabbed a box of tumblers to restock, worrying her bottom lip as she thought of all the work it would take to pack up the house. This freaking weekend.

She glanced at the ceiling. The little apartment upstairs had been her and her sons' fresh start a decade earlier. If memory served correctly, it was . . . cozy. And that was putting it nicely. She made a mental note to run up on her break and do an inventory of any repairs that might be needed . . . and to check that there weren't any critters vying to be her new roommates. She and the boys had moved in with Eli immediately after the wedding, and the apartment had been vacant ever since.

Her nose scrunched. She definitely needed to do a massive purge. There was no way two thousand-plus square feet of furniture and belongings would fit in the apartment.

And not only did she have to go through all her things, but there were the boys' rooms as well—

The boys.

She quickly placed the tumblers on the display shelf, then tossed the empty box in the back room and hustled to the counter to grab her cell phone. She shot a text to the boys, asking if they were free to chat.

Seconds later, her phone rang with an incoming video call.

"Hi, boys." Seeing them next to each other on the screen warmed her heart. She knew she should be okay with them leaving the nest—they truly were responsible kids—but she wasn't. She missed them desperately and worried constantly.

"Hey, Mom," they said.

"So . . . I was wondering if there was any particular reason why you were coming home this weekend." She had a feeling she knew the answer.

Silence. They glanced at each other before looking back at her. No doubt their twin telepathy was in play.

"I mean, you know that I'm always excited to see you guys and have you home, but I was just wondering if there was any specific reason you wanted to come home *this* weekend."

More silence. More quick twin glances.

Her stomach sank. If she was right . . . "Boys?"

Carter shrugged. "Well, we haven't been back since New Year's—"

"And it's the end of February," Dylan finished.

"So it's time."

"Yeah, Mom. It's past time for a visit. And we can do a belated birthday thing for you, too!"

She couldn't stop her smile. No matter how old they got, they were so stinking cute. But she stayed quiet. If she waited long enough, they'd crack.

A few more seconds of silence passed. Then Carter

heaved out a giant sigh. "Eli texted us yesterday that he sold the house."

I knew it! Eli fucking Walker. I. Hate. You.

She bit back a scowl. Damn him for putting Carter and Dylan in the middle.

"He told us we need to get our stuff out ASAP," Dylan said, using air quotes and mimicking Eli's smarmy smile. The impression was so on point, she had to laugh.

"We're not only coming back for our stuff, Mom," Carter added in a hurry, panic tinging his words. "I swear."

Oh, her sweet boys. "I know, honey."

"It's just . . ." Carter locked eyes with his brother for a moment.

"We're worried about you," they said in unison.

Poppy's heart squeezed, and she swallowed past the lump that popped up in her throat. "Who's the mama here, boys?"

They smiled. "You."

"And who's the one who's supposed to worry?"

"You," they said again.

"That's right. So don't worry." She wished she could hug them. "I'm excited to see you this weekend, no matter why you're coming home. Uncle Four said he's free to have dinner with us on Friday. Then you guys can all help me move on Saturday."

Dylan perked up. "You already found a place?"

"Where are you going?" Carter asked.

She paused, glancing at the ceiling again. The idea of moving back to where she'd started was humbling. "I've decided to move into the apartment above the shop."

"Our old place?" Carter's eyebrows rose in surprise.

"That's so cool!" Dylan exclaimed. "I haven't been there since we moved out."

That was one of the things she worried about. "You know, the apartment is a little small"—understatement of the year—

"so I'm sure you guys could stay with your uncle Four on Saturday and Sunday nights if you want."

"Nah, Mom," Carter said. He turned and slapped his brother on the chest. "Dude! We can build a fort like we did when we were kids!"

"Yeah, Mom. Don't worry about us. It'll be fun."

CHAPTER FIVE

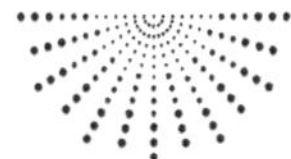

For the first time in Cade's memory, the Hudson Island gym was in a lull, and the usual go-go-go hustle that he had grown so used to was temporarily nonexistent. Coming off Jason's big fight, they were still a few weeks out from their next scheduled training camp, an eight-week camp for another one of their gym's elite fighters. Then in four weeks, another fighter arrived for a six-week camp. It wasn't unusual to have some downtime in between fight camps, but his near-empty calendar was shocking.

Usually, any extra time he had was consumed by their gym's partnership with Hudson Security—a world-renowned private security firm headed by a good friend, Gavin Frazier. Their new joint venture, uncreatively named Hudson Tactical, trained law enforcement and personal security types in hand-to-hand combat and different styles of fighting. It also provided tactical training in weapons, marksmanship, outdoor survival, and other skills. However, last month, they'd successfully passed management of the program over to another friend, Joe Buchanan, a former FBI agent who had plenty of experience handling the extensive paperwork and all the bureaucratic bullshit. It was safe to say that both Cade and Gavin had been more than happy to pass the reins of their pet project to him.

So, other than leading a jiu-jitsu class later in the afternoon, Cade had nothing to do today. His schedule was almost clear, and his Saturdays were *never* almost clear. Which was why he'd said yes when Four had called at the ass crack of dawn to ask if he could help unload some boxes.

He easily found parking in front of Monty's Tavern, since the street was practically deserted. Granted, it was only eight thirty in the morning. Also, the shit-tacular weather of gray skies and sputter—not quite mist, not quite rain—was likely keeping tourists from exploring their little island this morning.

Rounding his Range Rover, Cade walked to the restaurant's front door. A horn blared as he lifted his hand to knock, and he turned to see a truck approaching with its driver's side window lowering.

"Hey, man," Four called from the truck. "Thanks for coming to help."

"No problem." Cade noticed a young man in the front passenger seat and another in the extended cab. Poppy's boys. He lifted his chin in greeting, then gestured to the boxes and furniture in the truck bed. "We're unloading this stuff?"

Four nodded. "Yeah, but over at the Rainy Day building. You want to hop in or move your car over there?"

"I'll meet you guys over there."

A couple of minutes later, he parked in front of Poppy's store.

"Dylan, Carter, how's it going?" He greeted each twin with a handshake and a backslap. He knew they were solid kids. Well, young men who were nearly as tall as him. "Freshman year treating you guys well?"

"It's been fun so far," Carter said.

"Can't complain," Dylan chimed in.

Cade grinned at the duo. "You know, rumor has it you guys are taking some classes over at our Seattle gym."

"Hell yeah!" Dylan exclaimed, his face lighting up. "We're doing a boxing class with Jackie and a jiu-jitsu class with Oscar."

"It's so badass." Carter nudged his brother. "*We're* so badass."

"For fuck's sake, you guys are in the beginner classes," Four groaned, pulling a dolly from the back of the truck. "Even *I* could school you idiots."

Cade snickered as the twins howled and taunted Four with old-man insults.

"Well, C and D," Four said, chuckling at their ribbing, "since you're such tough badasses now—you know, after *two* months of classes—you guys are in charge of bringing all the boxes up. Cade and I will get the bigger stuff."

Instead of heading for the entrance to Poppy's shop, Four unlocked the discreet door between Rainy Day Boutique and Eli's real estate office—a door Cade had never noticed before. Four propped it open with a doorstop, revealing a long, narrow staircase. His friend darted up the stairs but was back within seconds.

Cade glanced at the boxes and furniture in the bed of the truck, then back to the narrow-ass staircase. Shit. No wonder Four wanted help. He frowned. "What? No elevator?"

"Yeah, right." Four laughed and turned to the twins, who both held medium-sized boxes. "It's the apartment on the left."

"Dude, we used to live here, remember?" Carter rolled his eyes, and then the twins disappeared up the stairs.

As he and Four unloaded a dining table, Cade eyed the staircase again. "Are you sure all this stuff is going to fit?"

"We'll find out soon enough, won't we?"

"Shiiit." Cade let out an exaggerated groan as he and Four grabbed the opposite ends of the surprisingly heavy dining table. With lots of creative maneuvering, they managed to fit the damn thing through the doorway. Barely. "Whose stuff is this, anyway?"

"Poppy's. Hold up," Four said.

Cade paused halfway up the stairs and took the brunt of the table's weight as his friend adjusted his grip.

"What do you mean, it's Poppy's?"

Four shot a glance up the stairs, lowering his voice as he said, "Her fuckwad ex sold the house, so she has to move. Apparently, the new owners take possession on Monday. Bastard didn't bother telling her until earlier this week."

"Seriously?" Cade asked as they continued up the stairs.

"Piece of fucking work, right?" Four grumbled.

No kidding. What a fucking asshole.

When they reached the small landing, it took more creative maneuvering to get the dining table through the door. If he'd thought the staircase was tiny, it was nothing compared to the apartment. They set the table down, and it damn near took up half the living room.

Four's phone rang, and he cursed as he glanced at the display. "I gotta take this," he muttered, heading back out.

A smart-ass comment was on Cade's lips, but it died when he noticed the boys. They were standing at the other end of the living room, staring into what Cade assumed was the bedroom.

"You two okay?" he asked, concern growing at their solemn faces.

Dylan shook his head. "It's smaller than I remember."

"A lot smaller," Carter said, his voice barely above a whisper.

Cade's gaze ping-ponged between the two. Unsure how to proceed, he said cautiously, "It's not the biggest place, but it's nice though."

Carter's hazel eyes shimmered.

Concern morphed to full-on worry, and Cade was next to the kid in seconds. "Talk to me, dude. What's going on in your head?"

Carter remained silent for so long, Cade wasn't sure he would answer. Until finally, he said, "We lived here before we moved into Eli's place. D and I shared this room."

"We had these loft beds," Dylan said, picking up his twin's thought. "One on each side with these little matching desks and beanbags underneath. Mom would hang sheets up, and it was like we had our own secret forts."

Carter sniffed. "It was so much fun."

Standing between them, Cade placed his hands on their shoulders. "That sounds like a great memory. Why are you guys sad?"

"There's only one bedroom," Carter said quietly. "*We* slept in this room. So Mom . . ."

"She didn't sleep in here with us. So she must have slept on the couch. Or the floor." Dylan's voice trembled on the last word, and he sniffed loudly. "We didn't realize what that meant when we were little, how much she'd given up for us."

Carter sighed. "She was barely older than we are now."

Matching looks of guilt and anguish filled their young faces, and Cade's chest clenched as his heart broke for them. At the same time, he found himself damn impressed that Carter and Dylan were aware enough to recognize their mother's sacrifices and humble enough to appreciate them.

"Hey," he said, squeezing their shoulders. "Even though

your mom and I don't know each other all that well, you know what I do know? I know that she loves you two. I know the last thing she'd want is for you guys to be sad or feel guilty."

Watery eyes stared back at him, and he prayed he was saying the right words. The last thing he wanted to do was upset them further. They were good kids. They really were. Boys on the cusp of manhood.

He remembered that time vividly. The excitement of spreading his wings, but deep down also still needing the support and guidance from his parents.

Cade cleared his throat and gave them a reassuring smile. "How about we get the rest of the stuff moved, pick up the next load, and then we'll go to the store and you guys can pick up some kind of treat or surprise for her? Does she like flowers?"

Carter and Dylan watched each other for a moment, then they took deep breaths in, squared their shoulders, and looked back at Cade, breaking out into matching wide grins. "Gummy bears," they said in unison.

Damn good kids.

"Gummy bears it is." He chuckled, slapping them both on the back. "But boxes and furniture first."

On their way out, the twins hesitated at the landing.

"Thanks, Cade," Dylan said, meeting his eyes.

"Not a problem, man." He shook his head. "You know, seeing your parent as an actual *person* and not your parent is . . ."

"A mindfuck?" Carter said.

Cade laughed. The kid was not wrong. At all. "You got that right. Eye-opening, huh?"

"Yeah," Carter agreed, leading them down the stairs in single file. "I don't know how she did it."

"I mean, really," Dylan said as they spilled onto the sidewalk. "Look how great we turned out."

Cade snorted. "You guys aren't even nineteen. Jury's still out on you two."

Four hung up his phone and slapped his fists to his hips. "Great, huh? You know what would make you jokers great? If you could figure out how the hell we're going to get this damn couch up those stairs and into that freaking matchbox-sized apartment."

Carter elbowed Dylan. "Come on, bro. Let's show these old guys how it's done!"

With a hoot, they unloaded the oversized couch and hauled it up to the apartment. When their laughter faded, Cade turned to Four with a smirk. "Smooth, my friend. That was fucking smooth."

"Damn straight." Four passed him a box. "We may be old, brother, but damn if we're gonna throw out our backs moving that fucking couch."

CHAPTER SIX

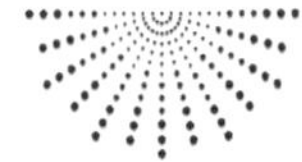

Poppy walked through the second floor of her house checking for anything she might have missed. She winced. No, not *her* house. Her *former* house. Well, if she wanted to get technical, it wasn't even that. It had always been Eli's house. But it didn't matter, not anymore.

As she made her way through the empty rooms, memories of her boys growing up here bombarded her mind. Her boys' high-pitched giggles when they'd been just little guys having pillow-fort campouts in the living room. Their voice-cracking embarrassment when she'd shown them how to appropriately slow dance with a partner for their first school dance. Their nervous anticipation and excitement as they'd opened one college acceptance letter after another.

Eight years they'd lived here. Her sweet ten-year-old twins had been ecstatic to move from their tiny apartment to Eli's home, which they'd thought was a mansion. Especially since Eli had doted on the boys in the beginning, spoiling them with all sorts of sports equipment and spending hours tossing footballs and baseballs with them.

It had been picture-perfect. She'd felt so lucky. For a couple of years, anyway.

Then the tension had crept in. Followed by the arguments. Most had been caused by her growing success with Rainy Day Boutique. Eli's real estate business had been thriving as well, but she'd realized too late in their relationship that he was only happy when the spotlight focused solely on him. The man was toxic. Still, they'd kept up appearances, hiding their marital issues from not only the town gossip, but from the boys. Him, for the sake of his reputation; her, for the sake of Carter and Dylan.

She'd wanted nothing more than to give her boys the stability of a two-parent household. Yes, Eli hadn't been the best stepfather toward the end, but he hadn't been awful, either. He'd shown up for them in his own way, like coming to their school and sporting events. Had it been in the manner she would have liked? No. But he'd been there. That meant something.

After the boys' high school graduation, however, she'd decided she'd had enough. The night she had moved them into their dorms—Eli, of course, had a prior commitment— she'd taken them out to dinner and told them she was planning on filing for divorce. She had expected them to have questions for her, to be upset. What she hadn't expected was their anger. At Eli. Or their sadness. For her.

The tears in their hazel eyes had at first confused her, then broken her heart. Because the boys had confessed they'd known about Eli's cheating for two years.

The revelation had been like a lightbulb suddenly illuminating a dark room. The boys' recent actions had finally clicked into place. They'd always been good students, but at the start of their junior year, they'd turned it up a notch. They'd also always been mama's boys, but again, they'd turned it up—sticking close to the house, inviting their friends over instead of going out, instituting a weekly mom-and-sons date night . . .

On the day they'd been born, despite being scared out of her mind, the moment the doctor placed both boys in her arms, Poppy had vowed to do everything she could to protect them. And until that dinner eighteen years later, she'd thought she'd been doing a good job. But taking in the stricken faces of her children, she'd realized she'd made some mistakes. So she'd reaffirmed her vow. Committed herself to doing everything in her power to make sure the mess with Eli didn't touch them again.

A few months later, everything had imploded, and the whole island had learned what kind of man Eli was. One who lied and manipulated. Who cheated countless times. Even with his wife's own cousin—

Nope. Do not *go there!*

That was another clusterfuck in and of itself. But cluster or not, she'd done everything she could to shield her boys. Yes, they were young men now—full-fledged adults in the eyes of the law—but if there was a chance she could protect them, she would. No matter what.

Poppy took one more look at their empty bedrooms and sighed. Her sons had grown from little boys to young men within these walls. She'd cherish those special memories forever, even if the bad memories threatened to outweigh the good. Her soul desperately clung to the good.

She trudged down the stairs, recalling Carter and Dylan laughing their butts off while packing up boxes the night before. Their goofiness and resilience warmed her heart. They had seen more than she'd ever wanted them to, and yet they could still laugh, could still joke around. She would forever be grateful for that.

The boys had been in and out all day, collecting everything the three of them wanted to keep and delivering it to either the apartment or Four's house. Four had a garage bay he was letting them use for the time being. Ideally, she'd have put the overflow in the storage room across the hall from her apartment, but the space was already packed with vintage items from the boutique. Items she'd been meaning to go through. For years. Another project for another day . . .

As for the stuff they'd decided against keeping, there'd been so much. Furniture, decorations, home goods, and various odds and ends. She had considered renting a storage unit but figured donating everything to Harlow's House, an amazing charity on neighboring Whidbey Island that helped domestic abuse victims get back on their feet, would be better. Luckily, she was friends with the charity's president, so she'd been able to call in a favor. Two reps from Harlow's House had come by a couple of hours earlier to take the remaining things.

Donning cleaning gloves, Poppy grabbed a washrag and a bottle of cleaning spray and got to work wiping down the kitchen counters and cabinets. There was nothing like a little therapeutic cleaning to keep her mind from spiraling.

Thirty minutes later, with the strong scent of lemon filling the air, she heard the front door slam open. Footsteps, like a herd of elephants, tromped in the living room.

"Mom! We're back!"

"I'm in the kitchen," she called out. For a split second, her breath caught. Was that the last time she'd be calling out those words? She rubbed her fist over her suddenly aching heart, then huffed out a breath, straightening her shoulders. *Get it together!*

After one last wipe down of the refrigerator's crisper drawer—just because Eli was an ass who'd sold the house as is, didn't mean *she* had to be an ass who left the place looking like a pigsty—she closed the fridge door and turned to greet the boys.

And froze.

What the hell was Cade de la Rosa doing in her kitchen?

"Uh, hi," she said, sounding as confused as she felt.

"Hey, Poppy. How's it going?" He placed a large brown paper bag on the kitchen island and smiled, lighting up the room with a wide grin that made the corners of his eyes crinkle.

All thoughts left her brain. Because there were swoon-worthy men . . . and then there was Cade.

"Hey, Mom!" Carter and Dylan said as they rushed into the kitchen.

Poppy blinked. Just like that, the holy-moly-there's-a-hot-guy-in-my-house spell broke, and she became acutely aware of her appearance. Wearing leggings and a ratty oversized sweatshirt, she'd pulled her hair into a messy bun that she was pretty sure resembled a bird's nest that was falling apart. She didn't have a lick of makeup on, and she hadn't showered since yesterday morning. *Fantastic.*

She peeled off the rubber gloves, placing them on the sink ledge, and took a deep breath before facing the trio.

"What's up, boys?" She nodded to Carter, who was holding a gift bag. "What's that for?"

"Well, Mom," he said, placing the bag on the island in front of her, "we know things have been stressful, so we figured you could use these."

The boys' sly grins piqued her interest. She glanced at Cade, who shot her a wink. Her belly fluttered, but she ignored it.

"Hey, Pop," Four said, entering the kitchen carrying two giant pizza boxes.

"Hi, Four." She'd never been more thankful for the distraction. She turned back to the sink and grabbed a roll of paper towels. "The dishes are all packed, but you guys can use—"

"Open it already!" Dylan said, pushing the gift toward her.

"Okay, okay," she mumbled, pulling the tissue from the bag. When she saw the contents, she laughed. A giant bag of gummy bears.

"They're your favorite *and* you don't have to share with us," Dylan said, pride tinging his words.

"Wait! We also got you"—Carter pulled a second bag of candy from behind his back while Dylan flashed ta-da hands—"the frog gummies you love!" He beamed at Cade and Four. "When we were little, these bad boys were our extra-special treats."

"You should probably share those with us, though," Dylan added with a smirk.

Oh, her sweet, sweet boys. Poppy smiled through misty eyes. The frogs had indeed been special treats. Money had been tight early on, but every now and then, she'd splurged. There were roughly twenty-eight of those gummy marsh-mallow frogs in a bag. And holy moly, could she make those little suckers last.

"Thank you," she said, going up on tiptoe to hug them both. They were so much taller than her now. "You guys start on the pizza, and I'll share the frogs. But only one each, okay?" She eyed the empty kitchen and grimaced. "I hope you guys brought drinks because, well, everything's been moved."

"D, go grab the drinks from the back of the truck," Cade said, opening the pizza boxes. "C, there are some paper plates in the bag."

Cade's use of their nicknames had her eyebrows rising. Four was the only one, aside from her, who called them that.

Cade caught her surprised expression and shrugged. "As you know, my brother's name is Dante. We call each other C and D, too. Besides, we're on a nickname-level basis now.

Right, C?" He glanced back at Poppy when Carter snickered. "Moving all day was a bit of a bonding experience."

"Yeah, right, Mom," Carter said with a roll of his eyes. "More like Uncle Four and Cade made me and D do all the heavy lifting. They just moved the smaller boxes and bossed us around."

Cade laughed. "Hey, we moved shit, too."

Carter scoffed, pulling a small stack of plates from the paper bag and placing them on the island. "Just the little shit so you wouldn't hurt your old-man backs."

"Ahem," Poppy said loudly, pinning her son with her best mom glare. "Language, young man."

Carter's jaw dropped, and disbelief painted his features. "But Cade just said the exact same—"

"Cade's an old man." She had to bite the inside of her cheek to keep from laughing. "You, my son, are not."

"Hey!" Cade protested while Carter and Four howled.

She pointed at Four as Dylan returned with a case of soda. "I wouldn't be laughing so hard, gramps. You're even older than Cade."

"You're not that far behind, lady," Four tossed back. He pulled a small bowl of salad from the paper bag and handed it to her.

She rolled her eyes but accepted the salad. "Dylan, honey, am I old?"

"No, ma'am." Dylan placed two slices of pizza on his plate, then hopped up to sit on the counter. "Not only are you young, but you're also the prettiest mom out there." He flashed a shit-eating grin at Four.

"Thank you, sweetie." She smirked at Four. "And thanks for the salad, old man."

Four threw his hands up. "See what I deal with, Cade? Not only these two smart-ass punks, but also their smart-ass mom. Fucking family, I tell ya."

"Well, the kid's not wrong." Cade passed Poppy a fork and gestured to her salad. "No pizza?"

Poppy shook her head, though she was stuck on his first comment. What had he meant by that? "It's salad and gummy bears tonight."

"Wait, you're not eating pizza because you're having gummy bears for dinner?"

She held up her bowl. "*And* salad. It's all about balance, Cade."

His answering grin had her belly fluttering again, and he toasted her with a slice of pizza. "Yeah, your kid's definitely not wrong."

Her fork hovered mid-air. Yup, she definitely wasn't sure what to make of that.

"So, Mom," Dylan said around a mouthful of pizza. "Cade said there's an all-level MMA class we can go to tomorrow at ten. Want to come with us?"

She snorted. "Uh, that would be a hard no. And stop talking with your mouth full."

"Awww, Mom," Carter complained. His ability to draw out those two little words was something else.

"Why not, Mom?" Dylan asked with a pout.

Her eyes widened. Lordy, no matter how old her babies got, good freaking god, could they whine.

"Yeah, why not?" Cade parroted from beside her. Thankfully, with a much-lower whine factor.

Glancing between her boys, Cade, and Four—whose eyes gleamed with mirth—she shook her head. "I go to the cardio kickboxing class on Saturday nights. Well, obviously not tonight, but still. That's plenty."

"But, Mom, that's a *cardio* class." Carter's face pinched, as if cardio were a heaping plate of boiled okra and brussels sprouts. "The MMA class will teach you how to kick some ass. It's important."

She stared at her firstborn—by a full minute—for a moment. "You've only been out of the house for like six months. How is this even possible?"

Confusion was etched on Carter's face as he grabbed another slice of pizza. "What?"

"It's Saturday night, C," Poppy said. "What am I *not* doing right now?"

Dylan chuckled, kicking his brother as he walked by. "Geez, *still*, Mom?"

She shot her youngest a playful glare. "Yes, *still*. Now, both of you, eat your pizza and stop badgering me."

Cade held up his hand and cleared his throat. Confusion was also etched on his handsome face.

Poppy bit back a laugh. God, he was cute. "Yes, Cade?"

"Seeing as I'm new to the group, could I get a little clarification on the 'still'?" He glanced at Four. "Do you know what they're talking about?"

Four shook his head. "No clue. They're an odd bunch, so you never know."

Cade turned his attention back to her. "So, 'still' . . ."

She placed her salad onto the counter and cleared her throat. When the boys snickered, she pinned them with a look, and they immediately quieted. They may have even squeaked. Score one for her. "It's my Saturday routine. It's like clockwork, really. Housework and errands during the day, then the early evening cardio kickboxing class. Most of the ladies go for drinks or whatnot afterward, but I come home for some self-care. I take an extra-long shower, then turn on *Forensic Files* and do my nails." Not exactly the most exciting way to spend her Saturday nights, but it was the only time she took for herself each week.

"But it's Saturday night now," Cade said, confusion scrunching his forehead.

"Yup," she said, popping the *P*.

Dylan let out a dramatic sigh. "When Mom misses her Saturday night routine, she crams it all into Sunday morning before work."

Poppy nodded and smiled. "Hence, I have zero plans to join you boys at that MMA class tomorrow. Besides"—she waved her now-chipped-nail-polished fingers at all the males in the room—"fixing these scraggly things takes precedence over throwing my body on the ground and grappling."

Carter and Dylan sighed in defeat and returned to inhaling their food.

Cade snorted at the boys' easy surrender. "I'm not trying to change your mind or anything, but you should know the MMA class isn't just grappling. There's also a lot of striking, which I know for a fact you're a fan of." Poppy arched an eyebrow, and he chuckled. "The last time I taught the cardio kickboxing class, I held the bag for you. And, babe, you walloped the shit out of that thing."

Excellent. She remembered that particular class a few weeks ago. Right before it, she'd walked in on Eli fucking some random woman. Their marriage had been over at that point—divorce papers had been filed and he'd shown his true colors to everyone—but why Eli had chosen to bring his "client" to the house was beyond her. Especially since he'd already been living at his family's damn vacation home. Of course, he was just an asshole like that. In any case, she'd taken out her frustration on the heavy bag, turning herself into a sweaty, huffing-and-puffing mess.

"That was simply stress relief. I don't actually want to punch anyone in the face."

Cade's eyebrow arched. "You sure about that?"

The corners of her lips twitched. The man had a point. After taking a bite of salad, she put on her best prim-and-proper expression. "Well, if push came to shove and I had to defend myself or the boys, I suppose I'd be okay punching someone."

"I'd pay good money to see you clock Eli," Dylan muttered.

"Yeah," Carter chimed in. "Go for the nose or throat, Mom. Usually I'd say go for the nuts, but you'd probably have a hard time finding those on that guy."

Poppy choked on her food, and for a moment, she could only blink.

Carter smiled at her sweetly, the picture of innocence. "What? Too soon?"

She burst into laughter, followed by Four and Cade.

Over the next half hour, the guys demolished the pizza. Another twenty minutes later, the mess they'd created was in the garbage bag by the door, the counters were wiped down, and her stomach ached from so much laughing.

"Well, we should get going." Poppy scanned the vacant house, and an air of melancholy surrounded her. They'd had some amazing times here. However, there had been some horrid and painful memories as well. More than she'd like to admit. So many tumultuous thoughts swirled in her brain, but she shoved them down. She had an audience. She would sort through her mixed feelings later. When she was alone. For now, she'd cling to the emotion that was inching its way to the surface: determination. To do better. To be better. For her boys. For herself . . .

Finally, for herself.

You've got this, dammit.

Clearing her throat, she turned to Four. "Are you sure you're okay having the boys stay with you?"

He rolled his eyes. "Don't be dumb, Poppy. There's no way in hell the three of you are fitting into that apartment."

Carter scoffed. "Unless one of us sleeps on top of the dining table."

"Yeah, hard pass." Dylan glanced at her, concern in his eyes. "You sure you're good, Mom?"

She reached out and pulled him close for a hug. He melted into her, and she squeezed him tight. "I'll be fine, honey."

As she locked the front door, everyone shuffled down the front steps. Following them, she refused to look back. What had made the house so special were the boys. And those boys were moving forward with her.

With her purse and tote over one shoulder, she walked to her Outback and waved at the boys as they headed toward Four's truck. "Text me in the morning when you're ready to get breakfast at Ray's."

"Will do. Love you, Mom!"

"Yeah. Love you, Mom!"

Her heart swelled.

"Here, let me get that for you," Cade said, opening her door.

"Thanks." She settled into the driver's seat and tried to ignore the hint of soap and woodsy aftershave tickling her nose. She left the door open while she placed her things on the front passenger seat. "Thank you for helping today, Cade. Seriously. I'm not quite sure how Four roped you into it, but I really appreciate it."

"Not a problem, Poppy." He watched Four's truck make its way down the drive. "You've got a couple of really great kids there."

Pride bloomed in her chest. "They're pretty special."

He caught her gaze and smiled. "So are you, you know." Before she could respond—hell, she wasn't even sure she *could* respond—he closed her door and patted the roof of her car. "I'll follow you out."

CHAPTER SEVEN

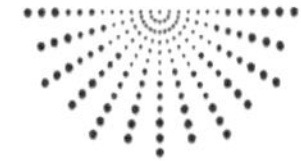

Cade wasn't quite sure what the hell he was doing following Poppy home. Yes, it was late and dark, but this was Hudson Island. Crime, for the most part, wasn't a big thing here. Still. She was a single woman out at night by herself. The least he could do was make sure she made it to her new place safe. What if she had car trouble or something?

Yeaaah, he knew his entire train of thought was mostly bullshit.

Truth was, Poppy intrigued him. She always had. Ever since he'd moved to the island a couple of years ago, he'd noticed her. She was a successful businesswoman with a solid reputation around town. And yet, despite having numerous friends in common, they'd never really spent any time together.

Granted, up until earlier this week, she'd been married to a man Cade had purposely steered clear of. Including the recent encounter at Poppy's boutique, he had only interacted with Eli Walker a handful of times. But that's all Cade needed. He knew people, and that guy? A complete dick.

Plain and simple. How Poppy had been married to that asswipe absolutely boggled his mind.

He followed Poppy's car to Hudson's quaint downtown and let out a content sigh. Spending the day with Four, Carter, and Dylan, and then the past couple hours with her had been nice. And eye-opening. He'd seen Poppy in an entirely new light. As fellow business owners, they went to many of the same functions. She was always reserved at those events, more of an observer than a partaker. But watching her interact with her sons and Four, he'd witnessed a side of her he'd never known existed. Hell, he was pretty sure most people on Hudson didn't know about it, either.

She was funny, sarcastic, and so damn cute. Quiet but surprisingly assertive. On more than one occasion tonight, she'd had her boys and Four backpedaling with one damn look. Impressive.

He could tell her confidence was a little shaky, which, again, boggled his mind. The woman was so damn beautiful. He'd seen her at her store, all dolled up and flawless, plenty of times. But seeing her without makeup? With her hair piled atop her head and dressed in an oversized sweatshirt and leggings? Absolutely fucking stunning.

He'd flirted with her because . . . well, how could he not? It was obvious to him that she hadn't known what to do with the attention. She'd deflected like a master. But that had just made him want to compliment her more. She was such a change from most of the women he interacted with. Well, the single women, anyway.

Cade wasn't an idiot. He knew what he looked like, knew how many women found him attractive. Problem was, the ones who approached him were usually looking for a good time or had dollar signs in their eyes. While there was absolutely nothing wrong with a consensual, no-strings affair, he wasn't interested in that.

God knew that hadn't always been the case. There'd been a period where *casual* and *no strings* had been his two main requirements for getting together with someone. Hell, they'd been the *only* requirements, really. But that was years ago, before everything had blown up in his face. Now, he liked to think he was more discerning.

He frowned. Not that he was looking for a relationship or anything. No. Not at all.

It's just that Poppy was so damn refreshing. When she spoke to him today, it wasn't about rehashing his glory days at the top of the MMA world. It wasn't about what celebrities and athletes he'd met. It wasn't even about how much money filled his bank accounts. It had been about everyday things, like how Dante and his family were doing and how much he loved being an uncle. About how the new assistant chef at Four's was going to make them all gain twenty pounds. About whether he liked the contractor who'd done the work for the gym.

Talking to her was . . . nice. Which was why, at nearly nine p.m.—the time Hudson Island shut down each night, even on Saturdays—he didn't want the day to be over. He'd been scheduled to teach jiu-jitsu today, but when he saw how much stuff needed to be moved, he'd called the gym and swapped with another coach for the MMA session tomorrow. He was looking forward to having the boys in class. He hadn't been lying to Poppy earlier. They were good kids. They reminded Cade of him and Dante at that age. While he was a few years younger than his brother, they'd always been close.

Speaking of brothers, he hadn't missed the warning look Four had shot him this evening. He knew his friend and Poppy weren't blood related, but considering how close they were, they might as well be. Maybe he could get Four to come to the MMA class tomorrow, too. Then he could school his buddy in front of the boys.

Chuckling to himself, Cade parked his Range Rover behind Poppy's Subaru and cut the engine. Getting out, he pocketed his keys and made his way toward her.

"When you said you'd follow me, I didn't realize you meant all the way here." Slinging her purse and tote over her shoulder, she opened her car's back door and grabbed a small box.

"I wanted to make sure you made it to your new place okay. I know Four's house is in the opposite direction." He grabbed a large box from the car, then took the small box out of her hands and placed it on the one he was already carrying, shooting her a wink. "Besides, those three would have my hide if anything happened to you."

"Well, thanks. That's really sweet of you." Her perplexed expression had him stilling. Was something as simple as making sure she got home in one piece a foreign concept to her? By the way she was staring at him, like she couldn't quite figure him out, he knew the answer. Damn. Eli was truly a piece of shit.

Cade cleared his throat and gestured to the doorway he'd lumbered through countless times today. "After you."

Tailing her into the tiny apartment, he placed the boxes on the dining table, then stepped back into the open doorway. He didn't want to crowd her. The place, stuffed with all the massive furniture, was beyond cramped.

"Thanks again, Cade," she said, dropping her bags on the couch. "It's been a long day, and it would have been so much longer without you. I really appreciate it."

"Not a problem, Poppy. I'll get out of your hair." But he didn't turn to go. For some reason, he was stuck in place. He shifted on his feet, shoving his hands into his jeans pockets.

And then he surprised himself by saying, "You know, we should get dinner sometime."

Poppy's jaw dropped open, and she gaped at him.

Holy shit, De la Rosa! For someone who's not looking for a relationship, that was kinda the fucking opposite.

Oh, shut the hell up!

Cade suppressed a cringe. Damn. A two-way conversation with himself? He'd gone nuts.

"Yeah?" A soft pink flush colored her cheeks.

Damn, she was pretty. Any doubts he'd had about asking her out vanished.

"Yeah," he said, smiling. "My schedule's kind of crazy—the weekends, especially—but maybe sometime during the week?"

She nodded, and her flush deepened. "Yeah."

Again, that one word had his smile growing. "Don't get me wrong, I'm a fan of *Forensic Files*, but I've been watching *Cold Case Files* lately, so we should definitely compare notes. See who knows more. Can I get your number?"

She smiled, and had they been outside, it would've damn near lit up the evening sky. He knew how sappy that sounded, but when Poppy reached for her phone, he didn't give a fuck.

Retrieving her phone from her pocket, she asked, "What's your number? I'll text you so you can have mine."

He rattled it off, and seconds later, his phone dinged.

"Perfect." He was pretty sure he was grinning like a loon, but again, he didn't give a fuck. Poppy Walker had just given him her number. He wanted to pump his fist in the air. "I'll give you a call. You know, so we can figure out which show is superior."

"Of course." Her eyes sparkled with humor. "Though we both know *Forensic Files* is the winner."

"Oooh . . ." He reached up and grabbed the top of the

doorframe with both hands, leaning into the room. "Those are some bold words. We may need to have a *few* dinners for you to convince me of that one."

"Whatever it takes, I suppose," she said with a shrug.

"For as long as it takes, then," he said. Her playful smile had him desperately wanting to stay longer. To banter with her more and see where it led. Instead, he reined in the urge and tapped the doorframe. Next time. Because there sure as hell would be a next time with this woman. "Have a good night, Poppy. Lock up behind me."

CHAPTER EIGHT

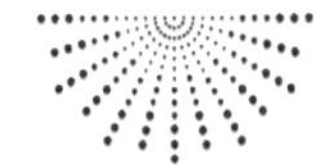

Throwing his arm over his face, Cade prayed the obnoxious buzzing would stop. On his next heartbeat, his eyes flew open. Holy shit, his phone. He shot up in bed and spotted it rattling on the nightstand. His brother's name lit up the display, illuminating the dark room.

Snatching up the phone, he caught sight of the time. His stomach dropped. It was just after six in the morning on a Tuesday. Dante never called this early.

"What's wrong?" he answered, scrambling out of bed and pulling on a pair of sweatpants.

"I need you at the gym."

He paused as he reached for a T-shirt. "Where are you?"

"Seattle. Can you come?"

His brother's brisk tone had the hairs on his arms rising. "Talk to me, D. What's going on?"

"I don't know, man. The fucking ceiling caved in."

"What?" There was no way in hell he'd heard that right. He waited for Dante to explain, but no words came. He pulled the phone away from his ear to make sure the call was still connected. It was. "Dante, what the fuck are you talking about?"

His brother blew out a breath. "Fuck, man. The five o'clock jits class was underway. One minute we're all rolling on the mats, and the next . . . the fucking ceiling collapsed."

"Holy shit," Cade murmured. He yanked on the T-shirt and stuffed his feet into a pair of running shoes. "Is everyone okay?"

Again, Dante went silent for so long, Cade pulled the phone from his ear to check if the call had dropped. When he saw they were still connected, ice skated down his spine.

Then Dante said, "I'm at the hospital."

Cade froze halfway to the front door. "Are you hurt?"

"Not me." Dante's voice was barely above a whisper. "Alexi and Pedro. They took the brunt of the damage. Others have minor injuries, but those two . . . Holy fuck. They're in surgery. The EMTs were talking about some spinal shit. I don't know . . ."

He grabbed his keys and locked the door behind him. "You said the ceiling caved in? The part over the mats?"

His brother grunted. Thankfully, Cade was fluent in Dante-speak, so he knew the sound was an affirmative.

"How the hell is that possible?" he asked, getting into his Range Rover. "That entire stretch was completely redone a couple months ago."

Over the holidays, a massive water leak had flooded the Seattle gym. The entire ceiling, pipes and all, had since been replaced. The company who'd repaired the damage was solid, and the repair work had passed all required city inspections. So what his brother was saying made zero sense.

"I don't know. All I know is we have two fighters who are in surgery. I need you in Seattle to work with Jackie on the insurance shit and to talk to the fire department and whoever else we need to fucking deal with. Jackie's at the gym now, and I'll meet up with you later. I'm going to stick around here and wait for the guys' families to arrive. I'll stay until they're both out of surgery so I can see how they're doing."

"Of course," Cade said, turning left toward Hudson's downtown. The group at the Seattle gym was a tight-knit group. While they had fighters come and go, that five a.m. class was a crew of regulars. "I'm on my way to the dock right now. Depending on the sailing schedule, I should be at the gym around nine, maybe a little later with traffic. Jackie and I will take care of the logistics. You take care of Alexi's and Pedro's families."

After saying goodbye, he hung up and pulled into the ferry line. His mind whirled as he waited. For the life of him, he couldn't picture how the gym's ceiling had not only caved in, but inflicted so much damage on the way down. The gym's ceiling tiles were just that—tiles. Standard, cheap-ass gypsum boards that should have left some bruises and some scratches at most. *Not* damage that required surgery.

Unease turned his stomach. What the hell was going on?

An hour and a half later, Cade tapped his steering wheel with impatient fingers. He loved the slower pace of island life, but it was times like now when he wished for the hustle of Seattle. Sure, there was a shit-ton of traffic in the city, but this? Catching the ferry from Hudson Island to neighboring Whidbey Island, then driving twenty-five miles through Whidbey to catch yet another ferry to take him to the mainland? It sucked. Especially when he still needed to drive another twenty-five miles down to Seattle after reaching said mainland. Meaning he had at least one more hour to go because, of course, it was rush hour.

The cars in front of him took their sweet-ass time disembarking, and Cade gritted his teeth while he waited. When it was finally his turn, the tension in his shoulders relaxed a bit. He got off the ferry and turned onto Mukilteo Speedway, pressing the gas. The faster he got to the gym, the sooner they would figure out what the hell was going on.

Brake lights flashed, and he growled as traffic ground to a halt. Ahead, he saw a car pulled partially off the road, its tail blocking traffic and its hazard lights blinking.

Motherfucking shit.

He inched forward with the line of cars, scanning the area for a drive-through coffee stand. It was much too early for all this shit. He had to get some coffee in his system if he wanted to survive the morning.

Nearing the broken-down Subaru, he saw steam rising from beneath the popped hood. He glanced over at the poor schmuck. Then did a double take.

Holy shit. No way in hell that's—

He swung his car to the side of the road, then cut the engine and hopped out. He glanced at his watch and knew he'd be even later to the gym than anticipated, but there was no way in hell he'd leave her on the side of the road.

Dressed in a long-sleeved black T-shirt, fitted jeans, and pink Chucks, the woman was petite. Slim. With her back to him, she could have been anyone. But he'd caught a glimpse of her face as he'd driven by, and it was one he'd recognize anywhere. After all, it was the face that had been stuck in his mind since Saturday night.

"Poppy?" he called out.

CHAPTER NINE

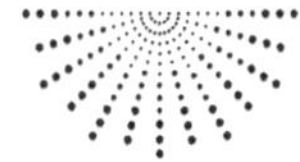

At the sound of her name, Poppy's heart jumped. She bit back a yelp as she spun from the open hood with her hand over her heart. Relief surged through her at the familiar face, though it did nothing to calm her racing pulse.

"Cade! Oh, thank god."

"Fancy meeting you here," he said, stopping beside her. "What seems to be the problem?"

Good. Freaking. God. It should be illegal to look as good as he did before eight in the morning. The casual sweatpants, T-shirt, sneakers, and jacket only enhanced his appeal. As for her? Yikes.

She'd started out looking human this morning. After her usual makeup routine, she'd even curled her hair. However, while spending the last twenty or so minutes dealing with whatever the hell was happening to her car, she'd devolved into something resembling a troll. Her makeup was smudged, and all her hard-earned curls were now piled atop her head in a messy bun.

Poppy waved at her smoking engine and sighed. Partially for her car, partially for looking like a hot mess around this man. Again. "No clue. I figured I needed to pop the hood because of the smoke, but I don't know what I'm looking at."

"Not a gearhead?" he asked, humor in his voice.

Peering up at him, she saw his lips were tipped in that half smirk he did so well. She shivered, and it had nothing to do with the frigid temperature. The man was ridiculously attractive. "To say I'm mechanically deficient would be a gross understatement. I'm lucky I figured out how to pop the hood." No joke. Cars were not her thing. At all.

"Have you called a tow truck?" he asked, shrugging out of his jacket.

"Not yet—" Her jaw dropped when he placed his jacket over her shoulders.

"Can't have you freezing now, can we?" he said, giving her a soft smile.

Another shiver tore through her as she slipped her arms into the sleeves, which were warm from his body heat. This time, her trembling was mostly from the cold. Mostly. "Thank you, but aren't you going to freeze?"

He shot her a get-real look.

Smothering a smile, she cleared her throat. "I had AAA, but it was under Eli's name, and he canceled it. I was about to call around for a tow when you pulled up."

Cade's jaw tensed, and he eyed her car. "Hop in. I can push you so you're off the road. Then you can make your calls from my car."

She hesitated at his expression. While she didn't know Cade all that well, she could tell he wasn't happy. "Um, are you sure?"

He tilted his head, and that half smirk returned to his lips. "So long as you don't hit the brakes, I'm one hundred percent certain I can get you and your car fully off the road."

Heat tore over her face. "Oh! Not that. I know you're plenty strong. I mean, you're practically all muscle and—"

She slammed her mouth shut. *Holy. Crap. Stop talking!*

There was no doubt the man could push her car, brakes or not, but she didn't need to go fawning all over the guy. Clearing her throat, she tried again. "What I meant is"—she waved at the traffic moving slowly by—"I'm sure you have somewhere else you need to be. I don't want to impose on your schedule."

Her heart stopped when he laid his hands on her shoulders and turned her to fully face him.

"Poppy. There's no way in hell I'm leaving you out here."

"But—"

He gently squeezed her shoulders, and butterflies took flight in her stomach. *Gah! It's just your shoulders, for god's sake! Get a freaking grip!*

"My priority right now is getting you out of harm's way. You can make whatever calls you need from my car, where it's actually warm—"

"Oh my god, you're cold!" She moved to take his jacket off, but his hands squeezed again, stilling her.

"Poppy, babe. I'm fine. You can figure out the towing situation, and then I can take you wherever it is you need to go, or you can hang with me. Bottom line? I'm not leaving you out here. The rest is just logistics."

Logistics. Easy for him to say. She'd gone from having an easy Tuesday morning to a mild panic attack while stranded on the side of the road. And now she was wearing the jacket of a man who tied her tongue in knots as he came to her rescue. All in the span of a couple hours. Plus, said gorgeous man had just called her babe again. Maybe that's what he called all women, but holy crap, even if he did, it was still . . . She didn't even know what. All she knew was it did something to her insides. Something she couldn't think about right now.

Poppy took a steadying breath in and—wrong move.

Cade's woodsy scent filled her nose. She fought a sigh. The man completely overwhelmed her senses. She couldn't remember the last time she had found anyone this attractive. Sure, she'd always thought Cade de la Rosa was shockingly handsome, but what had her tripping over her words now was the realization that he was honestly a nice guy. She hadn't expected that.

Yes, she recognized that someone's appearance didn't determine whether they were a kind person or not. She knew plenty of beautiful people who were wonderful. Just like she knew plenty who were complete dicks. However, the two men she'd been with—both of whom society deemed good-looking—had treated her horribly. Not at first, of course, but over time, their true colors had shown. And she'd been the one left looking like an idiot.

"Is that okay?" Cade asked, pulling her from her musings.

She shook her head. *Focus, woman!* "Sorry. My brain isn't firing on all cylinders right now."

"Understandable, Pop."

His use of her nickname had warmth flooding her face. Thankfully, before she could spew any more tongue-tied nonsense, he removed his hands from her shoulders, and led her toward her driver's door.

"Put it in Neutral. I'll push, and you can steer this bad boy to that spot over there." He pointed at an opening on the motorway's shoulder about twenty yards ahead. "That way it's completely off the road but still easy for a tow truck to get to."

"Okay," she said, ducking inside the Outback.

Cade shut the hood and went to the back of her car. When he called out, "Ready!" she shifted to Neutral and aimed for the clearing he'd indicated. Once she reached it, she put her car in Park and opened the door. Cade was already there, holding out a hand to assist her. Because of course he was.

Part of her wanted to balk. She was more than capable of taking care of herself. But another part . . . Well, it was a relief to have someone helping. Not only with her car issues, but with the little things, too. Call her wishful or wistful, but she found his compassion comforting. It had been a long time since she'd been able to lean on anyone.

"Thanks." She took his offered hand and climbed from the car, then collected the tote, purse, and backpack from the rear seat.

"Taking classes?" Cade asked, grabbing the backpack and slinging it over one shoulder as they walked toward his Range Rover.

She laughed. "No, this is Carter's. As book smart as that boy is, he's extremely forgetful. He left it at Four's and didn't realize until he got back to his dorm last night. And, of course, it has his laptop *and* his wallet in it. I got a frantic text right as I was falling asleep. Naturally, he has a test this afternoon and needs it ASAP."

"Of course," Cade said with a chuckle. He opened the front passenger door for her, and she bit back a smile. The small gesture was sweet, something no one had ever done for her. "So, being the wonderful mom you are, you hopped on the first ferry to deliver it."

"Yeah. But I think 'wonderful mom' transformed into grumpy mom when all the lights on my dash started flashing. The kid owes me big-time for this."

"No doubt." He shut her door, then went to the driver's side and settled in behind the wheel.

"Thanks again, Cade. Really." She eyed the time on the car's display. "His class isn't until one, so there's still plenty of time. If you drop me off in the U District, I can get him his stuff and then Uber back to Hudson."

He merged onto the road. "Do you have to be anywhere today?"

"No, not really. My ladies are covering the shop for me." After Carter's frantic texts last night, she'd placed her own frantic calls to her employees. Thankfully, they'd been available to cover for her.

They took the ramp onto I-5 South, and Poppy winced at the sea of brake lights. She'd forgotten how awful morning traffic was here.

"Yikes, I may have spoken too soon about there being plenty of time before his class started."

Cade chuckled and deftly maneuvered them into the HOV lane. "How about this? I have some stuff to take care of at our Seattle gym, but I can swing you by the boys' place now to drop off Carter's stuff. Then we can grab some coffee and maybe a quick breakfast in the U District, because I don't know about you, but I'm dragging right now."

She grinned at the dramatic face Cade made. Damn, the man really was adorable.

"Then after," Cade continued, "if you're up for it, you can come with me to the gym. We had a major building issue this morning, so while I deal with that, I'm sure we can find you a quiet spot to figure out the whole towing-your-car thing. And if you're okay waiting for me, we can head home to Hudson later today. Maybe grab dinner on the way. You can start making your case on why *Forensic Files* is the better show."

She snuck a peek at him. The grin on his face matched her own. "Only if you're sure. I'm serious, Cade. I don't want to impose on you."

"I'm serious as well, Poppy." He glanced over. "I wouldn't have offered if I didn't want to spend time with you."

She chewed on her bottom lip, not quite sure what to

make of that, and decided to take his words at face value. He wanted to be friends, and she was on board with that.

It might not be the smartest move. Her track record with men was abysmal. Not that she was jumping the gun by assuming Cade thought of her beyond friendship. But she wasn't going to lie to herself. She wanted to spend the day with this man. Get to know him better.

So what if she'd developed a teeny-tiny crush? She was an adult who could refrain from falling all over him. After all, as much as it sucked to admit, she knew Cade de la Rosa—a wildly successful, hot, ripped, and seriously kind guy—was way out of her league. Maybe if she reminded herself of that more often, her mind would stop going blank every time he looked at her.

"Okay. But you have to promise me that if I get in your way, you'll let me know. I have no problem taking an Uber back to Hudson." It was the truth. Even though the thought of how much that would cost, on top of what she knew was going to be a ridiculously steep tow charge and the cost of getting her car fixed, had her cringing inside.

"Deal. Now tell me about where the boys live. I'm a UW alum, you know, so new buildings and all, I'm pretty familiar with the area."

Cade maintained a steady stream of conversation as they made their way south toward Seattle's University District. With the way traffic was looking, they'd arrive just as Carter was heading to his first class, so it would be a quick drive-by drop-off.

Cade slowed as they wove through campus, staying alert for texting college kids oblivious to oncoming vehicles. He smiled as he approached the twins' dorm. McMahon Hall. The same dorm he'd lived in during his freshman year.

"Still looks like a concrete monstrosity." He chuckled. "Good times."

Poppy swung her gaze to his. "You lived here?"

"Yup," he said, popping the *P*. "Looked just as glorious and jail-like back then."

She laughed, and a pretty pink colored her cheeks. Before he could gawk, she pointed. "Oh, there he is."

Cade pulled up to the loading zone in front of Carter and cut the engine. He didn't miss the way the young man's eyes narrowed when he recognized his mom.

"Hey, honey," Poppy said, stepping out of the Range Rover.

Cade rounded the hood as Carter enveloped his mother in a hug. He tried not to wince at the look being thrown his way. "What's up, C?"

Carter's jaw clenched before his chin lifted. It was only when he released his mom did the young man look away.

"Your stuff's right here," Poppy said, retrieving the backpack from the car.

"Thanks, Mom," Carter replied, taking his things. "Sorry you had to come all this way."

"It's all right, honey. Just be careful with your stuff, okay?" She tugged him into another hug. "We'll let you get to class."

"I have some time." Carter's eyes hardened as he looked back at Cade. "What's going on, man?"

"Not much. Just giving your mom a lift."

"Oh really?" He crossed his arms over his chest.

Cade bit the inside of his cheek to keep from grinning. His respect for Poppy's eldest went up another notch. While the attitude was a bit over the top, he couldn't fault Carter for wanting to protect his mom.

"Ease up, C," he said. "It's not what you think."

"And what exactly am I thinking?" The snap in the young man's tone had Cade's eyebrow arching.

Yeaaah, he really could do without the attitude.

"Carter!" Poppy admonished.

"No worries, Pop," he said. Meeting Carter's suspicious glare, he added, "Your mom's car broke down on her way here, and I happened to be driving by. That's why she's with me this morning."

The tension in Carter's lanky frame eased. He held Cade's gaze for another moment before nodding and facing his mom. "Are you okay? You didn't get hurt, did you?"

"No, honey," she said, running her hand over his arm. "I'm fine. The engine started steaming, and the gauges went crazy. It was a little nerve-racking, but that's all." She gestured in Cade's direction. "I was lucky he stopped."

"Do you need to use our car? D has to work tonight, but I'm sure he can just bus it or something."

"That's a sweet offer, but no. I'll be fine. I'm catching a ride back with Cade this evening."

"But how are you going to get to work?"

"I live above the boutique now, remember? I have an easy commute."

"Sorry, I spaced for a second there." Shaking his head, Carter hugged his mom one more time. "Thanks again for bringing my things."

"Of course. Love you, honey."

Carter opened the front passenger door for his mom. When she was safely tucked inside, his gaze locked with Cade's. "Can I talk to you for a second?"

"Sure." Cade followed Carter a few yards down the sidewalk. He assumed the kid wanted to be out of earshot of his mom. "What's up?"

Keeping his back to the Range Rover, Carter stuffed his hands in his pockets. "I jumped to conclusions back there."

Cade nodded. He could tell the guy was working up to something, so he remained quiet.

"I'm sorry if I was a dick."

"Nothing to apologize for, C. She's your mom. I get it."

Carter's hazel eyes swung to his. "Do you?"

"If my mom showed up with some dude driving her?" He chuckled. "Yeah, I'd have flipped my shit, too. So you're good, man."

"It was just a surprise, you know? Caught me off guard."

"I'll bet. Seeing your mom this morning caught me off guard, too." Cade glanced toward the car and smiled at the worry on Poppy's face. *God, she's cute.* The thought gave him pause. Damn. He needed to give the kid a heads-up. "Look, C. You want full transparency?"

"Of course," Carter said, eyes narrowing.

"I asked your mom out the other day, and she agreed. She and I have a lot of friends in common, but we haven't spent much time together. I'd like to change that. At this point, we're literally just getting to know each other better. We'll see where things go from there."

Carter nodded. "Thanks for being straight with me. I mean, I saw the way you were looking at her when we had pizza the other night."

Cade's eyes widened. For a few heartbeats he could only stare at the kid. Then he sighed. "Fuuuck."

The corners of Carter's lips twitched. "Your poker face kinda sucks, by the way. I swear, Uncle Four was about two seconds away from clobbering you. But you've got that whole former-MMA-world-champion thing going for you."

Shaking his head, Cade grinned. "Well, thank fuck for that, huh?"

"For sure. Or else my money would've been on Uncle Four." Carter motioned toward the Range Rover. "But seriously? Thanks for stopping when you saw my mom. I know you didn't have to and—"

"The fuck, kid? Of course I had to stop."

"No, old man, you didn't." Carter chuckled, but there was no humor. "Eli would've driven right on by and told her to deal with it herself."

"You're exaggerating, right?"

Carter scoffed. "Nope. True fucking story. Happened a few years ago."

"That motherfucker," Cade growled, gritting his teeth.

"Yep." Carter started heading for the car, and Cade fell into step beside the young man. "Do me a favor, Cade?"

"Name it."

"Don't tell my mom about this conversation. She gets all, 'Who's the one who's supposed to worry here?'" Carter rolled his eyes, but the smile on his face showed his love and concern for his mom.

Cade gave Carter a chin lift as he reached for his door handle. "You got it, kid."

"Later, old man," Carter called out with a two-finger salute. Then he waved at his mom. "Bye, Mom! Love you!"

Cade laughed as he shut his door. *Fuckin' A, this kid.*

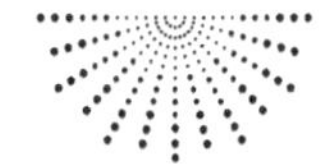

CHAPTER TEN

After leaving Carter outside his dorm, they swung into a local coffee shop on The Ave. Cade had received a call from the Seattle gym's office manager, so their quick breakfast turned into even quicker to-go coffees and pastries.

As Cade pulled back into traffic, Poppy took a sip of her vanilla latte and shook her head. "You're really not going to tell me what Carter said to you?"

"No, ma'am," Cade said.

She waited for him to say more, but he remained silent. The stubborn man had been deflecting since they'd left Carter. If she weren't so curious, she'd be impressed by Cade's resolve and insistence on keeping their conversation private.

Frowning, she said, "Well, at least tell me if there's anything I should be worried about."

"That?" He pointed at her face with his small bag of banana bread. "That's exactly what Carter didn't want."

Her frown deepened. "What?"

"For you to worry."

She picked at the cardboard sleeve on her coffee cup. "Yeah, but he was acting . . . off. I mean, he was downright rude to you, and that's not like him. Truly. He can be a little shit sometimes, but he usually reserves that for me or Eli. Should I be worried?"

"Poppy, babe. Cut the kid some slack. Yeah, his attitude was shit, but I can't fault him. Not really."

"Uh-uh. There's no excuse for him to be rude."

Cade heaved out a sigh, as if his resolve had finally cracked. He looked at her. "Kid's smart, right? So he knows that for you to get here when you did, you had to leave Hudson at the ass crack of dawn, right?"

She had no idea where he was going with this. "And?"

The corners of Cade's lips kicked up. "And when you showed up, you were with me. In my car. In my jacket. With the deduction being *we* left Hudson at the ass crack of dawn. Together. So naturally, he'd think . . ." He wagged his eyebrows.

Holy. Crap. There was no way Carter would think that. No. Way.

"Kid's eighteen, Pop. Of course he'd think that. And of course he'd be pissed."

Heat tore over her face. She didn't even care that she had just said her thoughts out loud. She quickly placed her latte in the cup holder and slapped her hands over her face. Bending at the waist, she hunched over and groaned. A moment later, when she'd composed herself, she sat up and eyed Cade. His mouth was split in a wide grin.

"Oh my *god*," she said. "This isn't funny."

"Oh, it kinda is."

She huffed out a breath and grabbed her drink. Taking a sip, she shook her head. "Why would he be pissed? He likes you."

"Yeah, as Four's friend. As a fighter and MMA coach. As

an acquaintance of his mom. But as the dude his mom's sleeping with?" His grimace was overexaggerated. "Probably not so much."

Her face burned as she swatted his shoulder. "I take it you set him straight?"

"Sure did."

Again, that smirk played on his lips. And again, she didn't know what to make of it. "Good . . . I think."

"Smart woman," he said with a soft laugh.

Driving with one hand, Cade used his other to pull the slice of banana bread from the bag on his lap. It was on the tip of her tongue to ask if he needed help, but the bag was . . . on his lap. Clarification: on his sweatpants-covered lap. Light-gray sweatpants that were loose and yet . . . not. So she held her tongue. Because yeah, that would be awkward.

Oblivious to her thoughts, he took a bite of his banana bread. His nose wrinkled as he chewed.

"What? Is it bad?"

He shook his head and took another bite. "It's okay."

Poppy reached for a napkin, but by the time she offered it to him, he'd already polished off the bread. Her eyes widened. "It's just 'okay'? Uh, you ate it in three bites."

He grinned as he switched lanes. "It was edible. Roxie's banana bread is a million times better, though."

She flinched, and her stomach dropped. Peeking over at Cade, she sent a silent prayer of thanks to the universe that he was concentrating on the road ahead of him.

After years of Eli comparing her to Roxie's perfection—of course, Poppy had always fallen short—flinching at the other woman's name had become an awful Pavlovian habit. One she needed to work on breaking, because none of it had been Roxie's fault. Hell, she was downright certain Eli and his wandering eye hadn't even been a blip on Roxie's radar. And yet she couldn't shake the lingering pain of never measuring up.

Maybe one day she would befriend Roxie. Yes, they were friendly when they encountered each other, but she gave the other woman a wide, wide berth.

From what all their mutual friends and shared customers said, Roxie was an all-around good person. But Poppy clearly had inner demons to battle before she could consider approaching her. Especially since she'd nearly ruined everything for Roxie a couple of months ago.

Right before the holidays, Poppy had recommended her younger cousin, Sheila, go for a job opening at Comfort Food. Like an idiot, she'd even personally vouched for Sheila. Her referral had set off an awful chain of events—for Roxie, for Poppy, and for the town. Her involvement had been inadvertent, of course, but still, she held some responsibility.

"We're here," Cade said. "You okay?"

Self-disgust soured her stomach, but she pasted on a smile and shoved her maudlin thoughts down. "Yeah, sorry. Zoning out." She held up her to-go cup. "Coffee hasn't kicked in yet. Is the gym—"

"It's around the corner. Parking's a bitch, so you gotta grab the first spot you see. Hang tight, and I'll get your door for you."

Before she could respond, he was rounding the hood. When he opened her door, she handed him her coffee so she could climb out.

"Thanks," she said, pulling her purse across her body. He returned her cup, and she gestured with it. "Lead the way."

"Now don't be surprised by what it looks like. You have to remember that this place was our first location, and it's strictly a fight gym. It's a lot smaller than our facility over on Hudson, and it's a lot older. Nothing fancy. At all."

Her eyebrows lifted at his rush of words. Studying him,

she noticed a slight flush tinging his cheeks. She was pretty sure it had nothing to do with the cool temperature. Grabbing his arm, she gave it a reassuring squeeze. "Cade, take a breath. I'm sure the place is great."

He paused mid-step and took her advice. "Sorry. I don't know why I'm so nervous. Dante called this morning and said there was some major ceiling damage, but I don't know . . . or understand the extent." He ran his free hand through his hair. "I guess I don't want you to think we run a hovel or anything."

She barked out a laugh and gave his arm another little squeeze. "Uh, I've seen the Hudson gym, remember? I know you guys aren't gym slumlords. It'll be fine, Cade."

He watched her for a moment, and she fought to not squirm. Then he let out a breath, looped her arm through the crook of his elbow, and started back down the street. "Well, I appreciate the positive thoughts, but just in case—"

Cade pulled them to an abrupt halt as they turned the corner. Worry shot up her spine when he paled.

"Holy shit," he whispered.

Following his gaze, she gasped, and her jaw dropped. The sign above the entrance to De La Rosa Gym was a simple blue-and-white design. On its own, it wouldn't have caught her attention. But the entrance was draped in yellow crime scene tape and surrounded by cracked windows.

"Oh my god, Cade. What happened?"

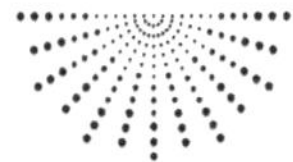

CHAPTER ELEVEN

Holy fuck. Cade couldn't believe what he was seeing. Yes, Dante had said the ceiling had caved in. And with Alexi and Pedro getting seriously hurt, Cade knew there must have been some major damage. So he shouldn't have been shocked at seeing two police cruisers and a fire truck out front. It shouldn't have been jarring to see the gym's front windows fractured like fucked-up spiderwebs. But it was. And then some.

"When you said you had building issues, I didn't know it was this bad," Poppy said.

He shook his head. "I didn't know, either."

Shock numbed him. It was as if his brain couldn't quite comprehend what his eyes were seeing. None of it registered . . . except for the small woman next to him, who wrapped her arms around his waist and hugged him tight. Her warmth, her empathy, her strength—they grounded him, and he let out the breath he hadn't realized he'd been holding.

Returning Poppy's embrace, he surveyed the scene again. The windows and glass front door were cracked and fogged with what he assumed was drywall and building dust. Holy hell. If it looked this bad from the outside, he couldn't imagine the state of the inside.

"Come on. Let's figure out what's going on." Cade stepped away, then took Poppy's hand as they hurried over to the gym. It wasn't the time nor the place, but he couldn't help himself from noticing how perfectly her hand fit in his, how naturally their fingers laced together.

They approached the Seattle PD officer standing guard at the front door.

"Holy shit," the officer said. "You're Cade de la Rosa! It's great to meet you!" He winced. "Sorry. Shitty circumstances. I'm sorry about your gym."

"Thank you." Cade nodded at the officer, trying to ignore the dread turning his gut. It must be *really* bad inside if the door needed watching. He glanced at the officer's name tag. "Is it safe to go in, Officer Litman?"

"Yes. However, the fire department roped off the area by the mats. Make sure you two stay to the right side."

"Thanks." He squeezed Poppy's hand. "Do you want to wait out here or—"

"I'll stay with you."

Her grip tightened, and a tiny bit of tension released from Cade's shoulders. He ducked under the crime scene tape, holding it up for her. Once inside, a rock lodged in his throat. He fought to swallow past it as he took in the giant chunks of cement and metal covering the mat, the water dripping down over the rubble.

He glanced up at the ceiling, and his lungs seized, as if he'd just taken a roundhouse kick right to the ribs. Because this was no mere ceiling collapse. No. He was looking at the fucking sky. An entire section of the building—ceiling, pipes, roof, and all—was gone. Like a bomb had detonated in the rafters. How was that possible?

"Cade!"

He spun around at the sound of his name.

Jackie Aria. Former Golden Gloves champ, stellar boxing coach, gym staple, and most importantly, Dante's right-hand woman. The gym manager was tall and lean and dressed in her customary leggings and De La Rosa Gym rash guard, with her long black hair pulled into a high ponytail.

"Oh thank god you're here," Jackie said when she reached them. Her eyes shimmered with tears, and she swallowed hard before waving at the pile of debris on the mat. "The majority of this fell after the EMTs took Alexi and Pedro out."

Cade's chest ached at his friend's distress. Letting go of Poppy's hand, he pulled Jackie into a hug.

"Holy shit, Cade," Jackie said, voice trembling. She sucked in a sharp breath. "If all of that fell on the guys when they were rolling, they'd have . . . died."

"But it didn't, Jackie. It didn't." He released her halfway, keeping an arm over her shoulders as his brow furrowed. He'd known this woman for a long time, but he had gotten to know her even better while they'd dealt with the water damage over the holidays. So he remembered she was particularly close with Alexi. "Any update on the guys?"

She shook her head. "Last I heard, they were both still in surgery. Alexi . . ." Her chin wobbled, and panic sizzled through every one of his nerves.

Swinging his gaze to Poppy, Cade nearly barked out a prayer of thanks as she took hold of Jackie's clenched fists.

"Let's go over there," Poppy said, nodding toward the beverage station on the opposite side of the room. "I'm sure we can find a clean cup. Maybe some tea will help? I know it won't take away what happened, but tea always helps calm me down." She linked arms with Jackie. "I'm Poppy, by the way."

Jackie let out a watery chuckle and smiled at the petite woman. "I'm Jackie. Thanks for stepping in front of that impending panic attack. I'm sure Cade will thank you for that as well. Because this guy?" She snorted and looked at him. "He doesn't do well with tears. Like, at all."

"Hey now," he said in a half-hearted attempt to defend himself.

Jackie's eyebrows rose. "Am I wrong?"

Poppy gave him a curious look as she began making tea.

His heart pinged. Her warmth, her empathy, her strength. All for a woman she didn't even know. God, Poppy was amazing.

"No, Jack. You're most definitely not wrong." He shrugged at Poppy. "Tears are like my kryptonite. I don't care if they're adult tears or little-kid tears. Either induces absolute panic."

"Well then," Poppy said with a smirk, bobbing a tea bag in a mug, "it's good to know you aren't perfect, after all."

He laughed. "I'm far from perfect, babe. Trust me on that."

"He's absolutely right," Jackie chimed in.

"Wait, what?" He aimed a playful glare at his friend. "You're on my side, remember?"

Jackie's eyes ping-ponged between him and Poppy before they rolled. Hard. "Oh, sorry." She dramatically cleared her throat. "Good ole Cade here is *amazing*! He's perfect. And yes, Poppy, even his aversion to tears is perfect and—"

"Okay, okay, brat," Cade groaned, knocking his shoulder into her. Of course, she knocked him right back. Laughing, he took Poppy's free hand in his and squeezed. "Don't listen to her. She's one hundred percent smart-ass."

Poppy grinned and leaned into his side. The little gesture, that extra contact didn't go unnoticed, and when he locked eyes with her, something inside him clicked into place.

A phone rang, interrupting the moment.

"Sorry," Poppy mumbled, digging in her purse for her phone. A soft blush colored her cheeks.

Cade wanted to pound his chest. He'd done that; he'd caused that blush. Call him a caveman, but satisfaction was coursing through his veins. It felt damn good to know he wasn't alone in whatever this . . . attraction was.

"Sorry, I have to take this." With an apologetic smile, Poppy pointed at the door and put the phone to her ear. "Hi, honey. What's up?"

One of her boys. Cade's gaze followed her until she ducked under the crime scene tape and exited the gym. He turned back to the woman beside him, and just like that, concern resumed simmering in his gut.

"Are you really okay, Jackie?" He frowned. "What even happened? I only got the bare details from Dante."

"It was terrifying, Cade." She closed her eyes for a moment, took a deep breath in, and sighed. "Class was going like usual, and then there was a loud boom. Everyone froze. Then a chunk of the ceiling came down." She placed her now-empty mug on the beverage cart and hugged herself tight. "Dante got to the guys and made sure they didn't move. Thankfully, the ambulance arrived really fast. The guys got loaded up, and Dante took off after them.

"The rest of us were just standing there dazed, you know? Then, maybe five minutes after the EMTs left, there was a loud, creepy-ass noise, like the building was groaning. Then the rest of it collapsed. Thankfully, most of the firefighters and cops were still here. There were some minor injuries. Cuts and bruises. Nothing like Alexi and Pedro, thank god. The firefighters got everyone patched up." She released a loud exhale. "It was so fucking scary."

Again, his arms went around her. The woman was a rock, but even rocks had their limits. He couldn't imagine how traumatic this morning had been for her.

"Thank you for handling all this, Jackie. I know it wasn't easy." For the millionth time since stepping inside, he surveyed the destruction. "As long as Alexi and Pedro are okay, nothing else matters. The building's just a building."

"Yup." Moving away, she scrubbed her hands over her face. "It's why you guys pay ridiculous amounts for insurance, right?"

"Exactly. I'm sure it'll take some time to figure out what went wrong. Then we'll rebuild." Cade tipped his head toward the pile of cement and metal. "That's all just stuff. The guys are what matters." He looked out the broken window, and his gaze caught on Poppy as she talked on the phone. "It's the people that matter, right?"

"Yup," Jackie agreed. She knocked him with her shoulder again, and he brought his attention back to her. His eyes widened. While there was some lingering sadness in her dark-brown eyes, he took in her shit-eating grin and waggling eyebrows.

"What?" he asked, feigning innocence. A lame attempt, but whatever.

"Sooo . . . you have a girlfriend." It wasn't a question.

He grimaced. Did he? Not really, right? "I'd say that label's a bit premature."

She scoffed. "Fuck you and your semantics. So you're dating, then?"

Was it dating if they'd never technically gone anywhere? "I don't know, Jack. It's all kinda new, you know?"

"Oh my god. You're so stupid, Cade." Her lips quirked. "You're already holding her hand."

He shrugged, and his eyes found Poppy through the window again. Fine. Jackie had a valid point. He liked Poppy. A lot. "She's not like any of the others, you know? She's kind and . . . special."

"Good." Jackie elbowed him in the side, and he didn't bother hiding a wince. The woman had some damn sharp elbows. It was a shame she'd never gone into MMA—he'd never been able to convince her to switch sides—because she would have done some serious damage with those things. "You know, Cade, after Alana, you sure as hell deserve someone kind and special. And I'm sure it doesn't hurt that Poppy's really pretty, huh?"

He would be lying if he said her looks hadn't caught his attention. They had, for sure. Poppy was fucking stunning. But he had dated pretty-and-stunning before. Hell, he'd married it. Back then, he'd been young and dumb and blind to so many things. Thankfully, his eyes were now open, and he knew how terrible Alana had been. If only it hadn't taken a career-threatening injury for him to see—

"Cade de la Rosa?"

His head whipped toward the police officer striding his way. Right behind the officer was a firefighter, but not one of the guys dressed in turnout gear.

Cade raised his hand in greeting. "Yes?"

"I'm Officer Arnoch with SPD, and this is Kenneth MacAllister from the Seattle Fire Department's Fire Investigation Unit."

Cade shook hands with both men, and his brow furrowed as he eyed MacAllister. "Did a fire cause this?"

"We're still investigating. However, I can tell you that after the second collapse, our guys went up to the roof and reported that the edges of the damaged area appear to be melted." MacAllister held up his hand when Cade opened his mouth. "We still need to investigate further. In the meantime, even though this part of the building doesn't appear to have sustained any damage, we're going to have to ask you to vacate the premises."

Cade nodded and scanned the gym. "How long do you

think we'll be shut down before we can start cleanup and repair work?"

MacAllister considered the question for a moment. "I can't give you an exact timeframe, but you're probably looking at a week or two. Minimum. Once our investigation is done and we've verified it's safe structurally, you'll be good to return."

"I understand," Cade said. "Safety and finding out how this happened are the priorities."

"Glad we're in agreement," MacAllister said turning toward the entrance.

"Wait!" Jackie pointed at the small office on the other side of the debris. "I need to get the laptop."

MacAllister shook his head. "I can't let you go back there, but if you let me know where the computer is, I'll have one of our guys retrieve it for you."

Jackie gave the fire investigator specific instructions on what she needed and where everything was located.

"Got it," MacAllister said. He gestured to the front door. "If there's nothing else, Officer Arnoch will escort you outside now."

As they exited the building, Cade's thoughts ran rampant. None of this made sense. Fire investigators? Melted edges? A whole section of the ceiling and roof gone?

He shook his head. Nonsensical or not, it was all bad news.

CHAPTER TWELVE

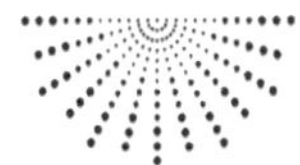

Cade blew out a weary breath and sank deeper into his couch. Poppy was curled up on the opposite end, and Dante was sprawled in the oversized chair across from them. Both she and his brother were talking on their phones, and SportsCenter was playing quietly in the background. On one hand, it was a bit surreal seeing Poppy in his Seattle condo, but on the other . . . it fit. *She* fit.

Today had been utter chaos. While they'd held vigil in the hospital waiting room this afternoon, his mind had been in a whirl—hell, it still was. He'd been antsy. Wound up from the lack of information. The police and fire departments didn't know shit. Or they weren't saying anything. As a result, his frustration had left him nearly clawing at the walls.

Then Dante had gone and opened his big, stupid mouth and told him that it had only been a few hours and to calm the fuck down. In response, he'd almost torn his brother's damn head off. Of course, Dante, being equally stressed as he'd been, had gotten right back in his face. They'd been ready to throw down. The time and place were completely inappropriate, but they'd been hanging on by a thread.

Until Poppy had stepped in. She'd reassured Cade that the officials just needed more time, and that she was sure they'd have some sort of update for them by tomorrow. Yes, Cade acknowledged that Poppy's words were basically the exact same thing as what Dante had said. But coming from her, it had been . . . different. It had gotten through. It had banked the frustration and turmoil and anger.

He was so damn thankful she'd chosen to come with him to the hospital. Her calming presence had kept him sane. She'd even taken care of Dante, too. Talking with them, reassuring them . . . hell, making sure they'd stayed hydrated. She'd claimed looking out for his brother was a no-brainer—the least she could do since Rebecca couldn't physically be there. That statement, that sentiment said so damn much about her.

Warmth, empathy, and strength. The woman was a miracle, and he wasn't sure how he'd have survived this day without her.

Poppy's grip on his hand in that hospital waiting room had also eased the panic that had been hiding and simmering in his gut while they waited for an update on Alexi and Pedro. Her embrace had kept him from falling to his knees in relief when the doctors had come in to say they were out of surgery.

Alexi and Pedro weren't just fighters who took classes at their gym. They were friends. Family, really. That's why hours later, Cade still felt like his chest was locked in a vise. The worry probably wouldn't lessen until both men made full recoveries. Alexi had a broken leg and three fractured ribs. Pedro had a fracture in his spine and four cracked ribs.

Thankfully, they were expected to heal with time and extensive physical therapy. Fighting again wasn't part of the discussion for either of them at this point, but regardless, Cade and Dante had vowed to do everything they could to help their friends get back on their feet, both physically and financially.

Exhausted, Cade pushed away the whirling thoughts of the day and watched the lights of downtown Seattle twinkle outside his floor-to-ceiling windows. The home he owned on Hudson Island was his permanent residence, but he'd kept this condo when he'd moved out of the city. It was one of two units on the top floor of a thirty-floor high-rise in downtown Seattle's Belltown neighborhood. The other belonged to his brother, who, like him, couldn't seem to part ways with the property despite calling Hudson Island home.

Cade used his condo for sporadic trips into town. Otherwise, it mostly sat empty. He was an extremely private person—in his experience, most people couldn't be trusted—so he rarely invited anyone to use the place when he wasn't here. Hell, he rarely invited anyone over when he *was* here. But having Poppy in his space felt right.

Another weary sigh overtook him, and he rested his head onto the back of the couch. He let her soothing voice wash over him, cleansing his remaining tension away. She was talking with her boys, and her soft smile was radiant. He couldn't look away.

"Yes, I did," Dante said into his phone, breaking Cade's focus. "Sure, please go ahead, but send it up to Cade's. Thanks."

He eyed his brother in confusion.

Dante tossed his phone onto the coffee table as he rose. "I ordered us some takeout for dinner. It just got here, so I'll be right back."

Startled, Cade checked his watch. Holy shit. How was it almost seven o'clock? He looked back at the twinkling lights outside his window and wanted to slap himself upside the head. Panic gripped his throat, and his eyes flew to Poppy.

The second she hung up with the twins, he blurted, "I'm

so freaking sorry, Poppy. I didn't realize how late it was." He glanced at his watch again, holding a tiny spark of hope that he'd read the time wrong. Nope. Seven o'clock. He hissed out a breath as he desperately tried to recall the ferry schedule. "I can still get you back to Hudson tonight. I'm certain we can make one of the later ferries. But we'd have to leave soon—"

He began to rise, but Poppy's hand landed on his thigh, preventing him from standing. "It's fine, Cade. Don't worry about it. I—"

"You're not taking an Uber back, Pop." No way in hell was he putting her in some rideshare when it was this damn late. Certainly not for a trip that damn long. No fucking way.

She pinned him with a look that had his mouth snapping shut.

Shit. He didn't know what he'd said wrong, but he had the distinct feeling he was about to get a verbal smackdown.

"May I finish speaking?" Poppy asked. She hadn't quite snapped the words, but her tone was most definitely stern and forceful. And sexy as hell.

"Sorry," he mumbled.

Reentering the living room, Dante set the paper takeout bag on the coffee table and slapped him on the back of the head. Spicy peanut goodness overtook Cade's nose as he flipped off his chuckling brother.

Clearing his throat, he turned back to Poppy. "You were saying?"

"Hope Thai's okay," Dante said, completely ignoring him. That dumb smile Cade hated appeared on his brother's dumb face. The fucker.

"Thai's great," Poppy said.

Dante began pointing at various containers, listing off the contents of each one as he made her a plate. When he handed it over, she beamed at him.

"Thank you, Dante. That's sweet of you." She dug into her food. "Wow, this is fantastic."

His brother caught his eye, and the fucker's smirk grew.

Cade bit his tongue. Fine. So a point to his brother. Not only had Cade forgotten about taking Poppy home, but he'd completely spaced on feeding her. After she'd spent the entire day dealing with his drama and making sure he and Dante were okay. He was an ass.

Giving Poppy a few minutes to enjoy her food, he fixed his own plate. When he finished, he repeated, "You were saying, Poppy?"

She set down her half-eaten food and looked at him, wiping the corners of her mouth. He quickly assessed her. She didn't seem pissed that he'd lost track of time and had forgotten to take her home. So that was good, right?

"I was going to say that I have Meredith and Bethany covering for me tomorrow, so there's no rush getting back home. Also, Charlie at the auto shop texted me earlier and said the tow truck dropped my car off. They were about to close, so that's a wait-and-see thing right now. If you're heading back sometime tomorrow, I'll catch a ride with you. If you need to stay here longer, it's not a problem. I can have one of the boys take me back after their classes are out. We can play it by ear."

"I have the condo across the hall, you know." Dante nodded toward the front door. "If you need a place to crash for the night, I have extra rooms."

Cade ground his teeth together. The fuck? "She'll stay here with me."

Poppy's eyebrow arched.

Shit. Fuck. Shit. "What I meant to say, Poppy, is you're more than welcome to spend the night here. I also"—he shot a glare at his brother—"have a guest room you can use."

"Thank you, Cade. I'll stay here." Poppy patted his knee,

then polished off her wine. After placing the empty glass on the table, she grabbed her plate and resumed picking at her food. The woman ate like a little bird compared to him and his brother, who had already cleaned their plates. They were both gigantic, though. "Dante, thank you, too. I appreciate your offer."

Cade snagged her wineglass. "Let me get you a refill."

He caught his brother's gaze and inclined his head toward the kitchen. Poppy hardly seemed to notice their exit, busy enjoying her meal and watching sports highlights on TV.

When they were out of earshot, he hissed, "What the fuck, man?"

Dante nudged him with his elbow. "Just giving you a push, little brother."

His eyes narrowed. Dante was just messing with him, but it was rubbing him all kinds of wrong. He grabbed the white wine from the fridge and filled Poppy's glass. "The fuck's that supposed to mean?"

Dante rolled his eyes. "It's obvious you like her, and you were taking your sweet-ass time asking her to stay the night with you. I'm surprised. It isn't like you to not jump right in when the chick's willing."

Before Cade could blink, he was in his brother's face, simmering with anger. "Don't be a fucking dick. It's not like that with her."

Dante cocked an eyebrow and crossed his arms over his chest, putting space between them. "I'll give you a pass for getting in my face *twice* today, but watch yourself. Don't fucking do it again."

He didn't back down. "If you fucking talk about her like that again, I'll do more than get in your damn face."

Dante stared at him for a moment, and for a split second, Cade regretted his words. Not because he wasn't ready to clobber his brother for saying or even *thinking* shit about

Poppy. No, he regretted them because while they were elite fighters in their own fields, they were evenly matched on a good day, and he was so damn tired right now. That would give Dante an advantage. And that was unacceptable. Plus, Poppy would no doubt step in and break up their fight. Again. Like they were a couple of unruly teenagers.

"Interesting . . ." Dante murmured. A slow smile spread across his face. All traces of hostility vanished. "Hoooly shiiit. You *like* her."

Cade fought to not roll his eyes. And failed. "Of course I like her. But it's not like *that*."

Dante scoffed, and that fucking smirk was back on his face.

"Okay, fine. It's like that." He let out an exasperated sigh. "But not in the shitty way you're implying. Poppy's different. She means something, you know?"

Again, his brother studied him for a moment, and it took everything he had not to squirm under the scrutiny. Then Dante nodded and slapped him on the shoulder. "All right, little brother. I like her. I didn't realize you liked her like that. And for what it's worth, I'm sorry for saying what I did about her. It won't happen again. You have my word."

With a chin lift to his brother, Cade grabbed Poppy's glass of wine and headed back to the living room.

***

"Sorry that took so long," Cade said, placing her wine on the coffee table in front of her.

Leaning forward, she swapped her plate out for the glass and took a sip of the tart, crisp wine. "Is everything okay?"

She'd heard grumblings from the kitchen but hadn't been able to make out any words. Both men had gone through the wringer today, and she knew tensions were high. The brothers had nearly gone at each other earlier, but luckily, sanity had prevailed. As much as the brothers had postured, she'd managed to help deescalate the situation. A gentle reminder of where they'd been—a hospital waiting room, surrounded by friends—had encouraged them to stand down.

"All is well," Dante said, striding into the room and smacking the back of Cade's head.

The look Cade shot his brother had her biting her lower lip to keep from laughing. Their dynamic was so much like Carter and Dylan's. Granted, the men were close to two decades older than her boys, but did brothers ever really mature past their teenage years?

For the next hour, she relaxed into the cushions and nursed her wine while Cade and Dante continued to tease each other. The only time they quieted was when Sports-Center flashed the boxing and MMA highlights from the weekend. Watching them, not only now but throughout the day, Poppy prayed her boys would remain close like these two. That they wouldn't let getting older and the slog of adulthood distance them emotionally.

"Well," Dante said, stretching. "I'm beat. I'm gonna call Rebecca and hit the sack."

"Thanks again for dinner," Poppy said.

"No problem." Dante looked at Cade. "Want to head over to the hospital tomorrow morning? Say around eight?"

"That work for you?" Cade asked her. When she nodded, he turned back to his brother. "Yeah. We can grab some coffee and food on the way. Text me when you're about ready to head out."

They bid their goodbyes to Dante and began cleaning up. While Cade gathered the plates from the coffee table, she snagged the empty takeout containers.

"Hope you don't mind," she said, stifling a yawn as she

followed him into the kitchen, "but I think I'm going to turn in early as well. Could I, uh, borrow a T-shirt or something to sleep in?"

For the span of two unsteady heartbeats, he simply stared at her.

She shifted on her feet and prayed the heat she felt spreading over her face wasn't turning her beet red. "Um . . . please?"

Cade startled, and a soft flush tinged his cheeks. With a shake of his head, he chuckled. "Sorry. I was picturing you wearing my T-shirt. To bed. It was a . . . distracting image." He shrugged and then shot her a wink.

Poppy's jaw almost dropped. Almost. That aw-shucks shrug mixed with that sexy wink? Yeah. Talk about a distracting image.

Cade stepped closer, and her breath hitched. Then he laced his fingers with hers, and her heart stopped. It was only when he tugged her out of the kitchen, and down the hall to where she assumed the bedrooms were, did she remember to breathe.

He led her into one of the rooms and hit the lights. She gasped. Holy. Crap. She knew her mouth was hanging open as she scanned the room, but she couldn't bring herself to care. It was like the fanciest hotel room she'd ever seen. Not that she'd ever seen anything like this in person, just in super fancy advertisements.

The wall on the left side was floor-to-ceiling glass. The entire thing! They were high enough to clear the neighboring buildings, and the wide expanse of Seattle's downtown was picture-perfect. To the west was an area void of lights—except for two ferries crossing Puget Sound—and she knew the sunset view of Elliott Bay would be spectacular.

"Wow, Cade." She shook her head in awe. "This room is for your *guests*?"

He stood beside her, admiring the lights of the city. "My room's across the hall and has the same view, but it's on a corner, so I've got two windows this size."

Good god, she couldn't wait to take in the view from his room. She glanced up at him. "Can I see?"

A devilish grin had his eyes twinkling. "Oh, I can guarantee you'll be getting the full tour, babe."

Poppy bit her bottom lip, but it did nothing to prevent her from smiling. There was an innuendo somewhere in there. She was sure of it, even if her brain was too worn out to connect the dots. She cleared her throat. "So, did you and Dante fight over who got which condo? Because this is spectacular."

Cade laughed. "Despite how my brother and I acted today, he and I *can* be adults."

She raised her eyebrows in playful disbelief, and he pulled her tight against his side.

The corners of his lips tipped up. "We tend to revert to being obnoxious teenagers when we're together, but we *are* able to agree and be mature when it counts."

Calling on all her bravery, she wrapped her arms around his waist.

His brown eyes heated, and he pulled her even closer. "To answer your question, though, Dante and I split this floor in half. Completely equal. We both got two bedrooms with water views and one with a city view. Dante's place is basically the mirror image of mine."

"You have *another* guest room?"

"Yeah. The door off the living room is the third bedroom." He traced the bridge of her nose with his finger, then tucked a lock of hair behind her ear. The butterflies in her stomach took flight. Drawing back, he gestured toward the open door on the opposite side of the room. "That's the bathroom, and it should be fully stocked. I'm pretty sure there are extra toothbrushes and that kind of thing in the drawers. Feel free to use whatever you want."

Retaking her hand, he walked them to a digital display mounted between the bathroom door and the walk-in closet. He tapped the screen, and it brightened. "Temperature control is here. Oh, and check this out." The boyish enthusiasm on his face had her laughing. He really was adorable. In a ridiculously, *ridiculously* sexy way, of course. "With this app, you can control the window."

Her forehead scrunched in confusion. "Control the window?"

"Watch." He tapped a button, and her jaw dropped. Again. The entire floor-to-ceiling window frosted. Some light still came through, but it was as if gauzy drapes had been pulled.

"It's so fucking cool, right?"

She laughed. "Yeah. Absolutely cool. I've never seen anything like it."

"And the best part?" He tapped the screen again, and a slider appeared on the display. "You can adjust how much visibility you want, from barely tinted"—he used his finger to drag the slider—"all the way to blacked out."

As the glass responded to his adjustments, her gaze ping-ponged between him and the window. "Not gonna lie, De la Rosa. That's pretty cool. Why the hell aren't you living here full-time?" She swept her arms out around her. "This place is gorgeous."

Cade stuffed his hands into the pockets of his sweats. "I used to live here before we opened the Hudson gym. Now, I stay here whenever I need to be in town. Or if I'm flying out of Sea-Tac, I'll come out a day or two early, so I don't have to be at the mercy of the ferries to catch my flight. But . . . I don't know." He shrugged. "I mean, don't get me wrong. This place is great and fun, but my place on Hudson is home. That matters more than all these cool gadgets."

Her heart squeezed tight. *Oh my god, this man . . .*

Cade leaned down and dropped a quick kiss to the top of her head. Her heart stuttered. "Come on," he said, again lacing his fingers with hers. "Let me show you the rest of this joint."

He walked her through the rest of the condo. The full city views were spectacular, but the water view was already her favorite. She wasn't going to lie, though. Seeing the opulent views and all the high-end kitchen appliances and electronics was intimidating. Sure, she'd always known he was extremely successful, not only as an internationally recognized athlete, but as an internationally recognized coach. Still, witnessing the evidence of his wealth firsthand was a lot.

Poppy's mind flashed to her tiny apartment, and she pursed her lips. Cade was grossly out of her league. She'd suspected it before coming here, but now she knew for certain. So what the hell was she doing hanging out with him?

She peeked down at their connected hands, and the sight sparked that flutter in her belly, the one that was becoming oddly familiar. Maybe she had no idea what she was doing, but holding hands with this man? It was comfortable. Exhilarating. Terrifying. All at once.

"You okay, Pop?"

Her attention went to Cade's sweet, handsome face, and she smiled. "I'm good. Just a little tired."

Whatever was happening between them, she would go with it. Yes, the man's net worth was probably ridiculous and more than a little intimidating. But Cade? *He* wasn't intimidating. He was one of the nicest men she'd ever met, and she couldn't remember the last time she'd enjoyed getting to know someone this much. So, even though it might be risky to her heart, she wanted to see where this led. For once, she was going to do something for her. Take a chance on herself. On her happiness.

"One last stop on the tour," Cade said.

When they entered his room, she came to an abrupt halt. He hadn't been lying, the corner view—the two full walls of windows—was breathtaking.

"This is stunning." Dropping his hand, she moved to stand in the corner and looked out. Her lips lifted into a broad smile, and she glanced over her shoulder at him. "It's got a very *Titanic* feel to it, you know?" She looked back at the skyline and threw her arms out. "'I'm the king of the world!'"

With a laugh, Cade wrapped his arms around her from behind, and her heart began racing. Putting his mouth to her ear, he whispered, "Hopefully, without the tragic ending."

She chuckled. "True. I'd scoot over and share my floating door with you, though."

His hands skimmed down her arms, from her shoulders to the tips of her fingers, causing her breath to catch. Enveloping her hands in his, he lifted her arms and placed her palms flush against the glass, his holding hers in place.

"I appreciate that." He stepped closer, and his breath warmed her neck, raising goosebumps. "You're infinitely more stunning than this view, Poppy Walker," he murmured. His mouth brushed the tender skin right below her ear, and she sighed. "Thank you for being my anchor today. You don't know how much it meant. How much *you* mean."

His words melted her heart, and the caress of his lips heated her blood. Tilting her head to give him more access, tingles tore through her when he gently nibbled that spot where her neck and shoulder met.

"Cade," she moaned, leaning into his body.

There was no mistaking the hard length against her lower back. She rolled her hips, and he growled into the skin of her throat. Feminine satisfaction surged through her. Before she could take her next breath, he spun her around, pulling every inch of her against every inch of him. Their mouths crashed together, and he devoured her, licking at the seam of her lips, requesting entrance. Which she was more than happy to grant. Their tongues tangled, eliciting a groan. From her or him, she didn't know nor care. She simply couldn't get enough of this man.

Raking her fingers through his hair, she was treated to another growl. She pressed closer, moaning as his hands ran over her, squeezing and stroking her breasts, her hips, her ass. She yanked his shirt up, desperate to feel his hot skin against hers. He was iron steel, muscle over muscle. With his shirt bunched up, she pulled away to look. And for the millionth time that night, her mouth fell open. Delicious. The man was absolutely delicious. And she wanted a taste.

Leaning forward, she pressed an open-mouthed kiss to his chest.

"Poppy." Cade's voice was gravel. Using a single finger, he lifted her chin until she met his gaze. "We have to slow this down."

Her forehead scrunched, and she pulled away, stunned. *What?*

His finger trailed along her jaw, then snaked into her hair. "I don't want to rush this. Not with you."

Old insecurities sprouted in her belly. Breaking his gaze, she looked down, and her stomach dropped. An apology was on the tip of her tongue. What it was for, she didn't know. But she must have done something—

"Oh hell no, babe." He tilted her head up and their eyes locked. "Hear me now, Poppy. I want you so damn much." With one hand still in her hair, his other wrapped around her waist, bringing her flush to him. He rocked his hips, and his thick, hard erection pushed against her stomach. "Can you feel how much I want you?"

For the life of her, she couldn't look away from his fiery brown gaze. Words failed her, and she could only nod.

Another rock of his hips. "I'm not going to rush this, Poppy. I'm not going to rush *us*. Yes, I'm ridiculously attracted to you. But I also want to do this right. Get to know you better first. So when we do finally come together, you'll know that it's not just an attraction. It'll be more."

Her heart tripped, and those butterflies returned. How could this man be real?

Be brave, Poppy. Be brave.

One side of her lips quirked up as she looped her arms around his neck. "Well, Mr. De la Rosa, what about what *I* want?"

His answering grin was downright predatory, and heat pooled low in her belly. "What would that be, Poppy Walker?"

She sent a quick prayer out to the universe that she wasn't about to make a fool of herself. "You," she whispered.

Cade growled and shut his eyes, sucking in a long, shaky breath. The man was practically vibrating beneath her hands. After a moment, he met her gaze. "Your opinion is duly noted." He dropped a kiss to her lips but stepped away before it heated. Then strode to his walk-in closet, pulled out a T-shirt, and handed it to her. Steering her into the hallway, he said, "Every part of me wants to see you wearing nothing but my shirt tonight, but I'm still not rushing us."

She chuckled, stopping outside the guest room. "Are you telling me, or are you telling yourself?"

He watched her for a moment, and his intensity had tiny seeds of hope sprouting in her gut. "You matter, Poppy. And I want to do this right." He kissed her. This time it was soft and slow, with the perfect amount of tongue. Her bones liquified. "Thank you again for being my anchor today." He placed one more kiss on the tip of her nose. "Good night."

Poppy stood absolutely still as he turned and crossed the hall. When his door closed behind him, she slumped against her doorframe and released the breath that had been stuck in her throat. Her entire body tingled, and she smiled, relishing every second of the feeling.

Yes, she had no clue what she was doing. And yes, these last few moments with Cade had been intense. But she couldn't wait to experience it all again.

CHAPTER THIRTEEN

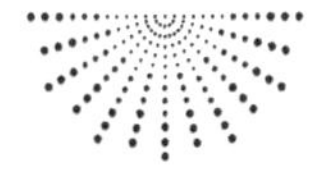

After waking early and answering a handful of emails and calls, Cade did one last walk-through of his condo to make sure everything was turned off. He could still hear Poppy in the guest room getting ready, and Dante had texted that he would be over shortly. They were going to grab a quick coffee and breakfast to go before heading to the hospital. Pedro was still in the ICU, but Alexi had been moved to a regular room late last night.

Cade double-checked that there was nothing in the fridge that would go bad, then gathered the trash from under the sink and put the bag by the front door. He and his brother shared a housekeeper who came biweekly, but the last thing Cade wanted was Thai takeout containers smelling up the place until her next visit.

Leaning against the kitchen island, he tried to imagine seeing his condo for the first time as Poppy just had. Aside from the fantastic view, his place was sleek and opulent. While he'd moved most of his personal mementos to his Hudson home, he'd left a handful of family photos and knickknacks so the space wasn't sterile. In his wildest dreams, he'd never imagined he would have this much. He'd fought for it all and was immensely proud of what he'd accomplished, not only during his fighting career, but especially now as a coach and gym owner.

Part of him hoped Poppy was impressed. Which was laughable since he had shied away from trying to impress anyone for years. Ever since his divorce. His ex-wife, Alana, had been a piece of work. The women who'd come after her had been nameless, faceless, warm bodies who'd scratched an itch. Did that make him an asshole? Maybe.

In his defense, he'd never lied to any of those women. Both parties had understood their interactions were about sex. Nothing more. And neither had minded. The women had sought him out for his fame and wealth, not love. Likewise, he'd known they weren't interested in him as a person. The experiences had been as shallow as they sounded. So, wanting to impress Poppy with the material things he possessed was ridiculous. But damn, he really wanted to impress her any way he could.

Poppy. He smiled as he pictured her exquisite hazel eyes. He'd noticed that sometimes they were more blue, sometimes more green. Either way, they were expressive as hell, blatantly showing when she was happy, nervous, annoyed, or —thank freaking god—turned on. It was sappier than shit, but he could stare into her color-changing eyes for hours.

God, she was beautiful. Kissing her last night . . .

Holy shit. She'd given as good as she'd gotten, and tasting her sweet lips had been exquisite. He'd nearly exploded. It had taken every ounce of self-control he possessed to not scoop her up, toss her over his shoulder, take her straight to his bed, and bury himself deep inside her. But he had held back because he'd meant what he'd said. As gorgeous as he found her, she was more than her looks. She was special. And he wanted to do this right.

"Morning."

Poppy's soft voice had him turning.

He took her in. From her long brown hair pulled into a high ponytail, to the light spray of freckles across her nose and cheeks, to another one of his T-shirts half-tucked into her jeans, to the bright-pink polish on her toes. His chest squeezed as a blush stole across her face. Stunning. Fucking stunning.

She shifted on her feet and dropped her gaze. Something flashed over her face. Embarrassment, uncertainty . . . He wasn't quite sure. But it was something he didn't like. He was in front of her in two seconds flat. Reaching out with one arm, he pulled her flush against him. With the other, he tilted her face up. A moment later, his lips were on hers.

Poppy gave a surprised squeak that was so damn adorable, then kissed him back.

Seconds, minutes—hell, it could have been hours—passed before he ended their kiss and rested his forehead on hers. "Morning. Did you sleep okay?"

She nodded, a hazy, satisfied look on her face. Unable to stop himself, he dropped a kiss on her forehead, then the tip of her nose—and then his mouth was on hers again. When her tongue teased his, he growled. Cupping her ass in both hands, he squeezed and lifted. Her legs wrapped around his waist, and he—

"For fuck's sake, come on!"

Poppy gasped, and she buried her head in his neck.

Glancing at his brother, who'd turned away from them, Cade sighed. "Ever heard of knocking, D?"

"I *did*, you little shit. I didn't hear anything, so I used my key and saw"—he waved in their direction—"*that*."

Lowering Poppy to her feet, he kissed her forehead, tucked her close to his side, and cleared his throat. "It's safe to turn around now."

With a hand slapped over his eyes, Dante turned and slowly peeked through his fingers, then gave an exaggerated, "Phew!"

Poppy chuckled, as Cade was sure his brother had intended. Dante had shitty timing for sure, but damn if the guy wasn't lovable.

After grabbing coffees and breakfast burritos at the café on the bottom floor of their building, they made their way to the hospital. He and Dante took turns visiting Pedro in the ICU, and all three of them visited Alexi in his regular room. Jackie was with Alexi, so when the nurses kicked everyone out to check on their friend, Cade and Dante caught up on some of the gym issues with her in the hallway.

As they said their goodbyes, with Jackie promising Poppy she'd visit Hudson Island soon, his phone buzzed with a text. When Dante glanced at his phone at the same time, Cade frowned and checked the message. It was from Gavin. His frown deepened.

GAVIN

Need to talk to you both ASAP

The ominous tone of his friend's message had the hairs on the back of his neck rising.

"Is everything okay?" Poppy asked, eyeing the text on his screen.

"I don't know," he murmured, attention still on his phone. As if looking at the text would magically make it say something else.

"Let's go in here." Dante slapped him on the chest and held open the door to an empty waiting room. Seconds later, his brother had his phone on speaker, and it was ringing.

"Are you on the island?" Gavin asked. He'd never been one for formalities.

"No," Dante said. "You're on speaker. I'm with Cade and Poppy Walker."

"I can step out," Poppy said in a rush, gesturing toward the door.

"No, babe. Stay. Please." Cade took her hand in his and squeezed. His gut was screaming that Gavin wasn't calling with good news, so he wanted Poppy with him. Holding his hand. Anchoring him. "What's going on, Gavin?"

"I ran into TJ last night—"

"He's one of our head coaches at the Hudson gym," Cade informed Poppy.

"—and he mentioned there was trouble at the Seattle location. Jackie told him the Seattle PD and FD were involved. Naturally, that piqued my interest, so I had Bean take a peek this morning—"

"Of course you did." Dante chuckled.

Smiling, Cade said to Poppy, "Bean is the brainiac IT guru for Gavin's crew."

"All true. So off the record," Gavin continued, "Bean says they're looking at a possible explosive device as the cause of the damage."

"Holy shit," Dante gasped.

"What?" Cade asked at the same time. Eyes wide, he glanced between Dante and Poppy. Utter disbelief rendered him mute.

Gavin cleared his throat. "Because of that, I wanted to check the cameras here—oh, on a side note, I think pulling Alvarez into this conversation would be beneficial. I'm not sure where the dude's at on returning to the force, but he'd be a great brain to pick for all this. Plus, his connections at SPD might be helpful. Anyway, getting back to the cameras, nothing's been tripped, but I wanted us to check for anything out of the ordinary."

Dante looked at Poppy. "On Hudson, we have

surveillance cameras all along our property line. It's like Fort Knox. No joke."

Cade nodded in agreement. Aside from partnering with Cade and Dante's gym for Hudson Tactical, Gavin was the owner of Hudson Security, a highly renowned and elite private security firm. Cade knew they offered private protection and cybersecurity services but was also pretty sure they were involved in other, more classified shit mere mortals like him weren't privy to. Which was one thousand percent fine by him.

Gavin's company was serious about protecting the land they leased from Cade and Dante, which surrounded the gym. The De la Rosa family had owned the roughly eight hundred acres that made up the northeastern corner of Hudson Island for multiple generations, and Hudson Security now used much of that land for their indoor and outdoor tactical and training facilities, plus their admin offices.

When he'd first moved his company in, Gavin had asked permission to put up a fence around the entire property. Cade and Dante had agreed, thinking it would be a simple wooden structure marking the property line. No. Hudson Security didn't fuck around. They'd installed an anti-climb steel palisade fence that included a specialty barrier so vehicles couldn't ram through. Of course, not on the water side, which was defended by a steep cliff, but he was pretty sure they monitored that area as well.

"Bean reviewed the camera feeds on the perimeter," Gavin continued, "and it looks like someone was scoping out the place."

Cade's gaze swung to his brother, and the shock on Dante's face reflected his own.

"What does that mean, exactly?" Dante asked. It was the same question on the tip of Cade's tongue.

"We have visuals on the entire property line, water line included—"

Cade nodded, and a small smile pursed his lips. He *knew* it, dammit.

"—and depending on the terrain, about nine yards out. At roughly two in the morning on Monday, we picked up beams of light—most likely flashlights—along the southeastern border."

That was the area closest to the gym. This development did not bode well for them. However, Cade decided to play devil's advocate.

"It could have been hikers at Jackson Cove with head-lamps or flashlights," he said. Jackson Cove State Park butted up against their southern property line and ran east all the way to the water.

"At two in the morning?" Poppy challenged.

"I agree with Poppy," Gavin said. "Hikers are highly unlikely. Plus, Bean pulled the cameras from the trailhead's parking lot and there were no vehicles. Of course, that doesn't mean anything for certain, but again, highly unlikely. Also, from the way the light bounced around, it looked like someone was checking the fence posts for cameras."

"Were you able to see who it was? Or if it was more than one person?" Dante asked.

"Negative. They stayed out of range, so we couldn't get a visual. But there were three beams, and they were spaced far enough apart that we're most likely looking at three individuals. At least."

Dante scrubbed his hands over his face, and Cade pulled Poppy close, putting her back to his chest. He tightened his arms around her and rested his chin atop her head. When her hands tightened over his forearms, he released a deep breath. What the fuck was going on?

"I'll have my people look into this. But I've gotta ask,

fellas. With this and a possible fucking explosive device taking out your Seattle gym, who the hell have you guys pissed off?"

"No one," Dante said, shaking his head.

Cade searched his memory for any recent drama and frowned. The fucking lawsuit. He'd shown it to his brother the week before. They'd concluded it was garbage and handed it off to their lawyer, who'd said he would handle it.

Releasing Poppy, he paced the length of the small waiting room. "What about the lawsuit?"

"What lawsuit?" Gavin grumbled.

Cade blew out a breath and dropped his hands on his hips. "A former fighter is suing me. Personally, though. The gym isn't named in the lawsuit."

Poppy's eyebrows rose. "Seriously? What for?"

Absolute bullshit, that's what. "For not training him. I barely remember the guy. I mean, it was a few years back, right after I retired and partnered up with Dante. The guy came into our Seattle gym after doing a few amateur fights. He thought he was hot shit and pre-paid for a bunch of personal training sessions with me." He shook his head. "I think we only did maybe a handful."

"Why?" Gavin asked.

Cade shrugged, though Gavin obviously couldn't see him. "He wasn't a very good fighter, and when I tried to train him, he wouldn't take correction. Overall, the guy had a shitty attitude. So I refunded his money. He bitched at everyone within earshot, and I told him to never come back."

"And this guy's suing you now? After all these years?" The disbelief in Gavin's voice was exactly how Cade felt.

"Yeah. But our lawyer said it was a bullshit case and that he'd get it dismissed."

"Do you remember the guy's name?"

"His last name is Justin." Cade recalled it from the paperwork. He pictured the fucker's arrogant face and frowned. "His first name is escaping me."

"I don't remember his first name, either," Dante said with a shrug.

"Timing's a little suspect," Gavin said. "Shoot me a copy of the papers, and I'll put Bean on it."

"Poppy and I are heading home now." Cade looked at her to verify, and she nodded.

"I'm staying another day or two," Dante said. "Pedro is supposed to get out of the ICU later today or tomorrow, and I want to make sure he gets settled."

Cade made a mental note to check on Rebecca and Rocco when he got back to Hudson. "Gav, I'll give you a call when the ferry docks. We can meet up later tonight or something."

"Sounds good. For what it's worth, I'm sorry this shit is happening to you guys. But trust me, between my crew and Alvarez, we'll get answers."

"You're for sure pulling Alvarez in?" From the moment Matt had stepped foot on Hudson Island for his recovery, Gavin had been circling. He wasn't shy about wanting to hire Matt. But Matt was Matt, and the fucker did everything on his own time.

"Hell yeah," Gavin grumbled. "If I have it my way, Alvarez will see what it's like to work with us, and then he'll tell SPD to fuck off. In the most polite way possible, of course. He'd be a great addition to my team."

Dante laughed. "Good luck with that."

Hanging up with Gavin, they left the waiting room. Dante went up two floors to the ICU, and he and Poppy rode the elevator down to the parking garage.

"Sorry about all this, babe," he said, bringing her hand to his lips. "Probably not the way you planned to spend your Wednesday morning."

Still holding his hand, she bumped her shoulder into him. "Do you hear me complaining?"

The elevator doors opened, and he paused to press a soft kiss to her lips. "Thank you again."

The sweet smile she shot him warmed his heart. How was it that in only a few short days, this woman had become his touchstone, his anchor? Things had been unbelievably crazy, and yet, with her at his side, it had all been bearable. Somehow, she made everything less bleak.

At his Range Rover, Cade opened the passenger door and waited until she was settled before shutting it. Blowing out a breath, he walked to the driver's side. He knew he should be wary, knew he should be doing more to keep his distance from her. Because he didn't trust easily. God knew he'd learned that lesson the hard way. But with Poppy . . . it didn't matter. He was jumping all in. He couldn't seem to help himself.

Cade just prayed he wasn't making a huge fucking mistake. Because if she decided she only wanted to be friends? He'd respect that, yes. But it would damn near rip him apart.

CHAPTER FOURTEEN

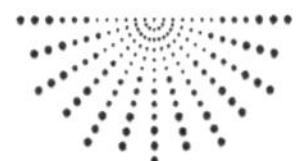

The trip back to Hudson Island was uneventful, comfortable, and . . . wonderful. With all the driving and two ferry rides, it took nearly two hours, but they didn't stop talking the entire time. From the twins' antics to their businesses to their favorite movies and sports teams, they used the hours to get to know each other.

It was nearing one in the afternoon when Cade pulled into a parking space outside Rainy Day Boutique. He walked her inside, holding her hand the whole way. As she waved to Bethany and Meredith, who were both helping customers, she knew a deep blush stained her cheeks.

Her earlier comfort in the confines of Cade's car had evaporated. What was she supposed to do now? How was she supposed to act? She still had no clue where she stood with him, but she knew he liked her. The way he'd fried her brain with that kiss last night—not to mention the kiss in the kitchen this morning—was definitive proof.

Poppy led him through the store, bringing them to a halt at the back counter.

"Thanks again for stopping to help a stranded motorist,"

she said. A grin had Cade's dark-brown eyes twinkling, and for a moment, she lost her train of thought. God, he was hot. She cleared her throat. "I know you have some stuff to take care of, so call me later?"

That sounded good, right? Mature. Sophisticated. Poised. Like she had her shit together.

His smile grew wider. "I'm going to swing by and check on Rebecca and Rocco. With Dante gone another day, I want to see if they need anything. Then I need to meet up with Gavin. But . . ."

He looked around the store. Her eyes never left his, so she had no clue what he was searching for. Then he placed his hands on her hips and pulled her against him. Her heart nearly jumped out of her chest when he kissed her.

"Let me take you to dinner tonight?" he asked, pulling slightly away.

She nodded, and her face warmed. It took two tries, but she found her voice. "I'd like that."

Cade's grin turned playful. He kissed her again. Soft, sweet, and quick. Like it was no big deal. "Great. I'll call you when I wrap up with Gavin."

With a wink, he turned and walked out the front door, waving at Meredith and Bethany on the way. The door shut, leaving them in complete silence for three heartbeats. Then her two employees squealed like teenagers, making Poppy jump. The women swarmed, peppering her with questions.

"Uh . . . what?!"

"Holy crap. Cade de la Rosa was kissing you!"

"When did this happen?"

"*How* did this happen?"

Poppy couldn't help but laugh. It had been quite the eventful last twenty-four hours. Taking in a shaky breath—because, yeah, Cade's kisses did that to her—she looked between the women and shook her head. *How did this happen, indeed.*

Poppy told them about Cade helping her move and gave them a recap of the last two days. She left out the stuff related to the gyms because, well, it wasn't her story to tell. She didn't mention the specifics of making out with Cade, either. While Bethany and Meredith were her friends, they were also her employees, and she wasn't *that* close with them. Even with the lack of steamy details, there were numerous sighs and nods of approval.

"Be forewarned, though," Meredith said when Poppy finished. "Mrs. Green was here when Cade laid one on you."

Her jaw dropped. How had she missed the woman? Mrs. Green was a lovely lady who'd been a loyal customer for as long as Poppy could remember. However, the woman was all about the gossip. If there was a juicy scoop to be had, Mrs. Green found it. And as the self-proclaimed First Lady of Hudson Island—her husband was the mayor—no one was in a better position to spread rumors than her.

"Your face right now?" Bethany's finger circled the air, indicating Poppy's expression. "Yeah. Don't be surprised if everyone knows by dinnertime that you were locking lips with that handsome man."

Usually, the thought of being the center of town gossip would have put Poppy in a panic. God knew she'd spent the last few years constantly worrying someone would find out about Eli's countless affairs and blast it around town. But this?

Yeaaah, she was okay being the center of *this* gossip.

A smile slowly lifted the corners of her lips, and the other women giggled.

"I suppose there are worse things that could happen." With a smirk, Poppy shrugged. "Now we should all get back to work."

. . .

Wednesdays were usually mellow, but that afternoon, they were especially busy as members of Hudson Island's gossip train paid her boutique a visit. Not that she minded, because the women, in all their sweet, nosy glory, each purchased something.

As early evening approached and the wave of shoppers died down, Poppy had left her employees in charge to run some errands. After finishing at the bank, she strolled down the sidewalk with her phone pressed to her ear.

"Six o'clock okay with you?" Cade asked.

"Sure," she said, waving to Mrs. Abbot and Mrs. Yoshida as she walked past. "Do you want to meet up at Monty's Tavern?" She frowned into her phone when Cade laughed. "Um, I take it that's a no?"

"Babe," he said, humor lacing his voice, "like I want your pseudo-brother chaperoning our first official date. Hard pass, Poppy. Hard pass."

She bit her lower lip but couldn't hold back a smile. He was right. If she showed up at Monty's for a one-on-one dinner with Cade, there was no doubt Four would pull up a chair and start an inquisition. It didn't matter that the two men were already friends; Four was meddlesome and protective. "You make a fair point."

"How about I pick you up and we head over to Watermark instead?"

She frowned. "That'd be great, but I don't think we can get a table."

Located inside the Pacific View Resort, Watermark was hands down the fanciest restaurant on the island. In fact, it was one of the top restaurants in the entire Pacific Northwest. With three Michelin stars, the place had a waiting list that was months long. Even on Wednesdays.

"Call me presumptuous, but I went ahead and snagged us a six-thirty reservation."

Her eyebrows rose in surprise. "How . . ."

"Their head chef is an old buddy."

"Of course he is." She chuckled, unsurprised—and excited.

She'd never been to Watermark but had always wanted to go. The closest she'd come to dining there had been during the Chamber of Commerce dinner party back in January. It had been held in the resort's ballroom and hosted by the mayor and his wife. While the hotel's catered food had been good, banquet chicken for close to one hundred people just wasn't the same caliber as the fare Watermark served. So yes, she was excited. Especially since she'd get to experience the meal with Cade.

"What can I say, babe? I know people."

She laughed at his playful words; she knew he wasn't bragging. "I'll see you in a couple hours, then."

"Can't wait."

The smile on her face lingered as she disconnected the call and made her way back to Rainy Day Boutique. During the walk, her mind returned to that Chamber of Commerce dinner. Her smile dimmed. It had been an awkward evening. Though Eli had already moved out a couple of months prior, their separation hadn't been public knowledge yet, and they'd still been pretending to be together. Why? She hadn't a clue. But hindsight was twenty-twenty and all that . . .

Now, she wanted to kick herself. Wanted to go back in time and shake her former self and scream for her to wake the hell up. She'd let a lot of things slide. Ignored countless issues in her marriage, like the way Eli had treated her, and the way she accepted it all. Because it had been easier than addressing the problems head-on. She hated confrontations, hated conflict, hated rocking any kind of boat. So she'd agreed to so many things she shouldn't have.

Passing Comfort Food, which was already closed for the day, Poppy's thoughts soured further. Her head-in-the-sand routine hadn't been limited to Eli. She'd done the same with Sheila. When her cousin had moved to Hudson at the end of last November, it had been easier to let everyone believe the lies Sheila had spewed. Including the one about them being extremely close—practically sisters—despite the nearly ten-year age gap between them.

None of it had been close to the truth. No, they'd never been close, and they sure as hell weren't "practically sisters." In fact, she had only recommended Sheila work for Comfort Food because she hadn't wanted Sheila working at Rainy Day Boutique.

Poppy winced. She still hadn't quite forgiven herself for passing her problem off to Roxie.

Had she known Sheila's true personality, she would have sent her cousin packing the moment she'd arrived to Hudson. But Poppy had thought Sheila was harmless. Then she'd walked in on her cousin and Eli fucking in her living room. Yes, she and Eli had already separated, but it had still hurt. When both Sheila and Eli had made it clear that their affair wasn't anything new, that it had been going on for years . . . Yeah. As horrible as that had been, she'd thought it was the worst damage her cousin could inflict.

She shook her head. No. There was no point in rehashing the what-ifs. What was done was done. No matter how much she regretted her part in everything—

Poppy gasped as she slammed into someone. "Oh, I'm so sor—"

"Still oblivious to your surroundings, I see."

She froze. God, she really needed to stop thinking about Eli. It was like some really messed-up manifestation or something. She tried to pass, but he shifted in front of her, blocking her way. Because of course he did.

Crossing his arms over his chest, Eli gave her that pompous smile he thought was so charming. "You know, I just heard the most ridiculous rumor."

Poppy rolled her eyes and stepped around him. She might not be a fan of confrontation and conflict, but she was so done with this man. "I really don't care what you heard."

Eli stepped in front of her again, knocking into her shoulder. "I was at Ray's Diner, and I overheard Mrs. Abbot telling her cronies that *you* are dating Cade de la Rosa." He threw his head back and howled with laughter. Like a freaking demented lunatic.

Shaking her head, she began to move around him again.

He grabbed her upper arm, wrenching her to a halt. "That's the funniest fucking thing, Poppy. *You* and Cade? No way in hell can that be remotely true. But on the off chance the guy is desperate, he obviously hasn't fucked you yet." He squeezed her bicep and yanked her up, high enough that she had to go up onto her tiptoes. "Because if he had, there's no fucking way he'd still be interested in someone as pathetic as you."

Shoving hard against his chest, she managed to put some space between them. Still, he held her arm tight.

"Let go—" Her eyes widened in surprise when he immediately released her.

Both of his hands went in the air as he stepped backward, away from her. His expression was the picture of innocence, but she saw the malice glittering in his eyes. Malice she knew all too well. He quickly leaned back toward her, and it took everything she had to not flinch.

"Oh, and don't be surprised if Cade drinks a lot when you're together," he said, lowering his voice. "God knows I had to be wasted to fuck you. And even then, I had to picture other women to keep it up. Because you? With your flabby gut and nonexistent tits?" Sneering in disgust, he gave her a once-over. "Nope."

With that, Eli turned and sauntered down the street. As if he weren't the world's biggest asshole.

Anger had her fists clenching, her stomach twisting. Every snappy comeback was now on the tip of her tongue. Every cutting insult was front and center in her mind. All five seconds too late.

She truly detested the man. Hated how petty and callous he was. Hated that he knew exactly what to pick at to make her doubt herself. To make her insecurities bloom and grow. Like the one that said if she hadn't been enough to keep Eli faithful, she could never possibly be remotely enough for a man like Cade.

"Everything okay, Poppy?"

Her heart jumped, and she spun around with a hand to her chest. Quinn O'Conner, Matt Alvarez, and Gavin Frazier. *Shit.*

Quinn's gaze was on hers. Matt and Gavin stood a half step behind the sheriff, their faces unreadable.

She shifted on her feet. "Um, hi."

"Sorry, I didn't mean to startle you." Quinn glanced at Eli's retreating form. "Eli giving you trouble again?"

So that's why he had left so abruptly. Why he'd let her go without more delightful remarks about how awful she'd been in bed. Shaking off his words, or at least trying to, she focused on Quinn. "Oh, you know Eli."

The sheriff's jaw tensed, and both Matt and Gavin crossed their arms over their chests.

Shit. Wrong answer. Get it together, Poppy! She cleared her throat. "Eli was just . . . being an ass." She shrugged. "I'll let you know if he crosses the line."

"Poppy, he had his hand on your arm." Quinn held up a

palm when she opened her mouth to speak. "To me, that's crossing the line."

Her mouth snapped shut. She had no response.

Of course grabbing her was crossing the line. Had Eli done it to someone else, she would be appalled. So what did it say about her that she hadn't even thought twice about it? That she was used to him grabbing her? Eli had never hit her. Not once. But he also hadn't had any problems pushing her around.

Her chest ached. There was no way to respond to Quinn without looking like a complete idiot. She tried anyway.

"Like I said, Eli's an ass. He likes to prove his little points and get in my face—" *Dammit!* Her eyes dropped to the ground, and she pinched the bridge of her nose. She needed to get it together. Now. "It's fine, Quinn." It really wasn't, but she straightened her spine and pretended. "Our divorce finalized last week, and he's been more . . . *Eli* than usual. I'm not making excuses for him, I'm just . . . stating a fact. I'll be sure to steer clear of him as much as I can."

Quinn held her gaze for a few moments, concern etched on his face. When he finally gave her a slight nod, she turned her attention to the men behind him, pasting on her best business-owner smile.

"Hi, I'm Poppy. I've seen you guys around town, but I don't know if we've officially been introduced." She thrust out her hand and prayed their manners would win out. They were friends with Cade, so they had to be nice guys, right?

There were a few seconds of hesitation, then both men stepped forward and took turns shaking her hand.

"Matt Alvarez."

"Gavin Frazier."

"Sorry about that." She waved her hand in the direction Eli had gone. "Probably not the best way to officially meet, but it's still a pleasure since I've heard a lot about you both."

They stared at her in question.

"Well, not *a lot* a lot. Just general stuff from Four. And Cade. Small town, you know?" Holy shit. She needed to stop talking. Immediately. "If you'll excuse me, I really need to get back to my shop." She looked at Quinn, who seemed a bit amused. "Thank you for checking up on me. Again." She suppressed a cringe. The sheriff had witnessed Eli being an asshole to her twice in as many weeks. "I don't plan on making it a habit. Trust me."

"Oh, it's not you I don't trust, Poppy." Quinn's eyes darted past her again, all signs of amusement gone. "Make sure to let me know if he keeps bothering you. Take care."

It required all her acting skills to nod at the men, turn, and walk away. Casually. Without scanning the sidewalks to see who was looking. With a pleasant, unbothered smile on her face. And with her head held high.

CHAPTER FIFTEEN

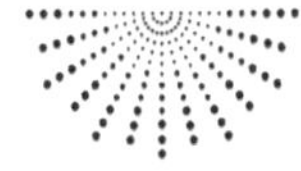

"Oh my god, Cade," Poppy moaned.

Cade's dick twitched. Holy shit. What he would give to have those words, that sound, come out of her gorgeous mouth when they weren't in the middle of a damn restaurant. Subtly shifting in his seat, he had to laugh. It was either that or groan. Because the absolute bliss on Poppy's face as she took another bite of her filet mignon was pure, lust-inducing torture.

"Cade, you have to try this." She held up a bite of steak on her fork.

Who was he to say no to the woman? He clasped her hand and brought it closer to his mouth. Keeping his gaze locked with hers, he took the bite and smiled at the heated twinkle in her eyes. The rich flavors of the red wine reduction played on his tongue, and the tender piece of beef melted in his mouth.

He leaned back in his chair. "Holy crap, you weren't kidding. That's amazing."

"Did you think I was just teasing you with the moaning and groaning?" she asked, arching an eyebrow.

"I was hopeful." He shot her a wink.

A pretty pink stole over her cheeks, and Cade knew it wasn't due to the wine she'd ordered. For one, she'd barely touched it, and for another, he'd noticed that beautiful blush every time he'd flirted with her. His mission tonight was to keep that gorgeous color on her cheeks all evening.

"You're ridiculous," she said, taking another bite. She swallowed and pointed at her plate with her fork. "Seriously, this is so good, but I'm definitely saving room for dessert. You?"

Cade knew what he wanted for dessert, and it sure as hell wasn't on the menu. He let his gaze wander down from her eyes. "Poppy, babe, dessert is my favorite."

The pink in her cheeks deepened, and she shook her head. Her soft laughter heated his blood, electrifying his insides. It demanded he call for the check and take her somewhere they could be alone.

Patience, dammit. He needed to exercise patience. Because he had a feeling that while she enjoyed his flirting and the sexy banter between them, she didn't quite believe he meant any of it yet.

On his way to pick up Poppy earlier, he'd gotten a call from Matt and Gavin. They'd told him about running into her downtown and said she'd had some sort of confrontation with her ex. They'd been too far away to hear anything, but they'd seen the fucker looming over her, yanking her around by the arm. Just thinking about it now had his blood simmering, but he made a conscious effort to unclench his fists.

"Is your food okay?" Poppy asked, forehead scrunched with concern.

He focused on the beautiful woman across the table from him. On the sweet smile she directed his way. His heart rate slowly returned to normal, and he nodded. "It's great. Do you want a bite?"

Poppy declined, and he took a moment to study her. Unbound, her long brown hair held a slight wave. She wore a simple black dress that showed off her fantastic figure. It was long-sleeved, and the V-neck hinted at her cleavage. He knew the dress hit a few inches above her knees and was pretty sure he'd seen the exact same dress in the front window display of her boutique. But it looked a million times more amazing on her.

"Have I mentioned how fantastic you look tonight, Poppy?"

Her gaze fell to her plate, and she let out a small chuckle, softly shaking her head. "You're very kind. Thank you."

She didn't believe him. It was plain as day. God, if he ever came across Eli again, that fucker better run.

Poppy had been quiet all evening. Still charming and sweet, and their conversation hadn't lacked, but she'd been subdued. Cade was certain her earlier encounter with that fucker had something to do with it. However, he'd avoided mentioning anything because he wanted Poppy to be the one to bring it up. So far, she hadn't said a word. But he could be a patient man.

"Gavin and Matt said you ran into them this afternoon." Yes, he could be patient. But that didn't mean he couldn't nudge things along.

"I did." She smiled. Her relief at the subject change was apparent. "It's crazy how even though we all have friends in common, I'd never actually met either of them before. Speaking of, were you able to meet up with Gavin today?"

Finishing his last bite of prime rib, he nodded. "Yeah. Gavin managed to pull in Matt, so I met with both of them."

"How did that go?" Poppy set her fork down. Taking a sip of wine, she settled back in her chair.

"Gavin showed us the video feed and . . ." A chill crept up his spine, and he fought a shiver. "I'm not gonna lie. Given what happened at the Seattle gym, seeing that video was creepy as hell."

She reached across the small table and covered his hand with hers. The warmth from the small touch wrapped right around his heart. "I'm so sorry. I can't imagine."

God, this woman . . .

"Thank you." Turning his hand over, he laced their fingers together. "Anyway, since I'm not exactly proficient in law enforcement-speak, I asked Gavin and Matt to meet with Quinn and let him know what's going on with the Seattle gym and the people scoping out our boundary here. Tell him we suspect that they're connected."

"Is there anything Quinn can do?"

Cade shook his head. "Nothing right now, but we all agreed it's a good idea to get it on Quinn's radar. Make sure he knows what's going on. Now we just need to be vigilant."

"Hopefully, with everyone on the same page, there will be some sort of resolution." The corners of her lips twitched. "I must say, seeing the three of them together this afternoon was a bit shocking."

His brow furrowed. "How so?"

"They make a formidable trio, that's for sure. If I didn't know Quinn was a nice guy, it would have been intimidating."

He could see that. Poppy was a teeny-tiny thing, and those three were giants, especially Matt.

"It helped that I assumed Gavin and Matt are good guys since they're friends with you. That brought down the scary factor a notch, too."

He smiled. "Two of the best guys I know." That was the god's honest truth. "They can be sarcastic assholes sometimes—well, most of the time—but they're solid guys."

"Pardon the interruption," a waiter said.

Cade flinched. Holy shit. Where the hell had the guy

come from? Poppy laughed at his shock, and he gave her a mock glare.

"If you're both finished, Chef Crawford would like to present dessert." The waiter waved at their plates. "May I?"

It was on the tip of Cade's tongue to tell the guy to fuck off. He couldn't care less about dessert, and the very last thing he wanted to do was let go of Poppy's hand. But seeing her face light up at the waiter's words made him bite his tongue. *Fine.*

Releasing her hand, he leaned back in his seat and crossed his arms over his chest. Was he acting like a toddler throwing a tantrum? Probably. Did he care? Not one bit.

The waiter and another server cleared their table with an efficiency that had Cade's eyebrows lifting. He opened his mouth to apologize for being a dick—because he was sure his poker face was shit right now, especially since Poppy looked like she was doing everything she could to not laugh at him —but a familiar face approached, cutting him off.

"Good evening, I'm Chef Micah Crawford." With a flourish, the man took Poppy's hand and air-kissed it.

Cade managed to stop his eyes from rolling. Barely. "Seriously, Micah?"

His friend was a charming flirt who could work a crowd like no one else. Six-five and shredded, the dude was an absolute beast. Multiple piercings dotted his ears and lip, and aside from his face and part of his neck, he was covered in tattoos. The guy looked scary as fuck, but as soon as he flashed that damn grin and those stupid dimples popped, everyone became putty in his hands. Everyone.

Micah wagged his eyebrows at Poppy, who'd gone from a deer in headlights to amused in three seconds flat.

See!

The chef nodded in Cade's direction and mock-whispered, "He's easy to rile up." But he released her hand.

Wise little fucker.

"Please try and keep your lips to yourself tonight," Cade told his old friend. "And what's this 'present dessert' business?"

"Fine. You got me." Micah winked at Poppy. "I wanted an excuse to meet you. It's not every day that Cade brings a lady friend to dine at my place." He leaned closer to her, and in another one of those mock whispers, clarified, "As in, never ever."

"Good to know." A rosy flush lit her face, and she cleared her throat. "You mentioned dessert?"

Accepting her redirect, Micah grinned and said, "We're thinking of doing a presentation thing for this particular dessert, so you guys get to be my guinea pigs." Micah looked over his shoulder. Seconds later, a cart was wheeled over. He lifted the silver dome atop it, revealing a mini mountain of meringue. "It's our take on a Baked Alaska." He held out a multipurpose lighter to Poppy and shot her what Cade knew to be his come-hop-in-my-bed-with-me smile. "Would you care to do the honors?"

"Seriously, dude?" Cade grumbled. "I'm, like, right here, bro."

Poppy laughed. "That's all right. I'll let you do your whole chef-presentation thing."

Cade's eyes rolled hard when Micah did another eyebrow waggle. Swear to Christ, the guy was ridiculous.

"We haven't done this yet, so fingers crossed it actually works." Micah brought the lighter to the dessert.

Poppy gasped as the Baked Alaska lit up in flames that went from blue to white, then to yellow, orange, and red before burning out. Cade tried not to gape. How the hell Micah had managed to create a rainbow flame was beyond him. The restaurant patrons dining around their table began clapping.

"What, no sparkles?" Cade asked with a straight face. The death glare Micah sent in response had him dissolving into laughter. "Okay, fine, asshole. You win. That was impressive."

His friend slapped him on the shoulder and sent another nod to the waitstaff. A server began slicing the dessert and plating it for them.

"So, our version of a Baked Alaska," Micah said, slipping into chef mode, "has a flourless chocolate torte as its base, then a homemade vanilla bean ice cream with cocoa nibs and a raspberry compote swirled in. And a cinnamon-vanilla meringue on top, of course."

"Oh my god," Poppy said on a sigh, her eyes glued to Micah. "That sounds divine."

The chef's smile grew, and Cade bit back a laugh. She was so damn cute.

"It pairs wonderfully with our house malbec, which is from Bellerose Family Cellars next door. Would either of you like a glass?"

Poppy shook her head as the waiter placed her dessert in front of her. "I'm good, Micah. Thank you."

"Thanks, man, but I'm driving, and I already had a beer tonight." Cade nodded toward Poppy as he stood. "Precious cargo, you know?"

"That I do, brother."

Cade hugged his friend with a hearty slap on the back. "Thanks for this, man."

"Anytime. I mean it." Micah turned to Poppy with an outstretched hand as Cade retook his seat. "It was lovely meeting you."

"You too." She shook his hand. "I've always wanted to come here. Dinner was so lovely. Thank you."

"I'll catch you this weekend, Cade?"

"Absolutely." Aside from being one of his very good

friends, Micah took multiple classes at the gym. "Be prepared, buddy."

Micah looked at him in horror. "Oh no. Remember our agreement? I get you in last minute, and you have to go easy on me when we spar."

Cade laughed. "Dream on, dude. Dream on."

CHAPTER SIXTEEN

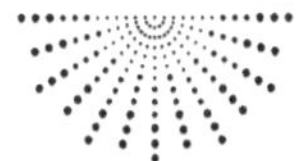

The evening had been as close to damn perfect as Cade could imagine. Dinner, dessert, a quick catch-up with his buddy, and the company of the most fascinating woman he'd ever met. A woman who was currently holding his hand as he drove her home.

There was a weird fluttering in his belly, and he wasn't sure what it meant. Twice, he opened his mouth to speak. Both times, he slammed it shut. He wasn't quite sure what to say now. He wanted them to do this again. To go out. Lunch, dinner, hiking, the movies—it didn't matter. He simply wanted to spend more time with her. But did he just ask? Was it that simple? Did he—

Holy shit. He was nervous. Stupid nervous. Middle-school-kid-with-his-first-crush nervous. After all, what if she hadn't felt a spark tonight? Or what if she'd realized he really wasn't all that cool? Holy shit, what if she liked Micah better than him? Holy fuck, that fucker. *I swear—*

She squeezed his hand, and her quiet chuckle filled the car. "You okay over there?"

Just like that, the budding panic crawling over his skin receded. Poppy was holding *his* hand. Not Micah's, dammit. He blew out an unsteady breath. "You know how your brain goes down a rabbit hole, and then it just . . . spirals to shit?"

"Uh, yeah." There was that soft, sweet chuckle again. "I'm the queen of overanalyzing."

"Well, queen." He brought her hand to his lips. "I'm pretty sure I'm the king, then."

Yeah. There was no way in hell he would admit he'd been insanely jealous of his friend. Who he knew would never try anything with Poppy. Micah was a manwhore, but he was a manwhore with morals. The dude didn't fuck around with other people's women. And yes, Cade was beginning to think of Poppy as his. So, nerves and all, he needed to be honest with her.

He ran his thumb over the back of her hand. "You know, Pop, I had a really good time tonight."

He fought a cringe because he could hear how dumb that sounded. "A really good time" was grossly inadequate to describe how much he'd enjoyed himself. Fuck, he had zero cool when it came to this woman.

"Me too, Cade," she said. He could hear the smile in her voice, and his nerves settled a bit. "Me too."

Before he could formulate his next thought, her building came into view. Parking in a spot in front of Rainy Day Boutique, he released her hand and shut off the car. He turned to her and—

"Would you like to come up?" Poppy froze, as if shocked by her own words, and her multicolored eyes went wide. In a giant rush, she added, "I mean, I don't expect us to do stuff, you know. I mean, we could, but we don't have to if you don't want to. No pressure or anything. It's just, I think it's been a really fun night, and I don't really want it to end yet. So, I figured we could just talk more or something and—"

Cade silenced her with his lips. She was so damn cute; he couldn't help himself. He kept the kiss soft and gentle, framing her face with his hands, angling her head so he could nip at her lower lip.

"I'd love to come upstairs," he said against her mouth, savoring her taste. Before their kiss got too heated, he pulled back an inch. "I want to do this again with you."

"The dinner or the kiss?"

"Yes."

Poppy's grin matched his. "I'd like that."

"Dinner tomorrow night? At Monty's?"

Her eyebrow arched. "You're willing to risk Four going all big brother on you?"

"For you?" He held her gaze, and though the interior of the car was dark, the streetlights illuminated that pretty flush along her cheeks. He kissed her again. How could he not? The woman was quickly becoming his favorite addiction. "You're absolutely worth the risk, babe. Now wait there a second, okay?"

Cade climbed out of the Range Rover and rounded the hood to open Poppy's door for her. They climbed the narrow stairs to her apartment. When the lights came on, he was taken aback by how much she'd accomplished in only a few days. Especially considering she hadn't been home for more than an hour since Monday night.

"Wow, Pop. It looks great in here," he said, impressed.

She hung up her coat on the hook mounted by the front door. "Well, the last time you were here, it was boxes and furniture on top of more boxes and furniture. So anything's an improvement."

"You're not wrong."

The apartment was as tiny as he remembered, but now it was homey. Neat as a pin, with decorations and framed photos on the bookshelves. A couple of art pieces rested against one wall, and he assumed she was in the process of figuring out which ones went where.

"Really, Poppy, it looks great."

"Thanks." Hands on her narrow hips, she surveyed the small space. "It's coming together. Slowly."

Poppy waved at the couch. He settled on one end, and she settled on the other. One cushion separated them.

"Oh, can I get you something to drink?" She began to rise.

He reached over, stilling her with a hand on her knee. "I'm good. Let's just talk. I want to get to know you better."

"Um, okay." She snuggled into the corner of the couch and placed a throw pillow on her lap. Fiddling with the pillow's tassel, she huffed out a breath. "Why am I so nervous all of a sudden?"

He grinned. "No clue. It's just me. Same boring guy you've been hanging with the last couple of days."

She rolled her eyes and snorted. "Riiight."

But she was smiling, and that anxious look was gone. Knowing he could calm her the same way she calmed him filled his chest with happiness. "Looks like you're settling in okay?"

"I'm getting there." Her shoulders relaxed, and her soft smile stayed in place while she looked around the apartment. "But the place is pretty tiny. It's tough getting used to."

"Can't beat the location, though."

"True. I think I've been able to get so much done and put away because I don't have to drive back and forth. Even though the house was only a few minutes away, the drive still took up a chunk of time. But I think I need to look for something a little bigger. Something with at least one more bedroom."

Even though he knew the answer, he still asked, "The boys?"

She nodded. "I know they're out of the house and all, but when they come home to visit, I want to have somewhere for them to stay. With me. I get that they're like a foot taller than me now, but they're still my babies, you know? It was nice of Four to let them sleep at his place last weekend, but that's not really a viable long-term option."

"I can see that. Besides, they come home to spend time with *you*." Carter and Dylan loved their mom. It was obvious to anyone who saw them all together.

"Yeah. They may not act like it at times, but I know it's true. The problem is everything around here's so expensive. I'm not quite sure I'm in a position to buy anything, especially now that I'm on my own."

He thought for a moment. "What about the door across the hall from you? Is it another apartment?"

Poppy shook her head. "No, it's a storage space. One giant room."

"Well, do you need the storage? If not, could you renovate it?"

Her lips pursed as she considered his question. "I hadn't thought about that. If I clear it out, I suppose it would be big enough for a couple bedrooms."

Cade shrugged. "I'm no architect, but maybe you could somehow reconfigure the floor. Make it one big apartment. It wouldn't be cheap, but I imagine a renovation would be less expensive than buying a house."

"Right?" She blew out a tired sigh. "This is why Eli selling the house for so cheap was so infuriating. If he'd just sold at market value, it would be easier to get a new place with my share of the proceeds. But . . ."

Disgust surged through Cade's entire being. That fucking guy. "I don't mean to speak out of turn, but your ex is a complete asshole."

Poppy laughed, but there was no humor in it. "You won't hear any arguments from me."

A contemplative look fell over her face, and she went quiet for a moment. Cade remained still, giving her time to collect the thoughts he saw turning in her head.

Just when he thought she wouldn't continue, she said, "I ran into him today. Literally ran into him, actually."

Relief flooded through Cade. Awe, too, at her decision to trust him. He'd do everything in his power to keep earning that trust.

"Eli heard a rumor that you and I are dating."

His eyebrows shot up. Damn. He knew the gossip train was speedy, but there had only been a few hours between him leaving her at the boutique and her encounter with Eli. "That was fast."

A smile lifted her lips. "Mrs. Green was at the shop when you dropped me off this morning."

He held his hands up. "Say no more."

"Exactly. Anyway, Eli was more than happy to share how ridiculous he thought the rumor was."

The fuck? "Why would it be ridiculous?"

Poppy simply stared at him. Like he was missing something obvious.

Frowning, he moved to sit next to her on the couch. "Babe, why would the idea of us dating be ridiculous?"

She scoffed. Honest to god scoffed. "Come on, Cade."

"What?" He truly didn't understand what she was getting at. They'd only had one official date, so he knew he was jumping the gun a bit, but in his mind, they worked. For the first time in forever, he had found someone he could just be himself around. No pretenses, no masks. He hoped like hell she felt the same.

"Cade, you're . . . *you*." Poppy waved her hands at him.

What the hell was *that* supposed to mean? "Is that a good thing?"

Her eyes rolled so hard, he winced. "You're stupid hot, Cade. Like, ridiculously so. I can't believe I'm going to admit this, but when we would run into each other before, like at Four's or something, you left me absolutely tongue-tied." He must have looked at her funny, because she shook her head and laughed. "Cade. To put it bluntly, you're so attractive, you make forming sentences difficult."

He still didn't know if that was a good thing or a bad thing. "You seem to be doing okay right now, Pop."

"Yeah. Because I know you better now."

He was at a loss for what to say. He wasn't a complete idiot; he knew some women found him attractive. Especially back during his fighting days. But those women didn't matter. He'd known that they'd only been interested in his bank account or had been looking for bragging rights.

"Poppy, I'm just a guy who owns a gym with his brother."

She pinned him with a get-real look.

"Okay, fine. I *used* to be famous-ish." He fought a shudder. Holy crap, he sounded like the biggest douchebag ever. "But all of that was just bullshit."

A cute, sheepish smile crossed her face. She shrugged. "Bullshit or not, it's a little intimidating."

"If anyone's intimidating here, babe, it's you." At her disbelieving look, he went with honesty. "When I asked you out last week, I was prepared to be shot down."

Her forehead scrunched. "You're kidding, right?"

"No, I'm not. You're the whole package, Pop." He took her hands in his and waited until she met his eyes. "I'm being one hundred percent serious here. You're successful, hilarious, obviously a great mom, and you can put up with fucking Four. I mean, come on."

She laughed. Just as he'd intended.

"On the shallow side," he continued, holding her gaze, "you look great all dolled up *and* without a lick of makeup on." Her head dropped, so he lifted her chin with a gentle hand. "Poppy. You're so damn pretty. I know you don't believe me, but trust me on this, okay? I think everything about you is so damn stunning. And the fact that you invited me up here? That you're sitting with me and letting me get to know you? I'm not taking that for granted."

"Thank you," she whispered. A tiny smile lifted the corners of her lips. She looked so adorable and so damn uncomfortable at the same time. "That's really kind of you to say."

He wanted to kick Eli's ass, because he knew that fucker was responsible for why she thought so little of herself. "Not 'kind,' Poppy. Just facts. So, when that dumbass says the idea of us dating is ridiculous, I say fuck Eli—"

"No, thank you." She smirked, and her eyes twinkled.

Cade grinned. There she was. The strong, sassy woman who flipped shit at Four and kept her boys in line with a simple look. "Eli's bullshit doesn't matter. Because that's what it is, babe. Bullshit."

No matter what Poppy thought of herself, this man had a way of making her feel beautiful. Which was crazy. Cade warmed something inside her, something that she'd thought had fizzled out a long time ago.

For as long as she could remember, her self-confidence had been shaky at best.

Throughout her childhood, her parents had been cool and distant. She'd never measured up to their expectations. So, as a starry-eyed teenager, she had fallen hard for the first boy who'd told her she was pretty. Four months into their relationship, she'd gotten pregnant. And dumped. Afterward, it had been pure survival. For years. She'd been too concerned with putting food on the table and keeping a roof over her and her boys' heads to give dating much thought. She'd still been a teenager, after all.

At twenty-five, when she had finally settled into a groove with the boys, she'd met Eli. He'd been her first attempt at dating as an adult. He'd charmed and wowed her. He'd made her feel wanted. Special. He'd built her up only to snuff her out later in spectacular fashion. Her confidence, her self-worth, her spirit . . . All had taken a hit.

So, Cade's compliments were hard for Poppy to believe, even if part of her really wanted to. She feared he was just messing with her, but she hoped that wasn't the case. Because she really liked him. And not for the mystique of him, but for who he was.

"I haven't felt pretty in a long time," she admitted with a wince. She couldn't believe she was saying it out loud. However, there was something about this man that felt . . . safe. "I appreciate you saying what you did."

His grin widened. "Well, I'm more than happy to remind you just how pretty I think you are. I can be very persuasive, you know." He traced his finger along her jaw, and she fought a shiver.

"Is that so?" Wait, was that flirty, husky voice hers? She gulped.

Cade's dark-brown eyes heated, making her stomach twirl with desire. Before she could second-guess herself, before she could overthink anything, before she could chicken out, she leaned forward and kissed him.

For a moment, Cade held perfectly still. Doubt and insecurity flared deep within her.

Then his hands buried in her hair, and he *devoured* her.

Their tongues tangled, and everything inside her sprang to life. She moaned when he pulled her astride him, hiking her dress up high on her thighs. A groan escaped when his erection pressed against her core. His slacks did nothing to hide his excitement. Knowing their only barriers were her damp panties and the thin material of his pants, she rubbed against him. The friction had her skin tingling. His hands gripped her ass, guiding her movements, grinding her harder against his cock.

"Fuck, Poppy," he growled, feasting on her neck. "You feel so damn good."

Delicious tension built inside her.

"Cade," she whispered, desperate to get closer to him. "Touch me. Please."

Abruptly, he pulled away, eyes blazing with fire. Then he crashed his lips onto hers again, claiming her with his mouth and tongue. It wasn't a gentle kiss. It wasn't a sweet kiss. It was hungry and desperate, and she couldn't get enough. Her hips never broke rhythm as she raked her fingers through his hair.

Cade made quick work of her dress, leaving her clad in only her bra and panties. Before she could become self-conscious, his mouth was back. Her heart raced as his hard body lowered her onto the couch cushions. She yanked up his shirt, and soon it was on the floor beside her dress. They were skin to skin now, and wetness flooded her panties.

The light hair on his chest was bristly, and heat radiated from him. When she scratched her nails down his back, he let out another growl. His lips trailed the length of her neck; his hands cupped her breasts. Pushing her bra aside, he rolled her nipple. Her back arched, and she groaned his name. She'd never wanted a man more.

"Look at me," Cade rasped.

Her breath came in pants as she obeyed. Desire and need stared back at her.

"You're so fucking beautiful, Poppy." He pinched her nipple, causing her to suck in a breath. His eyes twinkled. "You may not fully believe me yet, but I swear I will show you how much I want you." Without breaking eye contact, he took her breast in his mouth.

A slight nip had her quaking, flaming. Her pent-up desire threatened to explode. "More, Cade. Please."

He moved to her other breast, and her bra magically landed atop the pile of clothes on the floor. His fingers caressed and pinched while his mouth nibbled and savored. Every nerve in her body hummed with pleasure, and all she could do was enjoy each sensation he bestowed upon her. One hand wandered down her body, raising goosebumps on her skin. When he traced the seam of her panties, all the way to where her thong disappeared, her pulse skyrocketed.

With a single yank, Cade tore her panties off and tossed them aside. He skimmed her lower lips, his teasing touch lighting her on fire. "Fuck, babe. Look how wet you are for me."

She clutched his arm, and his mouth claimed hers again.

"Cade," she begged against his lips. Her insides trembled. She needed more. Needed him.

"I've got you, babe," he murmured. He spread her folds, and when his thumb slicked over her clit, she convulsed. "You're so fucking beautiful. I want to watch you come."

He sank two fingers deep inside her, and she cried out. Her hips rocked against his hand as he pumped in and out. His steady rhythm picked up speed, and her heart raced.

"That's it, beautiful girl. Come all over my hand, babe."

Oh my god, his touch, his words . . .

Screaming his name, she detonated. Her body clenched and throbbed around him.

"That's it, Pop. Fucking beautiful," he praised, dropping kisses along her jaw.

His fingers still worked, caressing and easing her back down until she trembled with aftershocks. Then, holding her gaze, he pulled his fingers from her body and licked them clean. With that ridiculously sexy smirk on his lips.

Holy hell. Who knew watching him do that would be so hot?

She drew Cade down to her for a kiss. Tasting herself on him, she moaned, roaming her hands over his hard chest and every dip and valley of his abs. When she came to the button on his pants, however, his hand settled over hers.

Poppy's eyes narrowed in confusion. There was still desire in his gaze. And his hard cock was straining the material of his pants. Yet . . .

Holy shit. Had she read something wrong?

She swallowed, suddenly nervous. "Do you not want—"

His lips silenced her. Then, in a voice like gravel, he said, "Oh, I want, babe. I most definitely want."

"Then why—"

Again, she was cut off. This time, by a soft press of his finger to her mouth.

"This isn't about me." His brown eyes held hers. "This is about you. I want you to know how gorgeous I think you are. And not just your stunning body. I mean, don't get me wrong, you're fucking exquisite, but I think *everything* about you is beautiful, Poppy."

Tears threatened to fall, and she blinked them back. Holding his face in her hands, she ran her thumb over the stubble along his jaw. This man had done the unimaginable. "You make me believe it."

"Good." He kissed the tip of her nose. "I want to make you believe it every damn day. Because it's true."

His words and gentle touches were a warm blanket over her heart and soul.

"Now . . ." Cade adjusted their positions so he spooned her, his hard cock nestling between her cheeks. He wrapped his strong arms around her, and she sank into his chest. "What do you say about me holding you for a little bit?"

"Not a bad plan," she said, stroking the coarse hair covering his forearms. "Not a bad plan at all."

CHAPTER SEVENTEEN

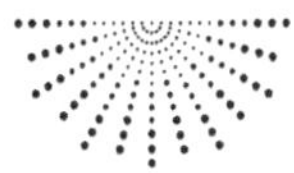

Cocooned in warm arms, a smile ghosted Poppy's lips as her eyes blinked open. She must have dozed off. Something buzzed nearby, and her smile faded. Her phone was ringing. At nearly eleven at night, according to the wall clock. Dread curled in her belly. No one called her this late.

She scrambled out of Cade's embrace and tossed on her dress. Without zipping it up, she grabbed her purse, which she'd set on the end table earlier and dug for her phone. Her heart pitched when she saw the display.

"Carter?"

"Hey, Mom. It's Dylan, actually. Now don't panic."

It was like all the air had been sucked from the room. Every horrible scenario—serial killers, car accidents, shootings—flashed in her mind.

"Honey, what's wrong?"

"C got arrested, but I promise it's okay—"

"What?" Her shriek had Cade's arms around her in an instant. "What do you mean, your brother got arrested?"

"Mom, look—"

"Don't 'look' me, young man. What's going on?" Her heart

raced. With Fear? Anger? She didn't know, but it wasn't good.

"Mom—"

Cade took the phone from her hand. In a hurry, he said, "D, it's Cade. Hang on a minute, okay?"

Dumbfounded, she looked at Cade. Before she could lay into him for taking her phone away, his hands gripped her shoulders and squeezed. "Babe, you have to breathe. You're gonna hyperventilate."

What the hell was he talking abou—

Her vision went hazy for a moment. He squeezed again, and she gasped. The influx of oxygen cleared her sight.

"There you go." Cade held her gaze, and her panic ebbed. A little. "I'm gonna put the phone on speaker, okay? Let's hear what D has to say. I'm right here with you. I've got you."

"Okay." She collapsed into the couch.

Cade tapped a couple of buttons on her phone and placed it on the coffee table. Grabbing his shirt off the ground, he yanked it on, then sat down beside her. His warmth and woodsy scent comforted Poppy as he tucked her close. She let out her breath and leaned into him.

"D, I'm here with your mom, and you're on speaker. You said your brother got arrested?"

"Yeah, he did." There was an odd note of pride in Dylan's voice.

Her eyes narrowed. More of the panic receded. "Tell us what happened, honey."

"Me and C were grabbing a late dinner on The Ave and ran into Jackie from Cade's gym. She's the boxing coach for our class. Anyway, we all left the restaurant together, and then this guy came out of nowhere and hit her with some kind of metal thing. C fought the dude, and I tried to help Jackie. She didn't get knocked out, but she was really out of it."

Poppy's blood chilled. "Oh my god."

"Holy fuck," Cade muttered, scrubbing a hand over his face.

"Someone called the cops, and C had the guy in a choke when they showed up. Then the asshole started saying C attacked him. I said that's not what happened, but the cops didn't listen to me. They arrested both of them!"

"Where are you now, honey?" She placed her hands over her heart. Holy crap, the damn thing was trying to pound its way out of her chest.

"I'm still in the emergency room with Jackie. She didn't want to go by herself. She was really scared, Mom." His voice broke on the last words.

Poppy's heart clenched. "When did all this happen?"

"A couple hours ago, I think."

"Thank you, D," Cade said, using a soothing tone. He took her trembling hands in his. "I know I can speak for my brother, too, when I say we really appreciate you staying with Jack. She's like our little sister, so it really means a lot, man."

Poppy heard Dylan take a deep breath. "Cade, Jackie had me call Dante when we first got to the hospital. He said he was going to figure out what was going on with C. So don't be surprised if he calls you—"

As if on cue, Cade's phone rang with Dante's name lighting up the screen.

"I'm gonna talk to my brother, D. You stay on with your mom." Cade kissed the top of her head and rose. Crossing the small room to the kitchen, he spoke in hushed tones with his brother.

Poppy took her phone off speaker and returned it to her ear. "Are you okay, honey?"

"I think so." Dylan blew out another loud breath. "But holy shit, Mom. It was so scary."

She nodded, not bothering to remind him about his language. Because holy shit, just *hearing* about it was scary. What she would give to hug her son right now . . . She glanced at the time. "I don't think I'll be able to get out there until morning, but I can be on the first ferry—" *Shit!* She dropped her forehead to her palm. "My car's still in the shop."

"It's okay, Mom. Oh, hang on a sec."

She strained to hear, but Dylan's next words were too muffled. Cade strode over to her and sat. He nodded at her phone in question.

"He's talking to someone."

Cade held out his hand. "May I?"

She gave him her phone, and he placed it back on speaker.

While they waited for Dylan, Cade said, "My brother's with C. SPD released him."

She sagged into the couch, relief flooding every nerve in her body. "Oh thank god. Is he okay? Are you sure?"

"Yeah, babe. They didn't charge C with anything. Dante has him, and they just got to the hospital. My brother's got the twins. I promise. How about you? Are you okay? Hanging in there?"

Poppy nodded, even though she wasn't close to okay. She wouldn't be until she laid eyes on her boys.

"Sorry about that, Mom," Dylan said. "A couple of guys from the gym showed up for Jackie. They said they saw Dante and C pulling into the parking garage."

"Good. I'm glad they're there. I want you both to call me when you get home, okay? I don't care what time it is."

"You got it. And, Mom?"

"Yeah, honey?"

"You don't need to come out tomorrow. I think me and C are gonna stick around the hospital, make sure she's okay, you know? But . . ."

Her forehead scrunched. "But what, Dyl?"

"I know we were just there, but is it okay if C and I come home this weekend?"

The slight quiver in her son's voice had Poppy's chest wrenching tight. Her eyes welled, and it took everything she had to hold it together. "Absolutely, honey. You never have to ask."

"Cool, I'll let C know. Call you in a little bit, then. Love you, Mom."

"Love you, too," she replied, though the three beeps indicated he'd already hung up.

Holding her breath, she stared at the ceiling and willed her heart to stop aching. Every fiber of her being wanted to pack up the boys and move them home with her. Forever.

"Come here, babe."

Before she could register what was happening, Cade scooped her up and placed her over his lap. Then his arms went around her, and she snuggled into his embrace. Turning her head, she buried her face against his neck. The first tear broke free.

"Holy shit, Cade." She let out a watery chuckle and sniffed. "I think I just experienced every single freaking emotion in the last ten minutes."

"I'll talk to Dylan about it, but I'm pretty sure it's a universal understanding that you never start a conversation, especially with your mom, by saying, 'Now don't panic.'"

"Right? I almost had a heart attack. Every horrible scenario ran through my mind." Just remembering the panic had her blinking away more tears. "The boys don't call. Ever. They text. Sometimes we'll do a video call, but that's usually after we've been texting. So, for one of them to call out of the blue . . ." She sat up and shook her head, wiping the remnants of her tears. "I swear, that was just too much." She held out her shaking hands. "See?"

Cade tugged her right back into his arms. "I've got you, Pop. I've got you."

He rubbed her back, up and down, over and over until her hands steadied. For the first time in what seemed like forever—but was probably only twenty minutes max—she felt like she could breathe again.

Cade's phone rang, and her pulse kicked.

"It's okay, babe. It's just my brother." Without letting her go, he reached for his phone and answered, putting it on speaker.

<hr>

"Hey, D. I have Poppy here with me."

"Hey, guys," Dante said, sounding utterly exhausted. "First, Poppy, the boys are okay."

"Thank you." The relief in Poppy's voice was palpable. More than anything, Cade wanted to wrap her in a damn bubble so nothing could upset her ever again. "How's Jackie?"

"She'll be all right. Luckily, there was no damage to her skull. She has a concussion and about eight stitches on the back of her scalp, so they're keeping her overnight to be safe." Dante chuckled. "Man, bro, you should have been there when Jackie found out they shaved the back of her head."

Cade smiled. He could imagine the ruckus their fiery friend must have made.

At Poppy's questioning look, he explained, "Jackie is tough as nails. Former Golden Gloves champ. Kick-ass boxer. Excellent trainer and coach." Talking about the woman who'd become part of their family, he smiled wider. "She's also the biggest girly girl there is. Loves getting all done up with the lashes, the glitter, the hair."

"I thought she was going to fucking throw down when

the doctor came in." Dante laughed, but his humor quickly faded.

Cade knew his brother was thinking the exact same thing he was: that they'd come too damn close to losing one of their own.

Bile surged up his throat at the thought of Poppy's boys getting hurt.

No. Fuck no. They are okay. Jackie will be okay, he told himself. And yet, trepidation still twisted his stomach.

"You know, D, I have a bad feeling about this. With what just happened at the Seattle gym and the shit here with the lights, this feels all kinds of wrong."

"Yeah. It fucking does." His brother was quiet for a moment. Then, with a loud sigh, he continued, "I was on the phone with Gavin before I called you. He and Alvarez got word that the fire investigator and SPD ruled it was an explosive device that took down the roof."

Cade's ears began ringing. A bomb? Holy. Fuck.

It shouldn't have surprised him. The possibility had been on all their radars. But it did. It fucking shocked him to the core, like an unexpected one-two punch straight to the chin.

Poppy hugged him tight, and he remembered to breathe. Damn. Her warmth, her empathy, her strength—they all brought his budding panic down a notch.

"For real?" Cade asked when he was finally able to speak.

"Yeah. Alvarez made some calls. SPD wants to meet tomorrow to officially go over the findings." A noise came through the speaker, like his brother was scrubbing his hands over his face.

"Do you need me with you? I'll be there."

"Nah, stay on Hudson. Alvarez said the police don't have much. They determined it was basically a homemade bomb of some sort, but that's all they know."

"What the fuck, D?"

"My sentiments exactly, little bro. By the way, thanks for checking on Rebecca and Roc today. I sure as fuck hate being away from them, so I really appreciate you stopping in."

"Always, brother." Rebecca and Rocco were part of his family, and Cade would do everything he could to look out for them, to protect them. Just like he'd do whatever he could to protect Poppy and her boys.

Cade stilled at that last thought. At the meaning behind it.

"I should be back sometime tomorrow afternoon or early evening," Dante said, pulling Cade from his thoughts. "My meeting with the investigator is at nine, but I want to check on everyone before I head back."

"Great. Want to meet up and hash it all out whenever you get home?"

"Yup. I'm gonna stop in and see Rebecca first, but I'll text you when I'm on the Hudson ferry. Do me a favor and round up Gavin and Alvarez for our meeting, too."

"You got it. I'll text them tonight. What has SPD learned about the guy that attacked Jackie? Do they know why he came after her? Was it random?"

"They're not saying anything, but that's another reason I want Gavin and Alvarez there when we meet tomorrow. They'll be able to get answers we can't."

"Sounds like a plan, D."

"Thanks, C. And, Poppy?"

"I'm here," she said, tensing in his arms.

Cade ran a hand down her back, as much to comfort himself as her.

"I've got the twins. Don't worry about them. I mean, I know you will because you're their mom, but I've got them. They're saying goodbye to Jackie right now, and I'll swing them to their dorm when they're done. And Carter's good. Getting thrown in cuffs pissed him off, but he held it together. I was able to talk with him on the way to the hospital, see where his head was at. Let me tell you, you've got a good kid in that one. Dylan, too. The way they stepped in to protect Jackie—" Dante's voice was thick. He cleared his throat. "We're indebted to them, Poppy. Jackie's one strong woman, but from what I've heard, that guy came out of fucking nowhere. God knows what would have happened if she'd been by herself."

Poppy shivered, and Cade resumed rubbing along her spine. When she leaned into his touch, satisfaction rushed through him. He knew she was struggling with her emotions. Hell, they all were. But these were *her* kids . . .

"Thank you again, Dante," she said. "Part of me is still petrified that they were involved in something like that. But the other part, especially since I know the boys and Jackie are all going to be okay . . . The other part's thankful they were there to help her."

"I know what you mean. Try to get some rest tonight, okay? C, we'll talk more tomorrow."

After disconnecting the call, they sat in silence. Until Poppy yawned.

Drawing her close, Cade settled into the couch cushions and kissed the top of her head. The citrus scent of her shampoo tickled his nose. "You should get to bed. You've been through the emotional wringer."

"True." She snuggled into him, and he felt her nod beneath his chin. "Some seriously amazing highs tonight"— she tilted her head up and smiled at him, then turned somber —"and some seriously frightening lows. I'm thankful you were here with me for the scary parts. *You* were my anchor tonight, Cade, and I can't thank you enough."

God, this woman.

"There's nothing to thank me for." He pulled her up his body so he could kiss her lips. "You going to be okay tonight?"

"Yeah, I'll be fine." She climbed off him with another giant yawn. "I'd invite you to stay over, but . . ." Her shy smile and shrug went straight to his heart.

"As much as I want to, babe, I'd decline. I really want us to take our time."

Poppy snorted. "I don't think I'd call what we did earlier 'taking our time.'"

He chuckled. Yeah. Maybe not. He could still taste her on his tongue. "Well, take our time-*ish*." His thoughts turned to everything that had transpired after their spectacular time together. He frowned. "Are you sure you'll be okay tonight? I can absolutely stay if you need me to. With the twins and everything, it was a lot."

Her eyes softened, and she gave him her sweetest smile yet. "I'll be fine. I think your persuasive abilities earlier exhausted me. I'm just going to crash."

Cade tucked a stray lock of hair behind her ear. "Anytime you have doubts about how gorgeous you are, just let me know. I'll be more than happy to use my persuasive skills on you." He kissed her, pulling away before it became any harder for him to leave. Spotting his dress shoes near the front door, he kneeled to put them on.

"Thank you again for tonight," she murmured, running a hand over his shoulders when he stood.

"Thank *you*." He gathered her into his arms and simply held her. "We still on for dinner tomorrow night at Monty's?"

She looked up at him. "Don't you have to meet your brother and the guys around then?"

"I do. But I want to see you. If our schedules get crazy, maybe we can have everyone meet us. Rebecca and Roc, too, if need be." He tipped her chin all the way up and kissed her again. "Nothing we have to discuss is top secret. You saw the destruction at the gym. Your boys were there when Jackie was assaulted. Besides, it would be good to have your perspective on things."

She nodded, yawning again. This time, it was contagious.

"On that note, I'll head out." As much as Cade didn't want to, he disentangled himself from her, put on his jacket, and opened the door.

"Text me when you get home, okay? So I know you made it."

"You got it." He smiled and gave her one last kiss. Because he could, dammit. "Lock up behind me. I'll see you tomorrow."

CHAPTER EIGHTEEN

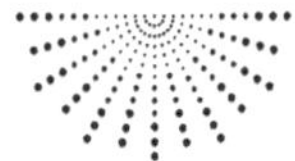

The bell chimed, and a giant bouquet of flowers in every shade of pink walked through Rainy Day Boutique's front door. A woman peeked out from behind the blooms, and Poppy laughed.

"Holy crap, Jenny, that has to be the biggest bouquet I've ever seen. For a second, I thought the flower arrangement had sprouted legs!"

Jenny, the owner of Petal Pushers, grinned from ear to ear. "Special delivery, my dear."

"Wait, since when do you do deliveries?"

"Since a certain resident hunk came in and placed one of the biggest single orders we've ever had. Where do you want them?"

Poppy's jaw dropped, and she studied the enormous bouquet with renewed interest. Peonies, roses, chrysanthemums, and other flowers she didn't recognize. "Oh wow. The counter would be great."

She walked with Jenny to the back of her shop. Heat tore over her face when she saw Mrs. Abbot, Mrs. Yoshida, and

Mrs. Green standing by the wineglass display, all smiling at her with knowing gleams in their eyes.

Jenny lowered the arrangement onto the counter, then placed a gift bag next to it. "This is for you as well."

She opened the small card first.

Poppy,
Even with all the craziness, I've enjoyed these last couple of days with you. I'm looking forward to spending more time together.
See you tonight,
Cade

With a swoony sigh, Poppy placed the card back on the counter.

"Gorgeous and sweet," Jenny said, wagging her eyebrows. "Doesn't get much better than that, does it?"

She grinned at the other woman. "It's a potent combination, for sure."

"I'll say. Now look in the bag! I'm dying to know what's in there."

Poppy pulled the tissue paper from the top and peeked in. Then laughed. A family-sized bag of gummy bears. Of course.

"Gorgeous, sweet, *and* remembers inside jokes." Jenny squeezed her arm. "Good for you, girl."

Poppy laughed again when Jenny turned to the other women and said, "All right, ladies, come on over and get your gossip straight from the source. And if you think this arrangement is pretty, I can give you fifteen percent off an arrangement of your own. Just stop by the shop sometime in the next few days and ask for the 'resident hunk' discount."

The women descended like vultures. Even Bethany, who'd been helping the ladies with their shopping. Jenny flashed a mischievous smile as she made her escape, and Poppy shook her head. Yes, the three women surrounding her were the gossip train leaders, but Jenny was no slouch herself. Being Hudson's only florist meant she was privy to not only birthdays and anniversaries, but also who was in the doghouse and who was wooing whom.

Speaking of which, she reached for the card. Mrs. Green snatched it up first, and Poppy's eyes widened. Wow. Who knew the woman had such ninja-like reflexes?

The trio fawned over Cade's message, passing the card around.

Mrs. Abbot looked at Poppy. "I don't know a lot about that fighting stuff, only what I've been told about the kick-boxing class, but those De la Rosa boys are good eggs."

Mrs. Green hummed in agreement. "They're great business owners, to boot."

Mrs. Yoshida nodded. "Goodness knows they're not hard on the eyes, either."

The women continued on about "the muscles on those young men," and Poppy worked hard to suppress her laughter. She grabbed her phone and waved it at Bethany in question. When her friend and employee nodded, shooing her away, Poppy walked to the front of the store and sent Cade a quick text.

> Thank you for the flowers. And gummy bears.

A smile lifted her lips when he immediately replied.

CADE

> I'm glad you like them. Did you know gummy bears are one of my favorites, too?

Hey now, mister, are you trying to get me to share?

CADE

I can be very persuasive, if you'll recall.

She shivered. Yes. Yes, she sure did recall.

Hmm . . . I suppose I'll consider sharing.

CADE

Excellent. What time do you close tonight?

6:30

CADE

Great. I'll swing by then and we can walk to Monty's for dinner. That work?

Perfect, see you then.

The smile on her face was beginning to hurt in the best way. Was this what dating was like? It had been so long, she'd forgotten.

"If that's not an über-gushy smile, then I don't know what is."

Poppy looked up at the familiar voice. Scarlet. The sweet, spunky woman was a waitress at Ray's Diner, and over the past year, she had become one of Poppy's closest friends. They both had their secrets, but when things with Eli had splintered and then shattered, Scarlet had been in her corner, supporting her. Hell, even holding her up at times.

While more than a decade separated them, they had so much in common. Like having been young single mothers and the new person in a nosy small town. Or like their love of jalapeño potato chips dipped in sour cream.

She studied the woman in front of her. From her long, dark-brown, almost-black hair that was pulled into a high ponytail, it's teal and pink streaks catching the light, to her bubblegum-pink waitress uniform, to the white high-top Converse on her feet. Poppy's heart squeezed. Scarlet was the younger sister Poppy had never had. One of the select few that she called family. That's why she knew, without a doubt, that she could be honest with Scarlet. There'd be no judgement. Teasing, perhaps, but never judgement.

"Scar," Poppy said in a whisper. She could hear the wonder and nerves in her voice. "I think I'm dating Cade de la Rosa."

"Uh, yeah." Scarlet waved at the flowers. "I'd say that's a fair statement."

"I can't quite wrap my head around it."

"Why?"

Poppy stared at her friend. "Because he's *Cade de la Rosa.*"

Scarlet rolled her eyes. "*Cade de la Rosa* is a hot athlete who has a ton of money and pseudo-celebrity status. Is *that* what interests you about him?"

"What? No! I don't care about any of that. He's sweet and funny and, yeah, stupid hot . . . but it's more than that."

Scarlet's eyebrows rose in challenge.

Poppy stepped closer and lowered her voice. "He listens, Scar. He asks me what I think about things. And he's great with the boys. He talks to them and not *at* them, you know? He doesn't act like he's better than them." And he made her feel so damn special.

"So why are you doing the whole 'Cade de la Rosa' thing? Why are you acting like he's better than you?"

Poppy *was* doing that, wasn't she? She sighed, shaking her head. "I don't know. Habit, I guess?"

"Holy Christ, Pop," Scarlet huffed. "Your self-esteem is total shit. You know that, right?" Poppy started to defend herself, but Scarlet held up a hand. "And I can say that because we're like sisters, so don't get your panties in a wad."

Poppy laughed. "You're right. But I'm working on it."

And she really was. First, by making a conscious effort to not automatically blame herself for everything that went wrong, from the demise of her marriage to her car breaking down. Second, she was trying to focus on the good—her boys, her business, and whatever this new . . . thing with Cade was. She had to admit that he was helping. A lot. His attention, the little things he did for her, the way he looked at her . . . like he valued *her* . . . It all went a long way in shoring up her dented confidence.

"That's great, Pop. Now tell me everything. I want *all* the spicy details."

Setting his phone down, Cade smiled. The sweet, flirty texts from Poppy had him wishing it was already time to pick her up.

A pencil smacked him in the chest, interrupting his thoughts.

"What the fuck?" He scowled at the two grinning faces across the conference table. Gavin and Bean. Matt was also watching, but he looked indifferent. Well, mostly. The corners of his friend's lips were twitching. The fuckers. Well, not Bean, she was nice. The other two though . . .

"Can we continue?" Gavin asked, humor lighting his eyes.

Cade tossed the pencil back at his friend. Gavin caught it mid-air. Because of course he did.

"Sorry, Bean," Cade said, shooting the IT guru a wink. "You were saying?"

"No worries." She pointed at the wall, where a copy of the lawsuit was projected. "Joshua Justin. Thirty years old. He pre-paid you for six months of personal training sessions roughly two and a half years ago. He only took four sessions, and two days after that last one, the full amount was refunded to him. He's suing you personally for defamation and is seeking two years of lost wages."

The lawsuit was replaced with a driver's license photo. White guy, brown hair, brown eyes. Super generic. Cade remembered coaching Justin, but he truly wouldn't be able to pick him out of a lineup. Aside from his shitty attitude, there'd been nothing worth noting about him.

So. Fucking. Nuts.

"Justin is saying that if it weren't for you, he would have made it big. Hence the lost wages."

"That's the stupidest load of bullshit I've ever heard," Cade said.

"Well, yeah. Any judge would dismiss this shit," Gavin said. "However, it made me curious. Why is this guy doing this? I mean, it's obviously a bullshit lawsuit. He has to know that. Unless he's an idiot. And why now? What's this guy been up to for the last two and a half years?"

God help anyone Gavin became *curious* about. But since this asshole had sued him, Cade was more than happy to green-light Hudson Security crawling up Justin's ass.

"I did a little dive into Justin's financials, because follow the money, right?" Bean said as she typed.

Cade nodded. Once, he had questioned Bean about the legality of "follow the money," and the look she'd sent his way had shriveled up his balls. So now he kept his mouth shut and just watched as she did her thing.

"It looks like Justin was a partner in a failed joint venture called Fight Club Gyms LLC," Bean continued, displaying more documents on the wall. "They opened in North Seattle at the beginning of last year and closed about nine months later. Have you heard of it?"

Cade shook his head. "No. But I don't really concern myself with other gyms. We're busy enough as it is."

"Fair. If I were the big dog, I wouldn't, either."

"Who are the other partners?" Matt asked.

Bean grinned in obvious approval. "You read my mind, buddy. You need to come work with us. It'd be fun." She turned to Cade, and the gleam in her eyes vanished. Unease crawled up his spine. "There was only one other partner listed in the formation docs. Alister Keys."

Cade's heart stopped. Holy. Fuck. "You're fucking kidding me, Bean."

"Sorry."

"Who the fuck's Alister Keys?" Gavin asked, eyes narrowing.

Cade shook his head. What the fuck was going on? "Former brother-in-law."

"Alana's brother?" Matt asked. "Is he the dumbass wannabe-fighter brother or the felon brother?"

"Dumbass wannabe-fighter brother," Cade mumbled, blowing out a breath.

"By felon brother, I assume you mean Adair Keys," Bean chimed in, fingers flying over the keyboard. "Adair has been locked up tight at the Washington State Pen in Walla Walla for the last nine years. Looks like he's not up for parole for another eight to ten."

"Interesting. Now back to the failed gym. Do we think it has something to do with the lawsuit?" Gavin asked, reining in the conversation.

Bean tapped her chin. "Well, even though the gym was only open for roughly nine months, Justin and Keys amassed an enormous amount of debt."

"Wait," Cade said. "I'm getting sued because this Justin fucker and my dumbass ex-brother-in-law can't run a business?"

Bean stretched her arms out in front of her. "When I say

an enormous amount of debt, I'm not exaggerating. They owe just over two million."

Damn. "Why don't they file for bankruptcy?"

"Because the debt they owe isn't to a bank. Hang on." The projection changed again as Bean began to type. He couldn't make heads or tails of the info flashing on the wall. "I can't tell for certain, but from the web of shell companies I tracked, it looks like they borrowed from either the Morozov family or the Kovalenkos."

"Fuuuck," Matt groaned.

"You're shitting me, right?" Gavin said at the same time.

"I'm not," Bean said with a grimace. "They're fucked."

Cade glanced around the table, and worry turned his gut. "Dude, I own a fucking gym. I don't know what you guys are talking about. Who the hell are the Morozov and Kovalenko families?"

"Russian mafia."

His eyes widened. Holy fuck. What world had he stepped into? "But how does a bullshit lawsuit get Justin and Keys their money? And assuming everything's related, why would they bomb the Seattle gym or attack Jackie or scope out the Hudson property?"

The room went quiet for a moment, everyone deep in thought.

Then Gavin sighed. "My guess is that the lawsuit is a shakedown attempt."

"Not a very good one." Bean snorted. "The lawsuit's ridiculous."

Gavin leaned back in his chair. "True, but we may not be dealing with the sharpest tools in the shed."

"They're still dangerous and destructive, though," Matt chimed in. "But yeah, maybe not the brightest guys."

Gavin nodded at Matt's comment. "My initial thought is that perhaps they're trying to intimidate you into giving them money. Maybe they'll say the harassment stops when you pay up."

"But why *me?*"

"Justin and Keys have both interacted with you. They know you have money. I mean, it's not a secret that you've done well for yourself. And they're desperate. They probably decided you're the fastest route to getting themselves out of hot water."

"Don't discount revenge," Matt added.

Cade's frown deepened. "How so? I barely remember this Justin guy."

Matt rubbed his chin. "Yeah, but if you look at Keys, you were that fucker's meal ticket."

True, but . . . "But I didn't leave Alana. She divorced me."

"Wow, what a dumb, dumb woman," Bean murmured.

Despite the gravity of the situation, the corners of Cade's lips tipped up. "Appreciate that, Bean."

"Okay. We've got these two guys," Gavin said, standing and writing both names on the whiteboard. "We have the lawsuit, the flashlights scoping out the property line, and the bomb at the gym. And the assault on Jackie."

"Don't forget the stuff from this morning," Bean said.

Wait, what? Cade whipped his head toward Bean, but before he could ask for clarification, Gavin asked Matt, "Anything more on the guy who attacked Jackie?"

"So far, it's a dead end. Homeless addict who was paid fifty bucks and some fent to hit her over the head with a steel pipe." Matt crossed his arms over his chest. "My old partner, Tran, peeked in on the interrogation and said the dude was a wreck. Crying, not understanding why 'that punk kid' attacked him. In and out of lucidity. Borderline hysterical. I don't think they're gonna get much more out of him."

Gavin stared at the whiteboard. "It's gotta be connected . . ."

A knock at the conference room door had everyone turning.

"Sorry to interrupt." The woman's expression said otherwise.

Natasha Silver. One of two female personal security officers employed by Hudson Security. Cade had met the highly skilled PSO on a number of occasions. She was somewhere in her thirties and a dead ringer for Wonder Woman. He'd sparred with her twice and quickly discovered she was dangerous. He didn't know her background, but he assumed it involved some sort of superspy shit. As far as Cade was concerned, the less he knew, the better.

"What have you got, Tash?" Gavin asked, gesturing toward the vacant seats at the opposite end of the long table.

Tash placed a file folder on the table and slid a thumb drive to Bean before sitting. While Bean plugged the thumb drive into her laptop, Gavin dialed out on the room's speakerphone.

"This is Dante."

Cade's eyebrows rose at his brother's voice.

"It's Gavin. Tash is about to give us an update on your situation, so I wanted to patch you in." Gavin caught Cade's stare. "The security cameras at D's house were tripped early this morning. Given Dante's out of town and Rebecca and Rocco are home alone, and in light of all the shit going down, I sent some PSOs over to keep an eye on things."

His stomach dropped. Holy shit. If anyone tried to hurt his little nephew and pregnant sister-in-law . . . He clenched his fists beneath the table.

While Cade's house was down the road from the gym and on their family's property—thus within Hudson Security's protective fences—his brother's place was closer to downtown. Dante and Rebecca had originally lived on property in a cottage, which they still owned, but once they'd had Rocco, they'd moved to a residential neighborhood. They'd wanted Rocco to have neighbors, and the central location was better for Rebecca's home-based day care.

Gavin swung his attention to the two women in the room and said, "Go."

"First off, D," Tash said, "I left Xander with Rebecca. He'll remain inside the house with her and all the kids until one of us—preferably not me—relieves him."

At the snickers coming from Dante, Gavin, and Bean, Cade looked around the room in question. He caught Matt's gaze, and his buddy shrugged, apparently at just as much of a loss as he was.

Tash rolled her eyes, the act such a contrast to the badass vibe she projected. "Don't worry, D," Tash continued. "Your family is in good hands. Besides, Xander is much better with kids than I am."

Bean burst into laughter. "The creepy-ass *Exorcist* chick is better with kids than you!"

"That's not a lie. Kids are just . . ." Tash shuddered. A look of abject disgust crossed her face, and she shook her head. "Not my thing."

"The ferry is pulling up to the Whidbey Island dock now," Dante said. "I'm an hour or so out of Hudson, but I'm gonna heading straight home to check on Rebecca and Roc first. So give me an hour and a half or two, and then I'll be in. What else do you have, Tash? I heard Wilson came with you and Xander to the house. Gavin said he was gonna scope out the area. Did he find anything?"

Bennett Wilson was Hudson Security's outdoor survival expert. Cade was pretty sure Wilson's credentials and previous experience were beyond his nonexistent security clearance. Again, the less he knew, the better.

Tash opened the folder in front of her. "He had to go

check a couple things out, but he wanted you guys to see these photos in the meantime."

She slid several printouts around the table. To Cade's untrained eye, the subject of the photos looked like a messy campsite.

"D, Wilson took photos of a makeshift campsite he found roughly a hundred yards from your backyard. You can check it out for yourself when you get home. Wilson will still be there." Tash leaned back in her chair. "Technically, we can't confirm the campsite was made by the same person who tripped the cameras, but it's in the right area. I don't see any reason why someone would set up in that location for fun."

"Looks like drunk backyard camping," Matt said, pointing at an empty plastic bottle of Black Velvet. It was filled with cigarette butts.

"True," Gavin said. "The person left trash and some of their camping supplies. They weren't hiding the fact that they were there. Clearly, they're either stupid or over-confident."

"Yes," Tash agreed. "Which tells us this person—or persons—isn't a professional. No one with a surveillance background would be that sloppy." She frowned. "But that doesn't negate the fact that someone's watching you, D. Wilson confirmed this little hiding spot has a direct line of sight into all the back windows of your home."

"Motherfucker," Dante grumbled. Cade could feel his tension through the phone.

"Dante," Gavin said. "You should seriously think about moving back to the cottage temporarily. It's more secure. We can keep one of the PSOs—one who's *not* Tash—with Rebecca at the day care until this thing is resolved."

His brother sighed. "I'll talk to Rebecca about it, but yeah. That sounds like a plan."

They hung up, and for the next two hours, went back to

the beginning, laying out everything they'd learned. When Wilson and Dante showed up, the process was repeated. As even the tiniest pieces of evidence were analyzed in excessive detail, Cade took in the determined faces of his friends and found himself damn glad to have this group on his side. He just prayed they figured it out before anyone else got hurt.

At the three-hour mark, Cade scrubbed his hands over his face and groaned. "Holy shit, I think my brain is bleeding. How the hell do you guys do this every day?"

"You get used to it," Bean said, taking a sip of her fluorescent energy drink. "Miss it, D?"

Dante glanced between Gavin and Wilson—he had served with both men in the military—and shook his head, laughing. "Fuck, no. I'll take training boxers and making them puke any damn day of the week. You guys can keep your cloak-and-dagger shit."

Tapping the conference table, Cade rose. "This has been fun, ladies and gents, but I need to head out."

"Hot date?" Bean asked.

"Just a normal date." He grinned. The hot date had been last night. "I'm taking my lady to Monty's tonight."

Matt choked on his water, spraying some on the table. Wiping up his mess, he said, "Wait, you're taking Poppy to Monty's?"

Cade raised an eyebrow. "Yeah, so?"

"You do know Four owns that joint, right?" Matt laughed and shook his head. "You must have a death wish, man. I swear, that fucker's liable to poison you or something."

Cade nodded. He knew Matt was right. "If any of you jokers happen to swing by tonight to distract the guy"—he sent a pointed look Tash's way—"say around six thirty or six forty-five, I wouldn't be opposed."

She laughed and flipped him off.

Giving everyone a two-finger salute, he headed for the door. Yeah, he was damn glad they were on his side.

CHAPTER NINETEEN

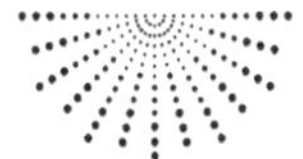

After thanking the customer for their purchase, Poppy returned to the mundane task of restocking a small display of locally made bath bombs and soaps. At this time of day, right before the lunch rush, she welcomed the mundane. And frankly, she wasn't sure she could handle anything that required her to actually think. Because, as cheesy as it sounded, her head was in the clouds.

Dinner with Cade at Monty's last night had been fantastic. She'd been nervous beforehand because she hadn't known how big of an ass Four was going to be. Yes, Cade and Four were friends well before she'd gotten to know Cade. And yes, Four had just lectured her the week prior about getting back into the dating scene. But Four was protective of her. However, her worry had been all for naught. Her pseudo-big brother had only stopped by their table three times, which was a lot less than she'd anticipated. Likely because he'd been distracted by a friend of Cade's. A Gal Gadot look-alike. Hell, if that stunning woman had come up and talked to Poppy, *she* would have been distracted, too.

Over appetizers, Cade had filled her in on the incident at

Dante's home and the possible connections between the guy who was suing Cade, Cade's former brother-in-law, and the mafia. The *mafia*! Talking about the stressful situation had seemed to lessen Cade's tension, so she'd tried her best to keep it together and remain calm for him. But holy crap, it had been a lot to process. By the time their meals had arrived, they'd moved on to lighter topics. And after dinner . . . Oh, after dinner . . . They'd gone back to her place and proceeded to have another amazing and intense make-out session.

Her body heated at the memory of his talented hands. Her mind turned to mush remembering his delicious mouth. What that man did to her was pure magic. Until this week, she'd had no clue her body could sing like that.

When she'd been ready to reciprocate—because, more than anything, she wanted to make him feel as amazing as he made her feel—her kids had texted, asking for a call. A *video* call. She'd never liked the term *cockblock*, but . . . in this case, it was apropos. Cade, bless him, had been understanding, and they'd made plans for tonight. A dinner date at her place. Because if things went according to her plan, she and Cade were going to get some quality one-on-one time in after dinner.

Thank god the boys weren't coming home until tomorrow morning. Because she was a woman on a mission, dammit. The take-it-slow sentiment she'd thought was a good idea just days ago no longer made her priority list. Not when she'd had the luxury of Cade's lips on her. Not when he'd brought her to such delicious heights. Fingers crossed, she'd figure out a way to seduce the man out of his patience tonight.

"Poppy?"

She startled, and her gaze swung to Meredith, who was standing beside her with an amused expression. Yikes, how long had she been zoning out? Clearing her throat, she resumed loading the small display tray with the pastel bath bombs. "Sorry, did you say something?"

Meredith grinned. "I said, if you need to cut out early to meet up with the boys, I'd be more than happy to close."

Poppy began arranging the soaps into a little pyramid. "I appreciate that, but the boys aren't coming out until tomorrow morning."

"If you still want to cut out early and hang with that handsome man of yours, I'm good closing."

Biting back a smile, she narrowed her eyes. "Why do I have the feeling you're trying to boot me out of here?"

"Because I am." Meredith waved to the flowers on the counter. "That man is so stinking sweet, and you, my friend, deserve sweet! Now, do you have plans with Cade tonight?"

Poppy laughed and rolled her eyes. "Yes, Mom, I do."

"Good! Then let me close. You go home and get dolled up and actually enjoy your Friday night like a single woman should!"

Poppy truly appreciated the offer. Still, she said, "I usually do inventory on Friday nights."

"Oh, believe me, we know." Meredith chuckled with her own eye roll. "It's been nice seeing you more relaxed these last couple of days, Poppy. And come on, when was the last time you had Friday night plans that didn't involve inventory or the twins?"

Poppy smiled. Her friend was right. She *had* been more relaxed since she'd started seeing Cade. Even with all the terrifying events that had occurred this week. Because he made everything less petrifying, less debilitating. Because he made her feel capable and calm and supported. When he held her hand, she knew she was safe.

The nagging voice in her head warned that things were moving too fast. That Cade was too good to be true. That she should slow down and prepare her heart for the day he wised up and realized she was a waste of time.

She hated that nagging voice. And she was making a conscious effort to ignore it. To trust how she felt about Cade. To trust *him* and how he treated her. That the care and respect he showed her was real. It was a minute-by-minute process.

Taking a deep breath in, she gave Meredith a nod. "You know what? You're absolutely right. If you're really okay with it, I'll see if Cade can meet up earlier." Baby steps, right? "I can't even remember the last time I took a Friday night for myself."

"If, for whatever reason, Cade isn't able to meet up earlier"—Meredith patted the bath bombs—"take some of these and let yourself relax for once! Now go call your new man, missy!"

"Thank you." Poppy hugged her friend, then reached into the pocket of her dress. Finding it empty, she frowned and walked back to the counter. No phone there, either. "Hey, Meredith? Can you call my cell?"

"Sure thing. It's ringing." Meredith held out her phone to listen, and her brow furrowed. "I don't hear anything."

Poppy sighed. "I probably left it upstairs. You okay here while I run up real quick?"

"Yup," Meredith said. "See? There's a bright side to Eli being a dick."

Poppy did a double take. "Excuse me?"

Meredith smirked. "Because Eli's a dick, you now have a super quick commute."

Snagging her keys from the drawer beneath the counter, Poppy shook her head and chuckled. A second later, she was out the door, calling, "Be right back!" over her shoulder. In a hurry, she hustled up the narrow staircase to her apartment and tripped on the top step. With a yelp, she fell hard on the landing, her knees and palms skidding across the floor as she caught herself.

"Holy crap," she groaned, slowly coming to her feet.

She unlocked the door with one hand, wincing at the scrape on her other. She stepped into her apartment and froze.

Something wasn't right. Something had the fine hairs on her arms rising.

Her racing heart kicked faster, and she sucked in a sharp breath. A chill slithered down the back of her neck, and she held herself perfectly still. Her eyes darted around the space, then focused on the mail she'd left on the dining table. She always sorted it into two piles: Rainy Day Boutique and personal. But the envelopes were currently in one jumbled stack. And there was a marketing flyer on the floor, under the chair she never used. As if someone had dropped it without realizing.

Her stomach pitched even as doubt tickled her mind. Maybe she hadn't gone through the mail yet. Maybe she had just . . . forgotten?

She spotted her phone on the small kitchen counter between the stove and the far wall. Her stomach dropped. Any lingering doubts she had evaporated. She hadn't been near the stove this morning or last night.

Fighting the instinct to grab her phone and run, she spun and closed the door behind her, locking it with trembling hands. Carefully, she made her way down the steps. The last thing she needed was to fly down the stairs, trip, and break her neck.

Once in the safety of Rainy Day Boutique, she finally took a breath. Meredith was assisting a customer, but she glanced at Poppy with a concerned expression. Poppy pasted a smile on her face and went to her small back office. Shutting the door and closing her eyes, she tried to settle her racing heart. Tried to tell herself she was imagining things.

Her stomach twisted again. She knew she wasn't.

With a shaking hand, Poppy reached for her landline and called the sheriff's department. It took a few seconds for her call to connect, and a few minutes for her to be assured that someone would come right over. She hung up and went back out on the floor. Meredith was ringing up a customer, so Poppy busied herself with arranging and then rearranging a display of Hudson Island logo wear.

The door chimed as the customer departed. Meredith was next to her in an instant.

"Are you okay? You look like you've seen a ghost."

Poppy rubbed her hands over her chilled arms. "I don't know."

The front door chimed again, and Quinn walked in.

"Um, I need to talk to him for a few minutes," she said to Meredith. "If you need me for anything, just call my—" She winced. "My phone's still upstairs, but—"

"It's fine, Poppy," Meredith said, voice full of concern. She nodded toward Quinn. "You do what you need to do. I've got the shop covered."

With a quick thank-you, Poppy approached the sheriff. "Hey, Quinn."

"Poppy." He looked around the store, then brought his gaze back to her. "What seems to be the problem?"

She chewed her lip, suddenly full of nerves. In the bright lights of her shop, she felt like a paranoid idiot.

The door chimed for the third time in as many minutes, and Gavin walked in. She nodded in greeting.

"Can we talk over there?" she asked Quinn, gesturing in the opposite direction of Gavin.

"Of course," he said, following her.

While Meredith assisted Gavin, she turned to Quinn.

"Well, um . . ." She eyed the shop again and dropped her voice, even though she knew she was well out of Gavin's and Meredith's earshot. "I think someone may have broken into my apartment upstairs."

Quinn's gray eyes hardened, and his muscles tensed. As if his entire body was now on alert. "What makes you think someone broke into your apartment?"

Poppy cringed. It wasn't like the man had shouted or anything, but he most definitely hadn't whispered, either. Her gaze shot across the store. Yup. Gavin was on his way over. His features were pinched and a little bit scary.

"Hi, Poppy," Gavin said, stopping next to the sheriff. "I'm sorry, I couldn't help but overhear."

Both men crossed their arms over their massive chests, and Poppy sighed. Whether she felt like an idiot or not, she needed to tell them her suspicion. If it *wasn't* all in her head, then these guys were her best bet at sorting things out. So she straightened her spine, and in one giant sentence, told them about the creepy feeling she'd gotten upstairs, the mail on her table, and her phone in the kitchen.

Afterward, Gavin and Quinn remained quiet, and she shifted on her feet. When she could no longer bear the silence, she added, "I mean, I know that's not a lot to go off of, and maybe it's just my imagination, but I could have sworn—"

Quinn held up a hand, shaking his head. "No. Trust your gut. Always." He glanced at Gavin. "In light of everything, you want in?"

Poppy frowned. In light of what? He couldn't possibly be referring to the issues facing the De la Rosa brothers. Could he?

Before she could say anything, Gavin replied, "You know I do."

Quinn looked at her. "Can we take a peek upstairs?"

"Of course." Poppy was numb with dread as she led the men out of her shop. Part of her hoped she was right, because she would feel terrible for wasting their time if she was wrong. But the other part—the jittery, scared part—was one thousand percent okay with some major embarrassment.

"Have you called Cade?" Gavin asked her while they ascended the narrow staircase in single file.

"No. He said he's going to be tied up today—" Her mouth slammed shut at the aggrieved look Gavin sent her over his shoulder. It wasn't quite pissed off, but it wasn't exactly approving either. Good god, she would hate to be on this man's bad side.

"Trust me when I say that Cade would want to know." His tone was so abrupt, she didn't know how to take his words.

Poppy plastered on her best business smile and aimed for neutral ground. "Well, even if I'd thought to call him, my cell is still in the apartment. The only numbers I know by heart are my boys'."

Gavin nodded.

"When you came up earlier, did you have to unlock your door?" Quinn asked as they crowded onto the landing.

"Yes." She prayed neither man noticed how her fingers trembled as she unlocked the door.

Gavin laid a solid hand on her shoulder and squeezed. "We've got your back, Poppy."

"You're all right," Quinn added. "You did the right thing by calling in."

So they *had* noticed how shaky she was. Great.

"Thanks," she whispered, turning the door handle. "Earlier, I only took a few steps in before it felt . . . off."

"I'm serious, Poppy," Quinn said. "Always listen to your gut. Now wait in the doorway, okay? Take a look around and see if you notice anything else that's off."

Quinn and Gavin made no sound as they entered the apartment, their imposing figures consuming the tiny space. Happy to stay out of the way, she watched them inspect her home, heart knocking hard in her chest. She was pretty sure she'd sorted the mail last night, and she was certain she'd left her phone on either the dining table or her bedside table. Definitely not on the far kitchen counter. So this had to be real, right?

A shiver tore through her.

When they were all crowded on the landing again, Gavin murmured, "I think you should scan the room."

Quinn scoffed. "Do you seriously think we have the budget for those kinds of toys?"

"Well, Sheriff, I suppose today is your lucky day." Gavin pulled a credit card–looking thing from his wallet and waved it in Quinn's direction.

"Do I even want to know why you carry one of those on you?"

"No, Sheriff. No, you most definitely do not." Gavin winked at Poppy, and her eyes widened in surprise. The little gesture was such a far cry from the serious—and somewhat scary—look he'd had on a few minutes earlier. "This won't take long."

Gavin circled her living room with the card held out in front of him. As he moved, a little light on the card flashed green and orange.

"What is that?" she asked Quinn.

"Bug detector," he whispered. His voice was so quiet that if she hadn't been standing next to him, she wouldn't have heard his reply.

The card flashed red. Gavin's scary face returned, and Quinn's expression grew equally grim.

She frowned. "A bug detector?"

Gavin shook his head and held a finger to his lips.

Her jaw dropped. Holy shit, they meant *surveillance* bugs? Someone was *listening* to her?

She glanced at Quinn and snapped her mouth shut at his nod. They held still as Gavin continued through the living room and kitchen. In some sort of silent communication with Quinn, he counted each red flash with his fingers and pointed. When Gavin finished scanning the common areas, he disappeared into the bathroom and then entered her bedroom.

He emerged shortly, face grim. Panic clawed up her throat as he returned a finger to his lips and pointed at the front door. She silently followed Quinn out of her apartment and down the stairs. From the sidewalk, they watched Gavin wave the card around the small landing. Thankfully, it flashed green.

Gavin shut her apartment door and came down, and the three of them huddled together.

"Five bugs in total," Gavin told Quinn. Turning to her, he asked, "Do you have an office in your store where we can talk?"

Incapable of forming words just yet, Poppy nodded.

"Excellent," Quinn said. He held out her phone. "I snagged it for you."

Worry turned in her gut. "Thanks. Is it . . . safe to use?"

"Smart question," Gavin said. "It's probably fine, but it would make me feel better if Bean ran a scan before you used it. She can check that there are no viruses or bugs. Pretty sure she can figure out when the last time it was accessed and all that, too. Would that make you feel better?"

Poppy swallowed past the rock in her throat. "Yes, please."

Reentering Rainy Day Boutique, she led them to her small office. Quinn halted her before she could enter, and they stayed silent as Gavin pulled out the bug detector and checked her office. When the card remained green, she let out the breath she hadn't realized she'd been holding.

Poppy settled into her chair and gestured toward the small loveseat across from her. Quinn sat, but Gavin came to a stop in front of her desk. He snagged a pen and scribbled something on a business card, then handed it over.

"It's Cade's cell. Do me a favor and give the guy a call when we're done here."

"Oh, no." Poppy shook her head. "He said he's going to be tied up all day prepping for an upcoming fight camp. We're meeting later tonight, and I can fill him in then."

Gavin pinned her with a stare that made her squirm like an unruly student.

"Right," she said with a nervous laugh. "I'll call him when we're done here."

The corners of Gavin's lips twitched as he pulled his phone from his pocket. His thumbs flew over the screen, and not a moment later, the device dinged with an incoming message. "Bean's on her way. She'll be able to get your phone figured out in no time."

"What did you find upstairs?" Quinn asked.

Aaand there was the nausea again.

"Like I said, five bugs in total. Fucker must have bought a starter pack or some shit. At first glance, they look to be basic, cheap-ass ones you can pick up online. No camera, just a mic, which is good."

Quinn crossed his arms over his chest. "Three, one, and one?"

Gavin nodded. His lips pressed into a tight line.

Poppy held up a hand. "Wait, what does that mean?"

"Three in the main living area, one in the bathroom, and one in the bedroom."

She was pretty sure her eyebrows hit her hairline. "What? Where?"

Gavin held her gaze and waited, as though asking if she was sure.

"Please," she whispered. "I need to know where they are."

He nodded. "In the kitchen under the cabinet to the right of the sink, in the living room on the shelf behind the framed graduation photo of the twins, and in the vent by the dining table. The one in the bathroom was on the top shelf over the toilet. The one in the bedroom was taped to the back of the nightstand."

At first, Poppy could only stare at the man. Then her stomach heaved. She clamped a hand over her mouth and reached for the trash bin beneath her desk. Bending over, she emptied her stomach.

CHAPTER TWENTY

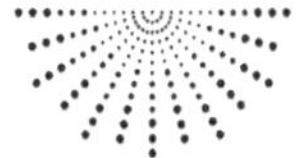

An hour later, Poppy was curled into the corner of her office loveseat with a damp towel pressed to her forehead. Bean had already popped in, snagged her cell phone, and taken off somewhere with Quinn. The woman, whom Poppy vaguely recognized from around town, had spouted some technical jargon before disappearing, but her brain had been too fried to register any of it.

In fact, there was only one thing her brain seemed capable of registering right now—someone had been in her home. Someone had gone from room to room and planted listening devices.

When? She had no clue. It could have been during the break-in this morning. It could have been while she'd stayed in Seattle. It could have been any one of the many times she'd left her apartment to run an errand or go to work or dine at a restaurant with Cade—

Her eyes widened. Holy shit, what if they'd listened to her make-out sessions with Cade? Chills skated over her skin, and she felt . . . repulsed. Violated. Terrified. Who would do something like this? And why?

"Poppy?"

She jumped, and her head whipped toward Gavin. Had he said something? "I'm sorry, what?"

"I said, I hope you don't think I overstepped."

Her eyes narrowed. Nope. The dots were not connecting.

Just as she was about to ask him what in the world he was talking about, Cade rushed through the door to her office. His eyes were wild as he strode toward her.

"Figured he'd want to know," Gavin said with a shrug.

Poppy considered balking at Gavin's high-handedness out of principle. But when Cade sat beside her and wrapped her in his embrace, she told her indignation to go the hell away. Because it didn't matter who had called Cade. She was just so damn glad he was here.

Cade pulled her across his lap and tucked her head under his chin. Pressing his lips to the crown of her head, he murmured, "Pop, babe, I got here as fast as I could."

She closed her eyes and nestled into him, breathing normally for the first time since she'd gone to find her phone. "Thank you for coming. I know you have a packed day. I really didn't want to bother you."

His arms tightened around her. "None of that crazy talk, babe."

Bean and Quinn reentered her office, and Poppy chuckled as they shuffled around the room, trying to find a spot amid the crowd. Quinn ended up hovering in the doorway, Bean settled behind the desk, and Gavin perched on the edge. Poppy was probably delirious with all the stress, but the claustrophobic conditions made her picture her office turning into one of those little clown cars.

"I think I need a bigger office," she joked.

"Nope," Cade said. "None of this shit is ever happening again. It's a one-shot deal, Pop."

God, she hoped he was right.

"Poppy, your phone is good," Bean said, passing it to Gavin, who passed it to Cade. The woman glanced down at her tablet. "It looks like someone tried to access your phone's passcode at nine thirty this morning. They tried five times unsuccessfully, then stopped. They must know you get locked out on the sixth."

Poppy shivered, and Cade's hands immediately began running up and down her arms.

"Quinn showed me the listening devices, and they're pretty basic," Bean continued. "Battery-operated and voice-activated. They do transmit, though, so that's a plus—"

"A plus?" Poppy asked, unsure how *anything* could be a plus.

"Makes them trackable," Bean clarified. "And trust me, I can track almost anything. Anyway, I think it's a safe assumption that whoever planted these didn't have a whole lot of experience, seeing as they were just placed all willy-nilly."

Poppy frowned. "How else would they have placed them?"

"Well, if I'm bugging a place—" Bean cut herself off and directed an angelic smile Quinn's way. "*If* being the operative word, Sheriff O'Conner. Then I'd attach them to light sockets or switch plates. Perhaps smoke alarms or outlets. Back of a remote control even. I would never just dump them behind a frame, you know?"

"Jesus Christ," Quinn grumbled, running a hand over his jaw.

"Do you know how long they've been there? Or where they're transmitting to?" Poppy asked.

"That's why we're leaving them. When I get back to my office, I can watch when they started transmitting and—"

"Hang on, Bean," Gavin said, silencing his employee. "Would you mind stepping out for a minute, Sheriff?"

"Oh, for fuck's sake," Quinn huffed, hands on his hips. "Try to keep it legal, guys."

"Always, Sheriff," Bean chirped.

Quinn rolled his eyes. "Riiight."

"Wait, Quinn," Poppy said. "Do you think this is related to the stuff going on with Cade's gyms?"

Quinn glanced at Gavin, then looked around the room and said, "I know we all have an idea who's behind this. However, I think it would be a mistake to automatically rule out a connection to Cade's ongoing issues. The timing is suspect. On that note, I'm out of here." His warning glare swiveled between Gavin and Bean. "But for god's sake, keep it fucking legal and admissible, got it?"

Gavin lifted his chin and smirked.

Sighing, Quinn shook his head. "Poppy, call if you need anything, okay?"

"I will, Quinn. Thank you."

Once the sheriff was out the door, Gavin nodded to Bean. "Find out when they started transmitting and to where. Then we can remove them. In the meantime, dig into Eli's financials and search history. See if that dumbass was stupid enough to Google this shit."

"You got it, boss."

Eli. Just thinking about her ex had her fuming. "Why would Eli do this?"

"Why does Eli do anything?" Gavin countered.

She stifled a frustrated growl. They were divorced, dammit. The house proceeds were the only thing left tying them together, and the funds distribution was supposed to happen next week. Then she would be done with that man once and for all. At least, she thought she'd be done with him. It was hard to know for sure, because Gavin was right—Eli did shit because he thought he could do whatever the hell he wanted. So, if he decided he wanted to keep harassing her, married or not, he would.

The strong arms around her squeezed, bringing her back to the moment.

"How are you holding up, Pop?" Cade asked as Gavin and Bean continued their discussion.

"I don't know what to think." She was angry, confused . . . and creeped the fuck out. But this man's mere presence did wonders for her blood pressure. Sitting up, she met his steady brown gaze. Then, before she could second-guess herself, she framed his jaw and brought her lips to his for a brief kiss. "Have I said thank you for being here yet?"

"Yes, but you never have to thank me for that."

She looked at Gavin and Bean, who were now huddled over Bean's tablet. "I know they're working on getting answers, but everything still feels so . . ."

"Fucked up?"

She blinked. "Exactly."

"What do you say we get out of here?" He checked his watch. "We can head over to Ray's Diner for milkshakes and fries?"

The mention of that delicious combo had her stomach growling. In the craziness of the day, she'd forgotten to eat. She was running on a single iced latte.

"Besides," Cade added, "on my way in, Meredith said I should steal you for the rest of the day."

Of course the sweet woman had said that. God, she loved her people.

Poppy hauled herself off Cade's lap, murmuring, "I had plans for us tonight, you know."

She froze, suddenly remembering they weren't alone in the small office, and prayed the words had sounded more innocent out loud than they had in her head. Even though her plans for Cade tonight were far from innocent.

A glance at her desk had her exhaling in relief. Gavin and Bean were oblivious, bickering over something on the tablet.

Cade rose and bumped her shoulder. "Oh yeah?"

She bumped him back with a smirk. "Yup."

He grinned. "How about this? You take all those plans you had for our dinner date at your place and move the location over to mine?"

"You still want to hang out tonight?"

He tucked a lock of hair behind her ear, then softly trailed his knuckles down her jaw to her chin. Lifting it with a finger, he gave her the sweetest, gentlest kiss. "Is that a real question, babe?"

Poppy couldn't fight the smile that broke out across her lips. Or the blush that spread over her face when she noticed they now had an audience. Bean's grin went ear to ear, and her hands clasped at her chest. Gavin grumbled under his breath, shaking his head.

When she looked back at Cade, he shot her that grin-smirk that made her stomach dance. "I suppose not, Mr. De la Rosa. Let's grab some food. But first . . ." She turned to Gavin. "Can I go up to my apartment? I want to pack up some things."

Gavin nodded. "Of course. I'll go with you if that's okay."

"I'd really appreciate that." Meeting Cade's eyes, she explained, "I don't want to stay there. Not with . . ."

"Of course not, babe. I can help you pack."

She grabbed her phone off the loveseat. "Let me call Four and see if I can stay with—"

Cade's hand covered hers before she could connect the call. "Why don't you hold off on that? I'm planning on making a case for you to stay with me, but over milkshakes and fries."

She arched an eyebrow. "Oh, is that so?"

"Yes, ma'am." His expression was serious, though his eyes

still twinkled. "My case is pretty good, so you better be ready. I mean, I have space for you and the boys when they show up tomorrow, and I also have an extra vehicle you can use since yours is still in the shop. Plus, you're already going to be at my place for dinner tonight." He draped an arm over her shoulders and tugged her close. "Those points are just a preview, Pop. I also have more . . . persuasive arguments to make over milkshakes and fries. What do you say?"

She laughed, blushing harder. The guy was too cute.

"Christ, De la Rosa, you're giving me a cavity," Gavin grumbled on his way to the door. "Let's go get Poppy's stuff."

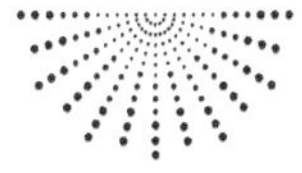

CHAPTER TWENTY-ONE

"Thanks, Scarlet," Cade said as the young woman cleared their empty plates.

"No problem." She pointed at their old-fashioned milkshake canisters. "You guys want those to go, or are you planning on hanging out?"

"Hanging out," Poppy answered at the same time as he replied, "To go."

"To go it is," Scarlet said with a laugh, sending a wink his way before hustling to the next table.

Cade leaned back in the booth and smiled at the woman seated across from him. Perfectly put together, she wore a flowy, long-sleeved floral dress that tied on one side and came to just above her knees. Like her dress from the other night, it was on display in Rainy Day Boutique's front window. One would never know the scare she'd received this morning just by looking at her. Poppy expertly hid a wealth of stress and nerves behind her beautiful, color-changing eyes.

But he knew how much the bugs had shaken her. Because he was equally unsettled.

He'd been meeting with his coaches, going over the upcoming training camp, when he'd gotten Gavin's text: *Come to Poppy's shop. Her apt was bugged. She needs you.* The to-the-point message had nearly given Cade a heart attack. He'd sprinted out of the meeting with little explanation and high-tailed it to Rainy Day Boutique.

Now, he couldn't do anything except sit and wait for Gavin and his team to work their magic. Not knowing shit was frustrating beyond belief. They all thought Eli was behind the bugs, but on the off chance that he wasn't, that it was somehow connected to the mess Cade was facing . . . Well, that was unfathomable.

So, rather than dwell on the worst-case scenarios, Cade had made it his mission to take Poppy's mind off the shit show in her apartment—and convince her to stay with him tonight. Somehow, he'd succeeded at both. For that, he was beyond grateful. And pleased, though he had no expectations for her visit. He still planned to take things slow, even if doing so became harder and harder with each passing second. Knowing what she tasted like, what she felt like . . . it made him want more.

Want all of her.

But she was under a tremendous amount of stress. The last thing he planned to do was add to it or take advantage of her situation. So, she was going to call the shots. And he hoped to hell that she'd let him hold her close. With all the craziness surrounding them, it was essential that she remained near him. He needed his eyes on her, needed her within touching distance, to trust that she was okay.

Reaching across the table, he took her hands in his. "Are you going to let the boys know what's going on?"

She winced. "Tomorrow. It'll be easier to tell them face to face instead of over the phone. Besides, it may smooth over the whole we're-staying-with-you-this-weekend thing."

He squeezed her hands. "You think they'll have a problem with that?"

For a moment, her lips pressed into a tight line. Then she shook her head. "I don't think so. But I'm also pretty sure they assume they're staying with Four, so they'll at least be surprised."

Cade nodded. That made sense. "Speaking of Four, are you going to tell him what's going on?"

"I really don't want to. He's gonna flip his shit."

He shrugged. "You aren't wrong."

His mind flashed to the glimpse he'd caught of Carter's face when the boys had video-called Poppy last night. As a lifelong martial arts practitioner, and in his career as a fighter and now coach, he was no stranger to injuries. However, seeing Carter's face—the bruising and swelling— had been like a powerful uppercut to the chin. For a moment, he hadn't been able to breathe. First, because it was Carter. Second, because the young man had gotten injured protecting Jackie.

If Cade had been that upset, he sure as hell couldn't imagine how Poppy had felt. How Four would feel once he learned about everything that had happened. He was Poppy's brother and the boys' uncle in every way that mattered. So yeah, Four was most definitely going to flip his shit. But the man needed to know about all of it. He was family. Plain and simple.

Cade squeezed Poppy's hands again. "Four's taking my class tomorrow morning. I can tell him for you if you'd like."

The relieved smile on her face made him feel ten feet tall. Holy shit, if only he could take all her stress away. Because that smile? An arrow right to his fucking heart.

"I know it's totally chickening out," she said, "but I'd appreciate that so much."

"It's not a problem at all, Pop. Now what do you say we

call it a day?" Cade paused as Scarlet returned, dropping off their to-go cups and the check. When she was gone, he nodded to their milkshakes. "Let's grab these, head to my place, get some popcorn going, and curl up on the couch with some movies for the rest of the day."

Poppy let out a breath that sounded part relief, part exhaustion. "Yes, please."

Thirty minutes later, Cade pulled his car into his garage. He released Poppy's hand—which he hadn't let go of since they'd started driving—to cut the engine. He reclaimed it as soon as they were outside the car.

"How about I draw you a bath?" he asked, leading her into his house through the mudroom. "After the morning you've had, I'm thinking a good soak would be nice and relaxing before we start our movie marathon."

When she didn't reply, Cade looked down at her. The heat and desire staring back at him made his eyes widen.

"I have a better idea," she said, dropping his hand. "Something that would be even more relaxing."

His heart tripped when she reached for the tie at her waist. His mouth turned to dust when she slowly pulled the bow free. His mind blanked when the panels of her dress parted, revealing creamy skin shrouded in scraps of pink silk and lace.

Mine, he thought. And then he lunged.

CHAPTER TWENTY-TWO

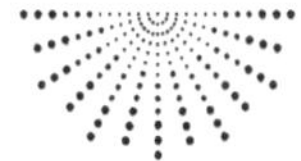

Poppy's pounding heart deafened her ears. Part of her couldn't quite believe what she'd done. That she'd dropped her dress in the middle of Cade's kitchen. But as he stared at her in wonder, desire and with heat flaring in his eyes, the other part demanded to know why it had taken her so damn long.

Then he was on her. His mouth consuming; his hands claiming. When his tongue requested entrance, she gladly welcomed him. And when they came up for air, her dress landed on the ground, along with his shirt. Clinging to one another, they stumbled out of the kitchen, into the hallway.

"I wanted to go slow with you, Poppy," Cade growled, pressing her against the wall, holding her up.

She gasped as he tore her panties off. Then the gasp turned to a moan as his hands began squeezing and molding her ass.

"We can go slow next time," she said, grinding against his hard length. The friction of his cock hit her in the most perfect spot, and she whimpered. Holy shit, she'd say whatever the hell he wanted to prevent this moment from ending.

"Thank god." He bit the delicate skin where her neck met her shoulder, causing her to groan. "Because right now, I need to fuck you hard and fast."

Wetness flooded her pussy. Pressing her harder against the wall, he plunged two fingers inside her. She cried out, trembling in his arms.

"You're so fucking wet for me," Cade murmured, fingers working in and out of her. "I can't wait to fuck you. To sink my cock into your tight pussy."

God, yes. More. She needed more.

"Please," she begged, riding his fingers.

"Tell me," he growled. "Tell me what you need. Tell me who you need."

"You, Cade," she panted. "I need your cock inside me. I need you to fuck me hard. Please." She clawed at his back, desperate for release. For him.

There was a crinkling sound, and on her next breath, his thick length stretched her in a way that stole the air from her lungs. She was so damn full she couldn't help but gasp and moan. It was borderline too much, but when Cade began thrusting his hips, she forgot everything except the pleasure he gave her.

"More," she begged, sparks zinging through every inch of her body. Delicious tension built in her core with each hard plunge.

"Fuck, Poppy, your pussy feels so fucking good," he murmured against her hair. His strained voice, his heated words—both had her insides clenching. "That's it, babe. Milk my cock."

Over and over, he pounded into her. The sound of slapping skin and their cries of pleasure echoed along the hallway; the raw, animalistic smell of sex filled her nose, her soul, her entire being. And then she shattered. Cade rode her hard through her orgasm, tensing only when she was on her way down. A moment later, he shouted his release within her.

When they stilled and the room fell quiet, everything was a bit hazy, a bit tingly. Poppy was still propped up against the wall, arms clutched tight around his neck. One of his hands was cradling her ass, supporting her, while the other was planted beside her shoulder, holding them steady. She had an ankle hooked over that arm. Her other leg was folded against her torso, leaving her spread wide open for him.

Damn. She hadn't realized she was that bendy. But holy hell, this position was the sexiest thing she'd ever experienced.

"Fuck, Poppy," Cade said, looking down at where they were joined.

Then his mouth crashed against hers, and he shifted them so that her legs were wrapped around his waist instead of twisted like a pretzel. His cock remained deep inside her, and she used her newfound leverage to rock against him. He let out a growl, so she did it again, grinning.

God, she couldn't get enough of this man. He made her absolutely ravenous.

"I lied, babe. Next time is gonna be hard and fast again. But the one after that will be soft and sweet. I swear it."

"No complaints here," she murmured, nipping at his shoulder. "I like how you do hard and fast. But a bed would be nice next time. Think you can manage that?"

He playfully smacked her ass, making her yelp. "Oh, Pop, you have no idea how I've imagined you in my bed."

Excitement stirred anew, and she rocked her hips again. "Yeah?"

He carried them down the hall and up the stairs, whispering in her ear, "I'm gonna spread you out on my bed and eat every inch of your sweet pussy."

Her breath hitched; her arousal dripped from her.

"Then I'm gonna play with that sweet ass and fingerfuck you until you come all over my hand."

She clutched his shoulders tighter, working her body up and down his hard cock.

"Then I'm gonna have you on your hands and knees on that bed while I fuck you from behind until you're screaming my name. That work for you, babe?"

Holy shit, she was on fire.

Before they made it to the bedroom, she was pinned against another wall, her legs spread wide. He thrust inside her again. Hard. Once. Twice. Three times.

"Come for me," he demanded.

She exploded. Everything shook—her limbs, her core, her soul.

"Good girl," he praised, pressing a kiss to her forehead.

Heat surged over her skin at his praise, and she could feel him inside her, still hard and pulsing.

"Now, what do you say we find that bed?"

"Yes, please," she said, grinning up at him. She wanted to wrap herself around him again, but her bones had liquefied.

So Cade picked her up and carried her down the hall.

CHAPTER TWENTY-THREE

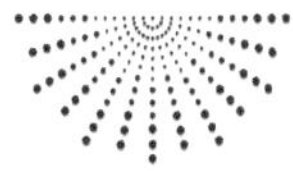

Poppy's sigh was one of pure satisfaction. She'd lost count of how many glorious orgasms Cade had given her tonight. Still, she couldn't quite believe that this was real. That they were naked. Together. In his bed. It was too good to be true.

"This has been the craziest week," she said, snuggling into his side. Goosebumps erupted on her skin as he traced a rough, calloused hand down her spine. She smiled and arched into him like a cat, then propped her chin on his sculpted chest. "However, I must admit that *this* is the best ending to any week. Ever. I can't think of a better stress reliever."

Cade grinned, but the humor in his brown eyes was short-lived. Turning serious, he said, "I hope you know this means more to me than just stress relief. Don't get me wrong, I one hundred percent agree. But this? Me and you?" He tucked a lock of hair behind her ear. "Way more than just stress relief."

His simple words wrapped around her heart and held

tight. This man didn't play games. He said what he felt, and she appreciated that more than he would ever know.

"For me, too, Cade," she whispered. "For me, too."

A bemused expression crossed his face. "I promise I had every intention of taking things slow with us."

She chuckled. So had she. "Well, we did give it a week. That counts for something, right?"

Suddenly, she was on her back. Her jaw dropped as she stared up into Cade's laughing brown eyes. Holy crap, this man's strength and speed were ridiculous. And so damn sexy.

Lying between her legs, Cade pressed a chaste kiss to each of her breasts, then rested his head on her chest. "There's something about you that snaps my control, babe."

Running her fingers down his back, she smiled at his shiver. "I was with you every step of the way, Cade."

"I know. I just want you—need you—to know that I'm serious about you." He lifted himself to hover over her. "I don't know what label to use for what's going on with us, but I like you, Poppy. A lot." His grin launched butterflies in her stomach. "Like *a lot* a lot."

She ran her hands along his sides, and satisfaction surged through her when he sucked in a breath. "Yeah, I kinda picked up on that."

"I hope so, but I've felt this way since before you let me touch you." He dropped his lips to her left shoulder. "Before you let me taste you." Then her right shoulder. "Before you let me feel what it's like to be inside you." He claimed her mouth in a searing kiss. "I really like you. So, at risk of jumping the gun, I want you to know I'm in this for the long haul, Pop. I don't want to date anyone else because I'm only interested in you. I want to see where this goes with us."

Her heart stuttered. She waited for the doubt and disbelief. But as she gazed into his eyes, they didn't come. Because the way he looked at her left no room for insecurity. His gaze reached down into the depths of her soul, to a part she didn't know existed, and told her the truth.

"I really like you, too, Cade," she whispered, chest swelling with emotion. "There's just something about *you*. Something about *us*. I want to explore it together."

"I'll take that." He placed another kiss on her lips, then turned her so they spooned. "Tell me more about you. From what I've seen and heard around town, Rainy Day is everyone's go-to gift shop. Did you always want to have your own business?"

"Uh, no." She laughed, snuggling into him. "I kind of fell into it, honestly. Then I fell in love with it, so that was a bonus. When I first moved to Hudson, having my own business was the furthest thing from my mind. The boys were just about to turn eight, and my only focus was getting through each day. Keeping them alive and fed and happy. I swear, those years were absolutely nuts."

"What brought you to Hudson in the first place?"

Poppy pressed her lips into a tight line. Where did she even begin? She was sure Cade didn't realize he had asked such a loaded question.

"No pressure, babe," he said, lips brushing her hair. "I just want to know everything about you."

"Everything, huh?" She chuckled. "No pressure, indeed."

"Definitely no pressure. It's just that you're one of the strongest women I've ever met, so I imagine your origin story is pretty kick-ass."

Her what? She twisted to look at him. "Origin story? Like a superhero?"

"Yup." He dropped another kiss to her head. "All badass people have some sort of origin story. I want to know yours."

She couldn't have stopped her smile even if she'd tried. When he put it like that, she supposed she did have an interesting backstory. Well, hindsight made it interesting. Now that the twins were somewhat grown.

"I was sixteen when I found out I was pregnant. Matthew was my first boyfriend." He'd been her first everything: First date. First kiss. First time. First heartbreak. "I was scared out of my mind, but I hoped my parents would understand and be there for me. Matthew's parents and mine were best friends and had been forever. I knew they'd be shocked, but I thought that maybe with time, they'd be happy for us."

His arms tightened around her. "I take it they weren't?"

"No, they definitely weren't." Her heart pinched. Even though nearly nineteen years had passed, her family's outright rejection still stung. "I dreamed that Matthew and I, with our families' support, would raise the baby together. I didn't know I was pregnant with twins until later. But that naïve dream didn't happen. He denied being the father, and both his family and mine sided with him."

Cade tensed, and she rubbed his forearms, as much to comfort herself as him.

"My parents kicked me out." *And called me a lying whore. A slut. A shame to the family.* Her mother's shrill screams still echoed in Poppy's ears. The shock of her mother spitting at her for "spewing these filthy lies about Matthew" was etched into her soul, just like the sting of her mother's palm across her face. Her stomach rolled recalling the punishing grip of her father's hand on her arm as he yanked her to the front door. With disgust in his eyes, he'd pulled out his wallet and shoved a wad of cash at her and said, "Never come back. You're dead to us."

Poppy took a breath to steady herself. Cade's woodsy scent filled her nose, calming her, pushing the horrible memories back. "I had no idea where to go, so I just hopped on a bus. I ended up in downtown Portland. It was getting dark, and I had no idea what to do. I mean, I was a kid from the suburbs. Really sheltered and not at all street-smart."

"Holy shit, Poppy," Cade said on an exhale. "What did you do?"

"I used the cash my dad gave me and found a motel. It was super sketchy, but it was dirt cheap. I remember lying in that creaky bed, petrified, hoping Matthew would change his mind and swoop in like a knight in shining armor to save me." She shook her head and scoffed. "But he was also sixteen, so there was no swooping. I stayed at that motel for two nights. Then I called my aunt Katy. She's my mom's younger sister. The black sheep of their family. My dad hated her, but she always made a point to come and see me a few times a year. She was always fun and so nice . . . and she actually listened to me."

"The cool aunt."

"Yeah." Poppy smiled, recalling how her aunt had dropped everything for her that fateful day. Tears prickled her eyes, and her throat grew thick. God, she missed her. "Yeah, Aunt Katy was the best. After I called her, she drove down from Seattle and got me. She took me in, no questions asked.

"Her best friend was Four's aunt Mirabelle. The two of them, and their circle of friends, helped me with my pregnancy and those first few years with the boys. It was so hard, but they somehow got us through it in one piece." A tear spilled down the side of her face. "Aunt Katy passed away a few days after the twins' seventh birthday."

"Oh, babe, I'm so sorry," Cade murmured, turning her. He tucked her head into the groove of his neck and ran a soothing hand down her back.

"She was riding her bike and got hit by a car. The teenage driver was on the phone and didn't see her. Aunt Katy was in a coma for a month before she passed. It was devastating all the way around." For Aunt Mirabelle. For the teenage driver. For Poppy and the boys. For everyone who loved her aunt.

"She left me and the kids her house, which was so kind of her, but I had to sell it to settle her medical bills. Afterward, it was all about trying to keep my head above water. Between the kids and work . . . It was a lot. I know that now. But at the time, it didn't seem like it. I think I was so terrified I was going to drown that I only focused on the next step in front of me."

"You didn't know any different."

Poppy nodded. "Exactly. Anyway, a year after Aunt Katy passed, Aunt Mirabelle approached me about moving to Hudson Island and becoming the manager of Rainy Day. She said I could live in the apartment upstairs for free if I accepted. The store had been in her family for a couple generations, but she wanted to retire and travel, so she needed someone she trusted to look after it.

"At that point, between the price of rent and the cost of day care in Seattle, I was barely getting by. So I figured, why not? I was already close friends with Four by then, so I knew there'd be at least one friendly face in town. And the apartment was small for the three of us, but I'd be saving so much money that it would be worth it."

Cade pulled away just enough to look at her. "You know, small apartment or not, you made amazing memories for your boys in that place."

Her forehead scrunched in confusion. "What?"

A soft smile touched his lips. "When we were moving your stuff in, the boys were talking about how awesome their bedroom forts were. How much fun they had in them."

She sighed, and this time, it was out of happiness. Resting her head back on Cade's chest, she said, "That so good to know. Half the time, I'm terrified I've done everything wrong." Which was why she'd be forever grateful that her boys were resilient. "After all, I brought Eli into their lives . . ."

"You are an amazing mom," Cade said, pressing his lips against her head. "Don't ever doubt that."

How could she not? Doubt was second nature to her. She had a lot of self-confidence to build before she could stop constantly worrying that she hadn't done enough for her sons, that Eli's jabs about her being a shitty mom and wife were true.

"I'm plagued by what-ifs," she admitted in a whisper. "What if I'd left Eli sooner? Would the boys have had a better, more stable life? What if I'd stood up for myself more? What if—"

"Babe, the what-if game will only drive you crazy." He sat up with his back against the headboard and pulled her between his legs, cradling her against his chest. She clutched his forearms. "C and D are doing well. Because of you. And even though you regret bringing Eli into their lives, the boys are also doing good, in part, because of him."

Her gaze swung to meet Cade's. She couldn't have heard him right. "What?"

"Poppy, babe. If that fucker taught the twins anything, it's what they *don't* want to be like. C and D are smart, kind, protective young men who have no qualms telling their mama how much they love her."

She smiled. It never got old hearing her boys call out, "Love you, Mom!" over the phone or in person. "You're right. I think it helped that C and D were older when I met him. They'd just turned nine. By then, we had a routine. A schedule. Finances were still day to day, but it was getting better. We were more than just getting by."

"You had gummy frogs."

"We sure did, and what special little treats those were." She grinned, then pressed a kiss to his forearm. "When I was a few months into dating Eli, Aunt Mirabelle gifted me the building and the business. The only stipulation was that no matter what—whether I got married or died or anything in between—the building would pass to the boys. And only the boys. The paperwork she drew up was very specific."

Cade chuckled. "Sounds like Aunt Mirabelle didn't like Eli, either."

"Gross understatement." Poppy frowned. "She saw what I couldn't . . . or didn't want to see. That Eli was all about Eli. That he would always put himself first. That even though he talked a good game, he wasn't a nice person."

"You have to give yourself some grace, babe," Cade said, hugging her a little tighter. "You were young."

"Yeah, I was. Young, hopeful, and desperate for affection." A disastrous combination. Good thing she was simply hopeful now. "When I met Eli, he swept me off my feet. I'd never had that kind of attention or help from a man before. In a way, he reignited that knight-in-shining-armor dream. Things were fine for a couple years. Then they weren't. But the more our marriage fell apart . . . the more I held on. Sinking ship and all."

"Why?" There was no judgement in Cade's question. Just curiosity.

She took a moment to collect her thoughts. "At first, I thought it was pride. But that wasn't it. Not really. I . . . I think I held on so tight because I was scared to be discarded again. My parents threw me out, and it was devastating. Matthew, my friends, my extended family . . . Everyone except Aunt Katy abandoned me." After all these years, the pain was still so fresh, so cutting and raw. But it was also mixed with revulsion. As a parent herself now, she couldn't imagine any scenario where she'd ever cast her children away like that. "I was trying to protect the boys from that kind of hurt. I didn't want them to ever feel abandoned the way I had. Eli wasn't what I wanted for them in a parent, but he was still their stepdad—the only father figure they'd ever known. I didn't want to steal that from them."

Her earlier conversations with the boys echoed in her mind, and she grimaced. "But now, after talking with them . . . I know that they saw more than I thought. More than I ever wanted them to see. So if anything, me staying with Eli for as long as I did hurt them more. It put this added guilt and responsibility on their shoulders and—"

"Hey," Cade said, running his hands over her arms. "None of that. You did what you thought was best at the time."

"Yeah, but I made things worse for them—"

"Poppy." Cade's chuckle was tinged with disbelief. "Have you met those boys? They're great. Not only are they smart as hell, they're happy, healthy, and they love you so damn much. *That's* what matters. Not what you could have done differently in the past, but what's happening now. You've done an amazing job with them."

Everything inside her warmed at his words. "You do such good things for my ego, Mr. De la Rosa."

"I hope so, babe," he murmured, adjusting them so she was on her back and he was settled between her thighs. "Because I think you're pretty damn wonderful. Spine of steel, brilliant businesswoman, and so damn sexy."

She buried her fingers in his hair and fused her mouth to his. Yup, this man did amazing things to all of her.

CHAPTER TWENTY-FOUR

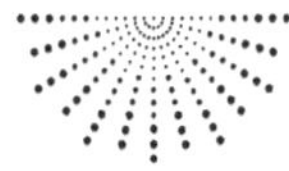

Cade collapsed with a moan. Holy shit, this woman. He couldn't get enough of her.

"Can't breathe," Poppy mumbled beneath him, her hand tapping his side.

"Shit. Sorry, babe," he said, rising onto his elbows.

Poppy's hair was a tangled mess, her cheeks were flushed, and pink marks dotted her delicate neck and chest where he'd nibbled and tasted every inch of her perfect skin. Her eyes were hazy, and the satisfied smile on her lips was that of a woman who'd just been thoroughly fucked.

With a growl, he claimed her mouth again. Still buried deep inside her, his dick twitched.

"Oh my god," Poppy laughed, pushing him away. "How can you be ready to go again?"

Cade had no fucking clue. It all had to do with this woman.

"Hold that thought," he muttered, pulling out and hustling to the bathroom. He made quick work of the condom before returning to the bed and pulling her back to his front. He'd never been much of a cuddler, but with Poppy? Yeaaah. He loved every second.

Her content sigh made him smile. He'd take a happy-and-satisfied Poppy in his arms any day of the week. The thought had him pausing, but not in the way he would have expected. Rather, it stunned him with just how right it felt.

"What were we talking about?" she murmured, tracing her fingers over his forearms.

"What?" He buried his nose in her hair. Damn, she smelled so good. Citrus and sex.

"Before you distracted me. What were we talking about?" She wiggled until her ass was snug against him, and his damn cock twitched again. See? Never enough with this woman.

"Keep that up, babe, and we'll be going for round four."

"Ooh, championship rounds," she said with a laugh and another wiggle. "I like."

His heart tripped. Yup, this woman was quite possibly the cutest and sexiest thing ever.

"You follow MMA?" he asked, interest piqued by her comment.

She twisted to lie on her back. "Not really. Though I do know the basics, like championship bouts being more than three rounds. The boys and Four are big fans, so I've seen my share of fights. Why? Did my knowledge impress you?"

"Maybe." He grinned. "You ever see me fight?"

Poppy's eyes narrowed, and it looked like she was fighting a smile. "Are you fishing for a compliment, buddy?"

"Maybe," he said again, his grin growing. "So have you?"

She laughed, smacking him playfully on the chest. "Of course I've seen you fight. *Everyone* who watches MMA has seen you fight."

She was probably right. But damn, this woman was starting to become the only viewer who mattered.

"What did you think?" He was genuinely curious. A huge

part of him hoped she'd enjoyed watching, that she'd found it exciting.

Cade knew many looked down on MMA—hell, combat sports in general—and considered it barbaric. He'd learned over the years that there really wasn't much you could say to convince those people otherwise. They usually weren't open to understanding what it took for a person to get to the top of such a demanding sport. All they saw were two people in a ring or cage beating the shit out of each other. They didn't see the focus, the drive, the hours spent in the gym building strength and endurance, or the countless years of technical training in numerous disciplines. All things considered, he didn't believe Poppy was one of those close-minded people, but you never knew.

"Honestly, aside from being happy for you when you won —since at the time, all I knew was you were friends with Four—I didn't really have much of an opinion either way."

Okay, he could work with that.

"However, since I started taking your cardio kickboxing class, I've changed my mind."

Cade stilled. *Oh shit, here it comes.*

"Every single time I go to your gym, I'm pretty sure I'm gonna die. Every time. So *now*, I can be impressed by your first-round knockouts and submissions." She ran her hands over his pecs and biceps, squeezing the muscles and waggling her eyebrows. "These aren't just for show."

He threw his head back and laughed, the tension draining from his body. "No, ma'am. They are indeed functional. I may not be competing anymore, but I still have to stay in shape if I don't want to get my ass whooped by the young bucks."

She snuggled closer, and everything inside Cade clicked into place. Holy shit, he wished he could stay like this with her . . . forever.

A comfortable silence fell over them for a while, and then Poppy asked, "Did you always want to be a professional fighter?"

His instinct was to say yes, but he pursed his lips in thought. He wanted to give her a real answer, not the canned response he'd given the media for years.

"It's a bit like you said earlier: I kind of fell into it. Dante and I grew up in Seattle, and our parents introduced us to martial arts when we were little. Kickboxing and jiu-jitsu, mostly. In middle school, we tried out wrestling and boxing. He kicked my ass at boxing, and I kicked his at wrestling. So he continued with that, and my coaches encouraged me to move over to MMA, which I did and obviously enjoyed. It wasn't ever anything serious. Just training and sparring at the gym. In high school, my coaches wanted me to do some amateur fights, but my mom was very much against that."

"You know," Poppy said with a nod, "as a mom myself, I can absolutely see where she was coming from on that."

"Yeah, it makes sense now, but when I was fifteen, it was grossly unfair." He chuckled as Poppy rolled her eyes. "I went to college at UW, so I was able to keep up with my jits, Muay Thai, and MMA classes, but like I said, it wasn't anything serious. Then a buddy dared me to enter this amateur MMA competition. I figured that since I was eighteen and an *adult—*"

"Oh good god," Poppy groaned.

"—it would be fine, and my mom would never find out."

Poppy's eyebrow arched. "How'd that work out for you, babe?"

"It didn't." He shook his head at the memory, grinning. "I won by first-round knockout, which was great, but what I didn't realize was *The Seattle Times* was doing a story on local up-and-coming fighters."

Poppy laughed. "Of course they were."

"They had photos of my fight on the front page of the sports section. My folks saw it, and to say my mom was pissed would be the biggest understatement in the world." He could smile about it now, but at the time, he'd been terrified of the severe bodily harm his mom would inflict on him when he got home. But he'd been prepared to take her wrath. What he hadn't been prepared for was how after the story had been printed, doors he didn't know existed began opening. Then, the course of his life changed.

"At least you won, though," Poppy said. "Your mom had to be happy about that."

"Yeah, but she was still pissed." Cade had been subjected to her disapproving glare for a long time afterward. However, when he really thought about it now, her look had been more worried than one of censure. "Due to the publicity from that fight, I was invited to headline another amateur show, and then another after that. My mom came to those fights, and thankfully, I won them."

"See? She came around."

He shook his head. "She had her hands in front of her face the entire time, but the fact that she even showed up meant a lot. After a couple more amateur fights, I had my first pro fight. It was a smaller promotion, but they were established and ran a tight show. I remember being so damn nervous that I puked before my walkout. I won by first-round submission and . . ."

"And?" she prompted, pinching his stomach.

Cade grinned like a loon. "And it was fucking awesome. I was hooked. I was ready to drop out of college and pursue fighting full-time and—"

"Uh, what did your mom have to say about that?"

He chuckled. "She said, 'Hell no, young man. You are *going* to finish your degree.'"

"Did you?"

"I did. I continued with school and trained and fought on the side. I had a few more pro fights with a few different promotions, all of them small, and then at the start of my junior year, I got lucky. I signed with the big dog, UFC. I fought three to four times a year, moving from the undercard fights up to the main card. Two months after I graduated with my business degree, I got my first title shot. And won."

"Was it everything you thought it would be?"

"Oh, it was. Hell, it was everything I'd ever imagined, plus shit I couldn't have ever fathomed. I was *the* rising star. It was a life of pure excess. I bought my parents a house and married a gorgeous girl and successfully defended my title countless times. I was unstoppable. I even had to get a fancy-ass agent to manage all the endorsements that were being thrown my way. Then Dante got out of the military and started tearing up the boxing world. I mean, life was unbelievable. By the time I was twenty-seven, I had everything I could possibly want."

"Then why are you frowning?" Poppy asked softly, tracing the line between his eyebrows.

Because I know what comes next.

Cade's heart raced. He wasn't sure if Poppy had heard his story or not, but the way she smoothed her hand over his chest, easing some of the pain and disappointment in his soul, suggested she had.

"Because after my eleventh successful title defense—I knocked my opponent out in twenty-two seconds—we all went out celebrating in Vegas. I'd been training so damn hard for so many months, and my coach had put me on a strict diet with no alcohol that whole time, so me and my crew were letting loose. Then the limo we were in got hit by a drunk driver."

Cade had been standing with his top half out of the limo's sunroof, screaming and hollering and rejoicing with the people partying on the Strip. Fans had shouted his name and cheered him on as he'd passed. At the intersection of Tropicana Avenue and Las Vegas Boulevard, he'd spotted a Ferrari SF90 Spider speeding their way. He recalled thinking that the car's color was so cool, that its iridescence picked up all the colors of the Strip and he wanted one just like it. Then . . . nothing.

In his nightmares, there was always the horrendous screech of metal on metal. The shouts of alarm and screams of agony. The stench of burning rubber and gasoline, and the sweet, coppery scent of blood.

Strong arms squeezed Cade tight, reminding him where he was. Here. Now. Whole. With Poppy, the woman he already cared so much about. She was holding him close, stroking her hand over his back. He breathed in her scent, the citrus of her shampoo mixed with . . . her, and relaxed into the pillows.

"The accident broke my right leg in two spots and pulverized my hip. I had a lower spine fracture, five broken ribs, and both my shoulders were dislocated, plus a collapsed lung and all sorts of internal injuries. Obviously, the doctors said I was lucky to be alive. The driver that hit us and our limo driver weren't so lucky."

"God, Cade. I'm so sorry." Poppy's voice was thick with sorrow. "I had no idea you were so badly injured."

"I didn't share many details with the media. I didn't want to talk about it." He swallowed hard. "The doctors said I wouldn't fight again. Every single medical professional who came into my room told me it wouldn't happen. That I had a very long road ahead of me, and it didn't look good. I was still in the hospital when my wife, Alana, served me with divorce papers."

"Fucking bitch," Poppy hissed.

His lips twitched in amusement, and he kissed her forehead before continuing.

"I lost all my endorsement deals, lost my star status, my wife, my friends . . . everything. It was a very, very dark time." He'd gone from the highest of highs to rock bottom. "But you know what? It was kind of a blessing."

She looked at him like he'd lost his damn mind.

"Hear me out," he said with a chuckle, dropping a kiss to her lips. "It took a while—and a really long-ass pity party— for me to realize what I didn't lose."

"And what was that?" she asked, caressing his jaw.

Cade leaned into her hand. This woman's touch made everything better. "My brother. My parents. My close friends. I didn't lose them. If anything, the accident made all of us a whole hell of a lot closer. They rallied behind me. So, losing everything actually showed me who my people were. And more importantly, who they weren't."

His chest clenched as he remembered the unconditional love and support he'd received from his family—both blood and chosen—during his recovery. They had thrown some tough love his way, too, but he'd needed it to get stronger, both mentally and physically. Without them by his side, cheering him on, he never would have defied the odds.

"My comeback two years later was billed as astonishing and miraculous. And it was. My first fight was to reclaim my middleweight championship belt. There was so much publicity and hype going into it, but no one really thought I had a snowball's chance in hell of winning. The Vegas odds were ridiculous. Like, insultingly ridiculous. But I knew I could do it. My family—my *true* family—believed in me."

"And you won. First-round submission, right?"

He leaned down and kissed her. "That's right. Then I went up in weight and won the light heavyweight belt, too."

"Of course you did." Her wide smile lit up something

inside him, something that had him needing to kiss her again.

"That's right, babe," he said against her lips. "I successfully defended both titles three times each, and my fame reached astronomical proportions as a result. Then I retired. On top and on my own terms."

"Why? Some would say you were still in your prime."

He shrugged. "I had nothing else to prove. Nothing else to reach for. I'd already reaped every reward and earned more money than I could spend in a lifetime. So, I figured the only thing left to do was give back to the people who helped me get to that point. All that hard work I put in? All the success I achieved? It wasn't a solo show. There was no way I could have made it to the top without the crew I had around me."

"Where are those guys now?"

Cade smiled all the way down to his core. "The head coaches at our Hudson gym are guys from that crew."

"Of course they are." Her eyes shimmered with tears as she pulled him down for a kiss.

"The other three guys from that group started their own gyms, but we collaborate all the time. Do joint training camps together. That kind of thing. We're all still tight."

"I'm so proud of you," she murmured, running her thumb over his lips.

His heart swelled at her words. This woman's opinion mattered more to him than she'd ever know.

It had taken Cade's dream shattering for him to realize what and *who* mattered. Alana? He didn't think twice about his ex-wife now. She'd jumped ship the second the money had stopped flowing. He didn't need that kind of shallowness in his life. Yes, his divorce and recovery had been a hard and, at times, dangerously dark road. But it was what he'd needed to become a better man.

Now that his fighting days were over, new dreams were

developing. They had started with opening a fight gym with his brother and friends. Now . . . they were evolving yet again to include the woman in his arms. Her kids. Maybe even one or two of their own.

He smiled. Jumping the gun? Maybe. But that's what dreams were for, right?

CHAPTER TWENTY-FIVE

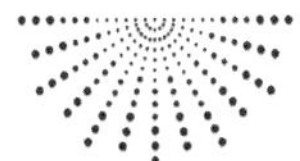

The ding of a text notification pulled Poppy from sleep. She rolled onto her side and snuggled deeper into the warm blanket. A second ding made her peek her eyes open. The space next to her was empty, but the indent in Cade's pillow remained. Reaching over, she found the sheets still warm, so he couldn't have been gone too long. A third ding, and she saw his phone on the end table, its display lighting up.

The door to the en suite opened, and Cade sauntered back into the room. She wiped a hand over her chin to make sure she wasn't drooling. Because yeah . . . the guy was that hot. He wore a pair of fitted boxers and nothing else. His chiseled chest, his washboard abs, that delicious *V* she'd had the pleasure of licking last night, that hefty bulge that was thickening by the second . . . She licked her lips.

A growl had her eyes shooting up. Before she could blink, the duvet was yanked away, and that delicious man was on top of her.

"Morning breath," she squeaked.

"Don't care," he murmured. His mouth covered hers, then trailed from her neck down to her breast.

On a sigh, she opened her legs, and he settled between them. Locking her ankles around his waist, she groaned when he tugged and rolled her nipples.

His phone dinged again. Then again.

This time, her groan wasn't one of pleasure.

"Cade," she said, tugging on his hair. "Your phone's been going off."

"Don't care," he repeated, moving his lips to her other breast. "I'd rather get you off right now."

She was inclined to agree with him—until his phone dinged *again*. "Cade, what if it's important?"

He released her breast with a pop and sighed, dropping his forehead to her sternum. "Fine," he huffed, rolling off her and reaching for his phone. "This better be fucking good." A glance at his messages had him chuckling. He sat up, adjusted himself, and ran a hand up her leg. "You need to get dressed, babe."

Her brow furrowed. "Is everything okay?"

"Everything's fine," he said, climbing off the bed. He grabbed his sweatpants from the heap on the floor and pulled them on. *Shame.* His T-shirt went on next. *Double shame.* "But trust me on this, babe. You'll want to put something on. The boys are gonna video-call soon."

Her gaze ripped away from his muscular forearms. Which she'd been ogling. "Wait, what did you say?"

With a smile that tempted Poppy to rip his clothes right back off, he handed her a folded T-shirt. "The boys will be calling you soon. They plan on coming to my MMA class this morning, but they said Four's out."

Rising from the bed, she slipped on the shirt he had given her, which fell nearly to her knees, and followed him out of the bedroom. Technically, what he'd said made sense. But it also didn't. She rubbed her forehead and groaned. "Oh my god, I think I need coffee."

A few minutes later, dressed in only a De La Rosa Gym T-shirt, Poppy leaned back against the kitchen island and let the hot, bittersweet coffee work its magic. "Okay, I'm ready now. Tell me one more time, please."

Cade grinned and took a sip of his own coffee. "Apparently, C and D talked with Four last night about my class. Even though Four can't make it, the boys are still in. They caught an early ferry, so they're already on their way."

She frowned. Why on earth would they do that? It was barely eight in the morning, and the boys were *not* morning people. Holy crap, was something wrong? Were they okay? Her lips pursed. Well, they must be okay if they were going to the MMA class . . . but why didn't they text *her*?

"Hey, now," Cade murmured, taking her mug and setting it on the island behind them. He pulled her into an embrace, propping his chin on top of her head. "I can see the worry turning in your mind. Everything's fine. We have some big-name fighters helping out with this class, so the boys are just excited, which is cool. I promise that between me and my coaches, we'll have eyes on them at all times, okay? And after what they went through on Wednesday, punching shit will be good for them. It's a great stress release. Relax, babe."

Poppy nodded with a loud exhale. Then she popped up onto her toes, wrapped her arms around his neck, and pulled him down for a kiss. "Thank you."

Seconds later, her phone rang.

Cade held her phone out to her. "I promise, Pop, they're good."

With a sigh, she hopped up on a backless barstool at the kitchen island and answered the video call. The twins' heads filled her screen. Sitting side by side in a booth, the utilitarian décor in the background showed they were on a ferry.

Studying her sons, she tried not to wince at Carter's face. He looked better than he had on Thursday night. Technically. But that didn't say much, since the bruising and swelling along his left side were still horrific.

"Hi, boys." She took a fortifying gulp of her coffee.

"Hey, Mom," they greeted.

Her eyebrow arched when Carter and Dylan glanced at each other with mischievous grins. They were obviously okay, but they were up to something.

"Morning, Cade!" they shouted in unison.

Poppy choked on her coffee, and she glared across the kitchen at Cade. He was shaking his head, hands held up in innocence, eyes wide.

"Nice place you got there, Cade," Dylan said as his brother guffawed.

Clearing her throat, Poppy brought her attention back to her phone and prayed her face wasn't as red as it felt. "Boys, how do you know where I'm at?"

Dylan rolled his eyes and moved the phone so his face was the only one on the screen.

"Mom," he said, and that one word held a world of exasperation. "The location tracking on our phones, remember? Before we moved out, we set it up so you'd know where we're at—and so we'd know where *you* are at."

Her jaw dropped. *Oh my god. Kill. Me. Now.*

"Whatever, Mom. It's cool," Carter said offscreen. Then he called out, "Hey, Cade, can I get a shirt like that, too?"

"Yeah, me too," Dylan added.

Cade coughed, but she was pretty sure he was covering up a laugh. He moved behind her to join the shot. "Uh, yeah. I don't see why not."

The boys' camera panned out, and Carter joined his brother on the screen again. "Cool. So, Mom, here's the plan: We'll be home in like an hour. You and Cade meet us down at the ferry dock. That way, we can leave you our car for whatever you need to do, and D and I can catch a ride with Cade back up to the gym for his MMA class. When we're done with class, maybe you can sneak away from work so we can all meet up for lunch or something. What do you say?"

For a moment, she could only blink. Then she grinned. Oh, these boys. "Well, it looks like you guys have it all figured out, huh?"

"Well, yeah," Dylan scoffed. "But does that work for you guys?"

She looked over her shoulder at Cade, and he laughed, giving her a nod.

"Okay," she said with a slight shake of her head. She wasn't quite sure how this was going to play out, but if the boys weren't going to act awkward, she'd try her best to do the same. "Cade and I will meet you at the dock. Text me when you get on the Hudson ferry. We'll figure out lunch later. I took the whole weekend off since you guys were coming home."

"Sweet!" Dylan said.

"Oh, shit," Carter muttered. "We gotta go—"

"Language," she sighed.

"Sorry, Mom. We're pulling up to Whidbey now. I'll text you soon."

"Don't speed through Whidbey, boys!"

"Of course not!" Carter was the picture of innocence. Well, if innocence also had a raging black eye. Still, she mom-glared into the phone, and he cracked up. "Don't worry, Mom. Old-man D's driving, so we're good."

Dylan rolled his eyes at his brother. "I'm a *cautious* driver, you dumbass."

"I'm not a dumbass. *You're* a dumbass."

"Boys," she groaned. "Language, please. You're in public."

They shot her angelic smiles and said in their sweetest voices, "Sorry, Mom. Love you." Then they disconnected.

Poppy stared at her phone for a moment, shaking her head. "They're good kids. I know they are. But I swear the two of them . . ."

Cade laughed and placed his hands on her shoulders. Lightly kneading, he kissed the top of her head. "They're fine, Pop. They're eighteen and brothers. Their mission in life is to give each other shit. And curse as much as humanly possible."

She leaned back against his chest and looked up. "Will they grow out of it?"

"Not necessarily. However, they'll learn when and where it's appropriate." He grimaced, and she bit back a smile. "Well, maybe. If you asked Jackie, since she's surrounded by dudes all day, she'd probably say no. We never outgrow being stupid."

Poppy gave up her fight and laughed. The man really was adorable. "Thank you for going along with the boys' plan for today."

"Nothing to thank me for, babe. It'll be fun to have the boys in class." He took her phone and tossed it on the counter, then spun her stool to face him and scooped her up. "Besides, those kids have this really hot mom I like."

"Is that so?" she asked, locking her arms around his neck and her legs around his waist. She nipped at his plump lower lip.

"Yes, ma'am." He took a moment to deepen their kiss. "Now, by my calculations, we've got just over an hour before we have to be at the dock."

He lowered her onto the kitchen island and pushed her knees wide. His hand gently circled the base of her throat, and her breath hitched. With a roguish grin, he pressed until she eased back onto her elbows. "Which is a good thing, babe, because I'm hungry for some breakfast."

. . .

Two hours later, Poppy scanned the playground and grinned. The little play area was a block from the ferry dock, nestled between Hudson's downtown public beach and the ice cream shop. Scarlet was beside her, and skipping in a circle around the swings was Scar's darling four-year-old daughter, Daisy. The temperature had dropped over the last few days, so even though it was the weekend, there were only a couple of other children playing. Not that Daisy seemed to mind. She had all the company she needed in her most cherished stuffy, Mr. Slothy, who was tucked under her arm.

Scarlet elbowed Poppy with a teasing grin. "So, you and Cade are *official* official, huh?"

Poppy pursed her lips. "I'm not quite sure what that means."

"Official means you're dating. *Official* official means you have the gossip train's blessing. And since I learned that difference directly from Mrs. Abbot, who was raving about you guys with Mrs. Green and Mrs. Yoshida at the diner yesterday, that makes you and Cade *official* official."

Poppy's eyes widened. "Wow. That's actually . . . kind of sweet. I think."

Scarlet laughed. "Oh, my friend, you should hear those women talk about your man. *Sweet* is not the word that would describe them. Sailors would blush, I tell ya!"

"Well, Cade is pretty amazing," she said with a shrug, grinning at her friend.

"Considering you climbed out of his car this morning, I'd say so."

Her smile dimmed. "Yeaaah, about that . . ."

"What's wrong?" Scarlet's brow furrowed. "Oh my god, please don't tell me he sucks in bed. That can't be possible."

She snorted. "Yeah, no. The man's fantastic. He's a world-class athlete who knows how to use his body. He has stamina for days."

Scarlet hooted, then grew serious. "So what's the problem, then?"

Poppy winced. She leaned toward her friend and dropped her voice. "Yesterday morning, Hudson Security found five listening devices in my apartment. Someone broke in and hid them."

Scarlet gasped, and her eyes darted around the playground before she whisper-yelled, "I swear to god, Eli is such a piece of shit!"

Poppy held up a hand. "We don't know if he's the one behind it. Not yet."

"Please," Scarlet scoffed. "He probably watched some spy movie or something and now he thinks he can find some dirt on you so he can stick it to you. Did you call the sheriff's department?"

"Yeah. Quinn came out right away. Gavin, the owner of Hudson Security, happened to be at the store too, so that's how he got involved and found the bugs. They don't have any answers yet, but they're working on it."

"You stayed with Cade last night, then?"

Poppy bit her bottom lip, but it was no use. A wide smile bloomed on her face. "Yeah. He showed up when things were all crazy yesterday and was just . . . there for me."

Scarlet eyed her for a moment, and though amusement played over her friend's face, Poppy still fought the urge to squirm under Scar's scrutiny.

"Promise me something, Pop?"

"Of course." There wasn't much she wouldn't do for her friend.

"Promise you won't let all the bullshit Eli has spewed over the years hold you back."

"I promise." She hooked her arm with Scarlet's and leaned in close. "Can I confess something?"

"Always, girlfriend."

"Cade . . . He makes me feel beautiful and strong. Like I really matter to him." She let out a sigh that she knew was sappy and swoony and all things dreamy. But she didn't care. Because she felt all those things. And more.

Scarlet squealed and pulled her in for a hug. "I'm so excited for you! The gossip train had it right—you guys are totally *official* official!"

Poppy was laughing when Scarlet suddenly spun her sideways. "Scar, what—"

"Fuck. Don't look," Scarlet hissed. "Eli is down the street."

"Fantastic," she groaned. "Just what I wanted this morning. Fingers crossed he doesn't see us."

They huddled together, backs turned in the direction Scarlet had spotted Eli, and continued to watch Daisy and Mr. Slothy play on the slide. After a few moments of waving to Daisy, then Mr. Slothy, then Daisy again, Scarlet said, "You know what I don't understand? Why doesn't Eli just leave town?"

"Holy shit. That would make life so much easier."

"I just don't get it." A look of revulsion crossed her friend's face, as if she'd smelled something rotten. "It's not like he has anything left here. Your house is sold, he's living at his parents' rental property, and no one wants to do business with him. At least, none of the locals. I mean, I'd be hard-pressed to find anyone in town who doesn't think he's a complete sleaze."

"I'd rather be a sleaze than a fucking whore like the two of you."

Poppy flinched at the malicious words. Whirling, she took two steps back.

"Look at the two of you," Eli sneered, face blotchy with

anger. "You think you're fucking better than me? Newsflash —*I* am someone in this community, and I always will be! You two are just little fucking whores hanging on to the coattails of whoever's dumb enough to support you." He turned his venom on Scarlet, looming over the petite woman. "And you, with your slutty tie-dyed hair, flaunting your tits and ass all over town—"

A large man stepped in front of Scarlet, knocking Eli back a step. "You want to say that again, motherfucker?"

Poppy's jaw dropped. Holy shit. Matt Alvarez. She could feel his barely leashed anger—it was that palpable. And that damn terrifying.

Apparently, Eli felt the same because the asshole paled.

"That's right, you piece of shit," Matt growled. "You go near Scarlet again, you deal with me. You go near Poppy again? You deal with me *and* Cade."

Eli sputtered, his mouth gaping like a fish. Then he straightened to his full height, which was still a handful of inches shorter than Matt's. "This is harassment, and I won't stand for it," he called out haughtily, loud enough for everyone nearby to hear. "There are witnesses—"

"*You're* a harassment, Eli Walker. To *everyone's* ears," Mrs. Green huffed as she walked over. The older woman linked arms with Poppy and Scarlet, glaring at Eli. "Would you care to repeat any of your delightful comments about these young ladies now that, as you said, there are witnesses? Because Scarlet here is correct. You'd be hard-pressed to find anyone in this town who doesn't think you're a complete asshole."

"Um, I actually used the word sleaze," Scarlet mumbled.

"Potato, potahto, my dear." Mrs. Green looked Eli up and down, disgust evident on her face. "I suggest you leave. Obviously, Mr. Alvarez was merely protecting these women from *your* filthy harassment. If you'd like, I can personally call Sheriff O'Conner and—"

Eli stalked off.

With a satisfied harrumph, Mrs. Green squeezed Poppy's and Scarlet's arms. "Don't let men like that intimidate you, ladies. They're weak. As for Mr. Alvarez here? You dig in and hold on to ones like him." She gave Matt a blatant once-over and shimmied her shoulders. Well, she'd ogled his back since the man was still standing guard, in full protector mode. "Now, I need to talk to the mayor about that odious man." Releasing their arms, Mrs. Green air-kissed their cheeks, patted Matt's shoulder, and hustled down the street.

"Wait, isn't the mayor her husband?" Scarlet whispered.

Poppy nodded, a little overwhelmed by all that had just transpired. "She likes calling him by his title. I don't ask questions."

"Mama?"

Poppy's gaze swung to the little girl who was now clinging to Scarlet's leg.

"Mr. Slothy is scared," Daisy said, her little voice shaking. She looked up at her mom with shimmering eyes.

"Come here, sweet girl," Scarlet murmured, picking up her daughter. Daisy immediately burrowed into her neck. "You tell Mr. Slothy there's nothing to worry about."

"Are you ladies all right?" Matt asked. His fury had dissipated, but his intensity was still in full force.

"Yes. Thank you for stepping in," Poppy replied.

When he turned his attention to Scarlet, the poor woman's complexion matched her name. Poppy couldn't blame her. Matt Alvarez was intimidating.

"Are you okay?" he asked Scarlet in his deep, rumbly voice.

Scarlet nodded, growing even redder, and Poppy had to bite the inside of her cheek to keep from laughing. Oh, her sweet, sweet friend . . .

Matt's attention moved to Daisy, and some of that intensity lessened. "Are you okay?"

The little girl remained silent, and simply stared at him.

"Is Mr. Slothy okay?" he asked, his eyes softening.

Daisy's lips curved into a sweet smile, and Poppy's jaw dropped. Daisy nodded and began wiggling in Scarlet's arms. "Down, Mama. Mr. Slothy wants to play on the slide."

They watched Daisy skip away, as if Eli hadn't just spewed vile shit in the middle of a playground.

Matt looked back at Scarlet. "If he bothers you again, you let me know, okay?"

When no response came, Poppy elbowed her friend.

Scarlet cleared her throat. "Um, thank you, Matt. I will."

With a lift of his chin and a quiet, "Be careful," Matt turned and walked down the sidewalk.

Once he was out of earshot, Scarlet gulped down a big breath and said in a rush, "Holy shit oh my god did that just happen?"

Poppy chuckled. How could she not? She slung her arm around her friend and squeezed. "It sure did."

"God, I can't even think about what a sleazeball shit your ex is right now, because that?" Scarlet waved her hand toward Matt, who had paused half a block away to answer his phone. "Holy shit. I mean, it wasn't just me, right? That whole alpha-male caveman thing was . . ." She fanned herself. "Right? And oh my god, when he asked Daisy about Mr. Slothy? I think I may have gotten pregnant from that alone. That was super fucking hot, right?"

Poppy's chuckle turned into a belly-aching laugh. There was one man—and one man only—who was super fucking hot to her. However, she also had a pulse. "Yes, my friend, that was definitely hot."

Scarlet's eyes bulged. "Oh shit, he's coming back."

"Eli?" Poppy asked, frowning.

"No, Matt. And . . ." She winced. "He's got that super-scary-but-kinda-still-hot look on his face again. Now shush!"

Matt pocketed his phone as he approached. "I'm sorry to interrupt. Poppy, I need you to come with me."

A chill crawled down her spine at the ferocity of his gaze. "What's wrong?"

"Cade asked that I escort you to the gym. Immediately."

Her stomach dropped, and she grabbed on to Scarlet's arm. "The boys?"

"They're okay, but we need to go now. Cade needs you."

CHAPTER TWENTY-SIX

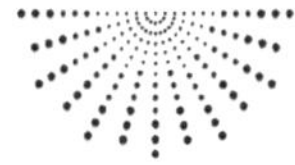

Tension filled the small car, thick enough to cut with a knife. Cade had decided to leave his Range Rover with Poppy and have the twins give him a ride to the gym, so he was sitting shotgun, Dylan was driving, and Carter was sprawled in the backseat. They'd been on the road for a solid five minutes. And no one had said a thing.

Cade genuinely liked Carter and Dylan. He really did. However, knowing that *they* knew he'd spent the night with Poppy was fucking awkward. He had no freaking clue what to say. But dammit, he was the adult here, right?

Aiming for casual, he asked, "So, how was the trip over? Uneventful, I hope."

"Yup," Dylan said, keeping his eyes on the road. "No traffic or anything."

More silence.

Fuck. Now what? He racked his brain for something else to say, but Carter spoke before he could come up with a single idea.

"The only eventful thing was seeing Mom still at your place this morning."

Cade's eyebrows lifted at the slight bite in Carter's tone. Oh hell no. As much as he liked the kid, there was no way he was going to let that snippy-ass attitude fly. He turned in his seat and met the young man's gaze. "Something you want to say?"

Carter shrugged, glancing away. But not before Cade saw the defiance and concern warring on his face. "Talk to me, C. What are you thinking?"

Carter blew out his breath and met Cade's stare. "You're not just messing with her, right? Like, you're serious about her? She doesn't need to be dicked around by another asshole. She had plenty of that with Eli."

Looks like defiance won. The tension in Cade's shoulders let up, and he gave Carter a chin lift of approval. There was no way he was going to fault the kid for being protective. "I'm very serious about your mom, and I've told her as much. This thing with us is new, but it's not casual. She's the only person I'm seeing, and honestly, I'm hoping to keep it that way for a long damn time."

Carter held his gaze for a few more moments before giving him a slight nod. Cade had to give the kid props. He wasn't one many would choose to go toe-to-toe with, but Carter had done just that for his mom.

"What do you think of Eli?" Dylan asked, his focus still directly on the road.

Fuck if that wasn't a minefield of a question. Swinging his attention to Dylan, Cade hedged, "What do *you* think of him?"

Dylan rolled his eyes but didn't answer.

Apparently, Cade's attempt at deflection was a no-go. He sighed. "You want honest?"

"Wouldn't have asked otherwise, man," Dylan said, deadpan.

Smart-ass. The corners of Cade's lips twitched. "I think the guy's a fucking worthless piece of shit."

"Same." Dylan's jaw worked.

He nodded. "You want to talk about it?"

Dylan shook his head, and Cade figured that was that, but the kid remained tense as he navigated around a bend in the road. When they were on another straightaway, he cracked.

"Eli didn't care one way or another about me and C. But Mom?" His hands gripped the wheel harder, making his knuckles turn white. "He treated her like shit. Mom didn't think we could hear, but we did. Eli ridiculed her all the damn time. He said the worst fucking things to her. Told her she wasn't as pretty as Roxie or her cousin, Sheila, who he was fucking on the side. Said she wasn't as thin as Scarlet or that hostess at Monty's he was *also* fucking on the side."

Carter let out a dark chuckle. "Eli's favorite activities were fucking anyone who fell for his bullshit and spewing hateful lies at Mom. She'd always yell back and act like it didn't hurt her feelings, but we know it did. It had to."

Cade saw red. If he ever saw Eli again, he'd knock the motherfucker out.

"Mom's a shower crier," Carter said, and everything inside of Cade froze. "Always says her eyes are red because she got shampoo in them. But it's bullshit. And when she's really stressed, she stops eating. So keep an eye out for that."

His breath locked in his chest. Holy shit, these guys . . . Poppy would be devastated if she heard the boys knew this about her.

It took two tries, but he finally found his voice. "I will do everything in my power to keep your mom happy. I'm sure she'll get pissed at me at some point because . . . well, that's relationships, right? Ups and downs. But I swear to you both, right here and now, I will never cheat on her. Also, I sure as hell will never call her names or ever touch her in anger. Ever."

They had to know that. Hell, *Poppy* had to know that.

Cade knew she was still a little hesitant, but he vowed he'd prove it to her every damn day of his life. That she could trust him, rely on him. Because that's what he wanted. To spend every damn day with her. And he could be a patient man when he needed to be.

"Do us a favor, though," Dylan said, turning onto the road that led to the gym. "Don't tell Mom we had this conversation."

"It's not that we want you keeping secrets from her," Carter clarified. "It's just that . . . if she knew we knew, it would make her sad."

Cade nodded. It sure as fuck would. "I promise you both that I'll look out for her."

"Good. She needs that." Dylan put the car in Park. "She's always looking out for everyone else. It'll be nice to have someone look out for her."

"She'll probably push back on you, though," Carter said, hopping out. "So be ready for that."

The boys slammed their doors, and Cade remained seated. Stunned. He'd known the twins were amazing kids. He just hadn't realized *how* fucking amazing.

"Are you coming?" Carter called.

"I can still have a shirt, right?" Dylan yelled.

"Yeah," Cade said, climbing out of the car. "Remind me after class." He slung his arms over their shoulders. "Seriously, you know your mom is so damn proud of you guys, right?"

At their solemn nods, he squeezed them both. "I can see why. Between the three of us, we've got her back. Agreed?"

"Agreed," they said in unison.

Then Carter's eyes twinkled with mischief. "So, old man, are we done with the kumbaya shit already?"

"Oh fuck, kid." Cade laughed and slapped them both on their backs, jostling them. "Trust me, you're gonna regret that one, buddy."

Thirty minutes into his MMA class, Carter and Dylan were drenched in sweat and glaring daggers at him. Well, Carter was glaring daggers at him. Dylan was glaring daggers at his brother.

"Again," Cade barked with a smirk.

Both boys flipped him off, and he howled. Nothing like some good ole burpee sprawls to get the blood flowing. *Old man, my ass!*

"Time!" he shouted two minutes later.

Carter and Dylan, along with the rest of the morning class participants, collapsed onto the mats, chests heaving, limbs sprawled out. From the beginners to the seasoned fighters, everyone was wiped. Cade grinned from ear to ear. Goddamn, he loved his job.

"Water break. Then pair up with someone at your level and work on takedown defense." He turned to face one of the elite fighters who'd dropped in to help with class. "Jason, can you work with Carter and Dylan?"

The twins' eyes bugged as Jason Rokovich approached them. Clearly, they recognized the current UFC light heavyweight champ. Cade had hoped the boys would get a kick out of working with the man, so he was pleased to see he'd been right.

After the water break, he and a couple of his coaches made the rounds, correcting and helping where they could. He walked by the boys often. Each time, he found them listening to every word Jason uttered in rapt fascination. The way their excitement had transformed into discipline filled Cade's chest with pride. More than a few times, he rubbed his sternum to quell the warmth growing there, but it was no use.

As the end of class neared, Cade checked his watch and prepared to call time. But a loud crash jerked him and everyone else to a stop. A millisecond later, the window to the left of their group exploded. A fireball landed on the mat, engulfing it in flames. The nearby fighters scrambled away. A second window shattered, and another fireball landed. And then another.

Chaos. Utter chaos.

The heat from the flames was immediate and oppressive. Black smoke filled the gym, and more glass shattered, more fire launched toward them. The fire suppression system kicked to life, raining water down on the mats. The flames continued to grow, undeterred. Blaring alarms drowned out the cries and curses of the fleeing fighters.

"Away from the windows!" Cade yelled, running to the fire extinguisher and tearing it off the wall. "Carter! Dylan! Get the fuck away from the windows!"

His eyes watered as he peered through the smoke, hurrying back to the flames. When he was six feet away, he pulled the pin from the extinguisher, aimed the nozzle at the base of the fire, and squeezed. A white cloud sprayed forth, blanketing the mats. Another extinguisher launched its attack from his left, and a few seconds later, a third joined the effort from his right.

Cade's pulse thundered in his ears as he and his crew worked on killing the flames with the fire retardant. Minutes ticked by, one heartbeat at a time. Then the extinguishers were empty, and the fire was out. As the smoke dissipated, the alarms stopped. Lucas, one of his coaches, had shut them off at the panel.

Apart from the hum of the sprinklers and the coughs of his friends, colleagues, and Poppy's boys, the gym fell quiet. Then a loud buzz sounded. Everyone tensed, but it was only a warning from the sprinkler system before it shut itself off.

Cade scanned the gym, and his blood turned to ice. Four panes of the floor-to-ceiling windows along one wall were shattered. White powder and shards of glass covered the floor, but they couldn't hide the charred and melted mats. The stenches of burned rubber and chemical spray lingered in the air.

"Holy fuck," Jason muttered before breaking into a hacking cough. He hunched over with one hand on his knee while the other cradled a fire extinguisher.

Holy fuck was right.

Cade stepped toward his friend, but Jason held up a hand.

"I'm okay," the fighter croaked as he straightened and swiped a hand over his face.

Desperately blinking against the painful grit in his eyes, Cade scanned the stunned faces in the room. "Is everyone else okay?" His gaze landed on the twins, and his chest locked. He was beside them in an instant. "Are you guys hurt?"

Their matching bloodshot eyes were owl-wide, and their faces were streaked with a mixture of soot, sprinkler water, sweat, and tears. Still, they nodded. "We're okay," they said in unison, their voices like gravel.

Thank fucking god. The vise gripping Cade's heart unclenched. He pulled them each into a bruising hug, then turned to the room. "Nobody touches anything, got it? Everyone needs to stay put until we know that whoever the fuck did this isn't still out there." He waved at the opposite end of the gym, which hadn't been damaged. "Get settled over there while I call—"

"What the fuck?" Gavin roared, bursting through the gym's front doors, three members of his security team right behind him.

"Was just gonna call you," Cade said, coughing. He motioned to Gavin, then walked toward the damage. When they were far enough from the group, he pointed at the scorched mats and destroyed windows. "Something that looked like fireballs crashed through the windows. They exploded when they hit the mats and burst into fucking flames."

"Motherfuckers," Gavin growled. Turning to his team, he ordered, "Secure the area, make sure the proper authorities are notified, and get Bean on the cameras." As his guys dispersed, he looked back to Cade. "Everyone okay?"

Cade glanced at the group huddled near the other end of the gym. Their initial shock seemed to have ebbed. They were talking amongst themselves now, their expressions and gestures animated. "I think so, but I'll double-check with everyone."

"Holy fuck," Gavin hissed. "Are those Poppy's boys?"

"Yeah." Cade heaved out a sigh, which set off another round of coughs.

"Holy shit, brother," Gavin said when Cade finally caught his breath. "I'll make sure Quinn and the EMTs are on their way. But fuck, man, are *you* okay?"

Cade's hands trembled as he scrubbed them over his face; the adrenaline dump had left him shaky. "I think so, but . . ." He linked his fingers on top of his head and grimaced. "Holy shit, if something had happened to them—"

"But it didn't, man." Gavin gave him two hard slaps on the shoulder. "It didn't."

Cade's exhale burned his chest, but he didn't care. The

boys were okay, and his friends and fighters weren't seriously hurt. That's all he cared about right now. They would figure out the rest one step at a time. Still, anger simmered in his gut as he scanned the destruction again.

Whoever the fuck was responsible for this . . . They were going to pay.

CHAPTER TWENTY-SEVEN

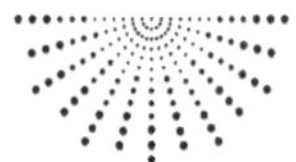

Nausea swirled in Poppy's belly as Matt drove her out of Hudson's downtown area in his truck. The buildings and roads were a blur. Her mind was in a whirl, and she couldn't concentrate on anything.

When Dylan had told her about the fight to protect Jackie, she had thought she'd known panic. But no, that had been nothing. That didn't hold a candle to the turmoil and terror running through her now.

"Matt, please tell me what you know," she whispered.

"I don't know much, Poppy," he said, his deep voice calm and steady. "I know for a fact that your boys and Cade are okay. There were no major injuries."

She twisted to face him, and her eyes widened in surprise. While Matt's voice was calm and steady, his appearance told a different story: His jaw was clenched tight. His face was hard and unyielding. His knuckles were bloodless on the steering wheel.

Poppy took in a deep breath. Letting it out slowly, she laid a hand on his forearm. He was worried, too.

"You said there was an explosion?" she asked, trying to

recall the rushed explanation he had given her when he'd hustled her into his truck.

Matt's nod was curt. "They don't know exactly what kind, but yeah."

Poppy willed her quivering insides to settle. It didn't work. She was still terrified.

Images of Cade's Seattle gym flickered through her mind—the destruction, the chaos, the injured men. Her heart knocked hard in her chest, and fear had sweat dotting her brow. She took another deep breath in. She couldn't fall apart, dammit. She needed to hold it together for her boys. For Cade.

More images flooded her mind. Carter and Dylan as precocious little rascals. Their excited faces when they'd driven off earlier today. The playful wink Cade shot her as he'd climbed into the car with the boys.

Her nose tickled, and her throat grew thick. She tightened her grip on Matt's forearm.

"They're all okay, Poppy," he murmured in that same calm and steady tone, patting her hand. "I promise."

She nodded, but she couldn't stop the first tear. Or the second. *Hold it together, dammit!*

After what felt like hours, Matt turned onto the road that led to Cade's gym. And immediately slammed on the brakes. She jerked forward but didn't feel the abrupt snap of her seat belt.

Fire trucks, ambulances, and police cruisers blocked their path.

Poppy unbuckled and jumped from the truck, heart in her throat. Vaguely aware of Matt calling her name, she didn't stop, couldn't stop. She raced toward the gym's front door. Nearly there, she stumbled to a halt at the sight of the devastation. The gym's wall of windows was a shattered mess.

Her lungs seized. *No. No!*

Someone grabbed her shoulder. She flinched and blindly shoved them away, bolting through the door. A sob tore from her throat when she spotted her boys. On her next breath, they were in her arms.

Though they towered over her, she clutched them close and inhaled their scents. Underneath the smoke, sweat, and grime, they still smelled like her little boys. Another sob escaped, and she gripped them harder.

"We're okay, Mom," Dylan said, though his voice cracked on the last word.

Oh, my sweet boy.

Reaching up, she placed a hand on each of her sons' faces and took them in. Both sported new cuts and scrapes, but they were in one piece. She straightened her spine and squared her shoulders. The last thing they needed to worry about right now was her. "You guys promise you're okay?"

They swiped at their eyes and nodded.

"We're good, Mom," Carter said.

Her throat grew thick again, and she pulled them into another hug. "You guys are my world. I love you so, so much."

"We love you, too," they murmured, stepping back to wipe their forearms over their eyes.

Dylan motioned toward the destroyed windows. "That was so crazy. I don't think I've ever been that scared."

Carter nodded. "Even when that guy was attacking Jackie, it wasn't as scary as this."

Clasping her hands together, Poppy pressed her knuckles to her lips. Her emotions were held together by a fraying string. She swallowed past the boulder in her throat and said, "But you guys are okay. That's what matters."

Her thoughts flashed to Cade, and her heart fluttered with panic. Where was he? Was he okay? Did he need her?

As if she'd summoned him, Cade entered her field of

vision. Fresh tears stung her eyes as she watched him stride across the gym toward her. He was covered in soot and beyond disheveled. Exhaustion, worry, and frustration lined his features.

The unraveling string holding her emotions together snapped. Without thinking, Poppy ran the length of the gym and launched herself at him. She crashed into his chest, and when his strong arms wrapped around her, tears flooded her eyes. Until this moment, she hadn't realized the depth of her feelings for this amazing man.

"I was so scared for you," she whispered. A tremble racked her body, and she buried her face in his neck, taking a deep breath in to prove he was real. Like with her boys, under the smoke, sweat, and grime, she found his familiar woodsy scent. It filled her nose and calmed her, gave her strength.

Even though Matt had said Cade wasn't injured, not seeing him with her own eyes, not feeling his strong arms around her, had been terrifying. They'd only been a part of each other's lives for a short time, but he had somehow snuck into her heart.

Cade set her back on her feet, and she framed his face in her hands. "Are you hurt? Are you okay? Are you—"

He pressed a quick kiss to her lips before wrapping his arms around her. "I'm good now, babe."

Thank god he's okay. Running her hands up and down his back, she propped her chin on his sternum and looked up at him. "Anything I can do to help? Anything at all? I'm here for you."

Cade buried a hand in her hair and pressed his lips to her forehead. "Thank you, babe. I just need to hold you for a little bit."

"It's my turn to say it now, Cade." Poppy squeezed him tighter, and for the first time in what felt like forever, she smiled. "I've got you."

CHAPTER TWENTY-EIGHT

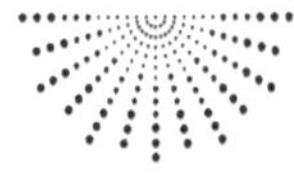

By mid-afternoon, the fire department was finally gone and Quinn and his deputies, accompanied by two of Gavin's team members, were on their way to meet with the feds. The gym's fighters and staff had cleared out long ago, all heading home except for three of Cade's coaches, who had hopped on the ferry to Whidbey Island. They planned to hit up the big-box home-improvement store to buy blower fans for the water-damaged floors and boards for the windows.

Since the gym was surrounded by yellow crime scene tape, everyone else had moved to Hudson Security's building, which was located down the road from the gym. The twins were hanging out with Rebecca and Rocco in the employee lounge at the opposite end of the facility, to decompress in front of the television and various video game consoles. The rest of them were gathered in a large conference room to debrief the situation.

Cade sat with Poppy next to him. On her other side were Dante and Matt, and across the table were Bean, Wilson, and Gavin. On the large video screen wall were Joe Buchanan, the head of Hudson Tactical, who was conferencing in from

Montana, and Oliver MacKay, Hudson Security's second-in-command, who was conferencing in from . . . Cade frowned . . . god knew where.

After Gavin introduced everyone to Poppy, Cade leaned back in his chair and let out an exhausted sigh. "Please tell me you guys have an idea of what's going on?"

"Wilson," Gavin said.

Giving both Cade and Dante a chin lift, Wilson stood and walked to the Smartboard on the wall opposite the video screen. "We canvased the area across from where your gym sustained damage and found the launch point. It was a small clearing about ten yards past the perimeter fence."

"Out of view of the cameras," Bean added. "I'll be scoping out any other blind spots on the property and installing additional cameras over the next few days."

Gavin nodded. "Good. Keep me updated."

Wilson tapped the Smartboard and a couple photos popped up.

To Cade's untrained eye, one was simply a clearing between two trees. However, the other chilled his blood. It was the same clearing but from a different angle, this time with a direct line of sight to the gym's main windows.

"Unfortunately, whoever did this"—Wilson waved at the Smartboard—"made a quick exit. Fortunately, because they made such a quick exit, they did a shit job cleaning up their mess."

Nerves fluttered in Cade's gut, and he clutched the arms of his chair. Holy shit, had they actually found something? Did they have something to go on? Some sort of clue as to who was behind all this mayhem?

Poppy's hand settled over his and squeezed. The breath that was lodged in his chest left in a soft whoosh. Rotating his hand, he linked their fingers and shot her a grateful smile. As she smiled back at him, he noticed she also had a supportive hand on Dante's shoulder. His heart pinged, and he brought the back of her hand to his lips. Goddamn, this woman. Her warmth, her empathy, her strength . . .

He was so damn grateful for her.

"Fifteen yards from this spot, deeper in the forest, we found two crude, old-school launcher-type devices," Wilson continued.

"What?" he and Dante exclaimed at the same time.

"They were like the old Cuban M-16s," Wilson clarified.

"You found fucking assault rifles?" Matt asked, surprise and fury evident in his tone.

"No," Bean interjected. Her fingers flew over her keyboard, and then another photo appeared on the Smartboard. It showed a . . . Hell, Cade wasn't sure what it showed. "Cuban M-16s were, in essence, Molotov cocktail launchers from the 1950s and 60s. It's basically a sawed-off, 16-gauge, break-action shotgun that's modified to launch Molotovs."

Matt whistled. "Holy shit, that's a thing?"

Bean nodded. "It's said they were developed during the Cuban revolution, hence the name. And they're surprisingly accurate even from about a hundred meters out."

Wilson nodded. "Which explains how the perps—I found two sets of tracks—were able to cover the distance and stay out of the camera's view. Now, if you look closer at this second photo, you'll see it appears they misfired a couple times." He pointed at two spots along the security fence where the greenery was singed. "There was broken glass here and here, along with a flash burn of the immediate surrounding area. At least these assholes were smart enough to tamp out the flames before they started a fucking wildfire."

"Damn," Dante muttered, shaking his head and staring at the photos in wonder. "As bad as the damage is, it could have been even worse."

"We gave Quinn this information a few hours ago, which is why he called the meeting with the feds," Bean said, crossing her arms over her chest. "Officially, the Hudson Island Sheriff's Department is handing this case off to the FBI and the US Bureau of Alcohol, Tobacco, Firearms, and Explosives. They can get into a pissing match on jurisdiction."

"And unofficially?" Cade asked.

"Unofficially, Hudson Security is taking point on this." Gavin nodded to him and Dante. "This is all connected. They've hit both your gyms now, and they scoped out your home, D. But you know what? This is our fucking home, too. Between me, Bean, Wilson, and the rest of our crew, we'll get whoever the fuck's behind this."

Cade nodded, pulling Poppy closer.

"May I make a suggestion?" Oliver asked from the video screen.

"Forgot you were there, fucker," Gavin said, smirking when Oliver flipped him off.

"I'm sure it doesn't need to be said, but close ranks," Oliver said. "Dante, I know you've already moved your family back onto the property and Xander's with Rebecca and Rocco during the day, but my suggestion is to lock it down even more. Assign PSOs for the Seattle gym, but call everyone else back in. Keep everyone on property until this is resolved."

There were murmurs of agreement around the room.

"Done," Gavin said.

"Hey," Poppy whispered, squeezing his hand.

"What's up, babe?" he asked, voice low as Gavin and Dante began talking logistics for the Seattle gym.

"When they take those bugs out of my place, if you need me to, I can get out of your hair."

His brow furrowed. "What?"

"Get out of your hair. With all this going on, I'm sure the last thing you need is me distracting you from everything that needs to get done and—"

"Poppy," Bean interrupted. "The bugs were removed this morning."

Poppy swung her attention to the other woman, lips parted in shock.

"What can I say? I have really good hearing." Bean shrugged and shot her a wink. "I gave Quinn the paperwork this morning—with all evidence obtained legally and completely admissible in the court of law. And since I still have the key to your place, I went with him to remove them."

"Oh, wow, um," Poppy stammered. "Thank you."

Cade's eyes narrowed, and he growled, "Who was it?"

"Down, killer," Bean said, grinning. "You know, I was at the sheriff's department with Quinn this morning, helping him get his ducks in a row for the warrant and arrest, when everything went down at the gym. That's why I took a while to get up here."

Cade's blood simmered. "Who, Bean? A name."

The woman's eyes went to Poppy, and a split second later, he felt Poppy's soft hands on his jaw.

"Look at me, Cade," she whispered.

Begrudgingly, he met her hazel gaze.

"Let Quinn do his job, okay? You cannot—no, *will* not—do anything that might get you in trouble."

He didn't want to agree. Not at all. Because if Eli had bugged Poppy's home? Invaded her privacy like that? Holy shit . . . "If that motherfucker comes near you, I swear—"

"He won't," Bean said, bringing Cade's attention back to her. "He'll be arrested as soon as the warrant comes through. There's no way he's getting out of it. Not only does his search history back it up, but Eli purchased the damn things on his credit card *and* registered the devices to his email and cell.

On top of all that, he had them transmitting to his phone and iPad."

Motherfucking shit!

Poppy cupped his jaw again, this time more forcefully. "Cade, please. Let Quinn do his job. Eli isn't worth it. Don't get arrested for beating him up."

"Would be satisfying as fuck, though," Matt grumbled.

"Not helping," Poppy said, glaring at Matt. She brought her focus back to Cade and ran her thumb along his jaw. "It would be extremely satisfying. But, babe, I'd rather you not get into trouble over him."

Babe. She'd called him babe. In front of everyone. Sure, there were probably more points to unpack from everything she'd just said, but that's what stuck in his mind. Cade took her hand in his and pressed a kiss to her palm. "Fine. But on one condition."

Her eyes narrowed. "Go on."

"You're part of the lockdown, too. You stay with me at my place."

For a moment, her mouth just opened and closed. More than anything, he wanted to kiss those sweet, luscious lips, but he was aware they were in a full room. A full room shamelessly listening to their conversation.

"But I have to work, Cade."

"I can assign a PSO to you," Gavin said. "Then you'll be protected wherever you need to go."

Poppy's confused gaze ping-ponged between him and Gavin. "PSO?"

"Personal security officer," Gavin clarified. "Rebecca has one with her during the day. It wouldn't be a problem to assign one to you."

Poppy shook her head. "I don't think that's necessary."

"I do," Cade said. "Someone's targeting us. Both of our gyms. Dante's home. I can only assume the reason they haven't targeted mine is because it's secure." He lived well within the property lines. The perpetrators would need something closer to a rocket launcher to hit his home from outside the perimeter fence. But Poppy's apartment was an easy target. Even Eli fucking Walker had infiltrated it. And Rainy Day Boutique was open to anyone. Frowning, he turned to Gavin. "I want Poppy protected. The boys, too."

His friend nodded. "When do they head back to school?"

"Monday." *No one is going to touch them, dammit.*

"Bean, check and see who's available. We'll need three in Seattle—one for each of the twins and Jackie."

"On it, boss." She shot Poppy a wide grin.

Gavin nodded at Matt. "Tell Four what's going on. Make sure he's prepared in case shit hits the fan."

Poppy gasped. "Do you think Four needs protection, too?"

Chuckles came from around the room.

"I'm sure he'd love having a certain tall brunette personally assigned to him," Wilson snickered, "but trust me, Four is more than capable of taking care of himself."

"Don't worry, Pop." Cade squeezed her hand, then met the eyes of each person at the table. "No one's gonna hurt Four, and we've got the best of the best at our backs. We're not alone in this."

"Damn right," Gavin said, nodding at him and Dante. "You two are family. We'll handle this." He looked at Poppy. "And like Rebecca and Rocco, we've got you and the twins. I promise."

CHAPTER TWENTY-NINE

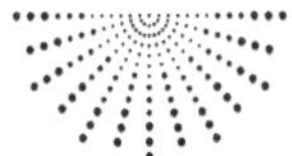

After finishing up in the conference room, their group made their way to the parking lot. Poppy was still overwhelmed by everything, but from what she'd witnessed, Gavin and his crew were rock solid. They'd get to the bottom of who was going after Cade and Dante.

She glanced at the De la Rosa brothers as they huddled with Gavin, Matt, and Bean in the building's entryway. Her heart hurt for them. She knew how much their gyms meant, how much of themselves they'd put into each one. Without a doubt, Cade and Dante were relieved no one had been seriously hurt this time . . . but she knew the damage to their new facility still weighed on them.

Rebecca, carrying a sleeping Rocco, walked up to Dante, and the man immediately wrapped his arms around his family. The tension visibly eased from him as he held them close. A small smile ghosted Poppy's lips as she watched the interaction. She could be that for Cade. No, she *would* be that for him. The man worked so hard. The love for what he did was apparent, and though he was projecting a calm exterior, she saw his frustration, concern, and underlying anger behind his turbulent eyes, behind his strained smile.

Without thinking twice, she approached the gathered group, careful not to interrupt Gavin. She moved to Cade's side, invaded his personal space, and wrapped her arms around his middle. And just held on.

One of his arms encircled her instantly, and he released a long, slow breath. When he finished replying to something Gavin had said, he pressed a kiss to the top of her head.

After a few moments, their discussion wrapped up. Gavin, Bean, and Matt said their goodbyes and went back inside.

Turning, Cade hugged her hard. "Thank you, babe."

Still in his embrace, she propped her chin on his chest and looked up at him. "Nothing to thank me for."

His dark-brown eyes seemed calmer. The worry and frustration were still there, but the anger had diminished significantly. If anything, her man looked exhausted.

Yes. Her man.

Smiling, she asked, "What do you say we—"

"Mom!" Dylan called, pulling her attention to the parking lot. The twins were standing outside their car, waiting. "Uncle Four is gonna drop off food for everyone at Cade's."

She glanced at Cade. "I was going to ask if I could make us dinner at your place, but it looks like Four, the little punk, beat me to it."

Cade chuckled and dropped a kiss to her forehead. He laced his fingers with hers and tugged her toward the parking lot. "Let's get out of here."

They pulled up to Cade's house—Cade in his Range Rover and her in the boys' car—and when Dylan cut the engine, she turned to her sons.

"I hope it's okay with you guys, but instead of staying with your uncle Four this weekend, I'd like it if you guys stayed here at Cade's."

"Are you staying here, too?" Carter asked, pinning her with his hazel eyes.

Oh my god. Hello, awkward. She cleared her throat. "I am. For a couple reasons."

"Cool," Dylan said, opening his door. He popped the trunk. "Grab your stuff, C."

She walked with them to the trunk of the car and slung one of their backpacks over her shoulder.

"So, you like the guy?" Carter asked, tightening the strap of his duffel bag across his chest. When it was secure, he reached for the backpack she'd taken. "I got it, Mom." He snagged it before she could protest. "D and I think Cade's pretty cool, by the way. He's a good dude."

The corners of her lips twitched. God, she loved watching her little babies act all protective and mini man-ish. "I'm glad you think so."

"What's the other reason?" Dylan asked as they made their way through the open front door.

She heard the murmur of Cade's deep voice as they entered the living area. A quick scan revealed he was in the kitchen. *Sorry,* he mouthed, pointing at the phone he held to his ear.

God, he was so damn sweet. And—

"Mom?"

She startled, and her gaze flew to Dylan. "Sorry, what was that?"

"You said there were a couple reasons why you're staying here. One is"—he shuddered with great exaggeration—"you obviously like the guy. What's the other reason?"

Her stomach sank, and she sighed. Shit. She'd meant to tell them when they arrived this morning, but they'd basically said hi and then bye as they'd sped off to Cade's class. How was she supposed to . . . ?

Rip it off like a Band-Aid, dammit!

She looked over her shoulder at Cade. He was still on the phone but had moved out to the back deck. Taking a deep breath, she succinctly explained how they'd found listening devices in her apartment and how Gavin's team had tracked them back to Eli. At first, the boys stared at her in shock and disbelief. Then their expressions went blank. The whole story took less than five minutes, and they said nothing that whole time.

"Gavin and his team gave all the evidence to Sheriff O'Conner," she said, hoping to reassure them. "I expect everything with Eli will be handled in the next day or two, so there's nothing for you guys to worry about. Okay?"

Silence.

Poppy's brow furrowed. She couldn't read their faces right now . . . and she could *always* read their faces. Stepping forward to hug them, she jumped when they suddenly exploded.

"What the fuck, Mom?!"

"He bugged your apartment? What the hell?!"

"I'm gonna fucking kill him! How dare—"

Before she could pick her jaw up from the floor, Cade was standing between her boys, his hands on their shoulders. Voice cool and firm, he said, "C, D, ease up."

Carter shook off Cade's hand and spun toward him, ready to pounce.

Cade shook his head. "Trust me, man. A few hours ago, I was right where you're at. Believe me. I was ready to hunt that fucker down and beat the living piss out of him." Wincing, Poppy started to interject, but Cade met her gaze and rushed on, "*However*, there was a voice of reason, a voice of sanity, that calmed me down. That reminded me that getting tossed in jail wouldn't do me any good. If anything, it would let that cocksucker win. And Eli is *not* fucking winning."

Again, her mouth opened and closed, gaping like an oxygen-deprived fish. When she managed to get it under control, she tapped Cade's shoulder and said, "Um, Cade? I don't think that's what I actually said."

Cade met her gaze, and with an aw-shucks grin, he shrugged. "Really? Well, that's what I got out of it."

Shaking her head, she studied her sons. They were both frowning, but some of the tension in their postures had lessened. Oh, her sweet babies.

"C, D, you guys remember what we talked about in the car?" They nodded, so Cade continued, "Well, it's not just us three who have her back now. Gavin and his crew do, too."

Carter's chin lifted, and he huffed out his frustration. "We'll keep it together."

"I know you will." Cade patted their backs. "Now why don't you guys go get settled. When you head upstairs, turn right. There are three guest rooms. Take your pick."

Fifteen minutes later, the boys had selected their rooms for the weekend. Sounding like a herd of elephants coming down the stairs, they paused when the doorbell rang. Rushing to the front door, they swung it open and let out a cheer.

"I brought dinner from Ray's," a familiar voice called out.

Poppy grinned, taking in Four as he walked into the kitchen carrying three overflowing bags of food. "Not that I'm complaining or anything," she said, taking one of the bags from him, "but why didn't you bring food from your own place?"

He gave a chin lift to Cade, then placed the remaining two bags on the island. "Because I value my life."

Dylan snorted. "Whose shitlist did you get on?"

"Haha," Four deadpanned, flipping off her son.

Poppy rolled her eyes at the two as she unloaded the containers. Her stomach growled at the warm biscuits, mac and cheese, mashed potatoes, coleslaw, and potato salad. Then the smell of fried chicken filled her nose, and her mouth watered.

"It's a madhouse at the restaurant right now," Four said. "We're down a line cook, two servers, and a hostess. So, as much as I want to, I can't stay."

She gasped. "Four! You didn't have to come all the way out here—"

He engulfed her in a hug. "Don't be dumb, Pop. I had to see you guys with my own fucking eyes. I love you. And I know you're strong and capable and all that shit, but *please* listen to Gavin's crew."

Her heart squeezed, and she met his indigo gaze. "I will."

"Good." Four turned to the boys and hauled each one into a back-breaking hug. "Love you guys. Look out for each other, yeah?"

Carter and Dylan nodded, their eyes misty. He turned to Cade. "Talk to you outside?"

Poppy opened her mouth, but Four held up a hand and smirked. "Don't worry, Pop. I won't hurt him. Much."

Less than five minutes later, Cade strolled back in.

"Everything okay?" she asked.

He pressed a quick kiss to her lips, and a blush tore over her cheeks. The boys groaned.

"Four loves you and the boys," Cade said. "He just wanted to . . . reiterate how much."

"Of course he did." Her eyes rolled, though she bit back a grin. Then she waved at the food. "Let's eat."

It took nearly twenty-five minutes for her guys to demolish the food. Poppy pushed the remaining pieces of her dinner around on her plate, then sat back to survey the almost-empty takeout containers.

"Not hungry?" Cade asked, eyeing her plate.

She shrugged. "It's been a crazy day."

The guys exchanged a look she couldn't read.

Cade rose and went to the pantry. He returned with an unopened bag of Haribo frog gummies. "At least have some of these." He winked as he retook his seat. "You don't even have to share."

A grin spread over her face. "Thanks."

Poppy was sure the guys were up to something, but at the moment, she couldn't bring herself to care. Opening the package, she popped one of the gummies into her mouth and let out a happy sigh. As she savored its sweet, marshmallowy goodness, she took in the three faces around her. Two, she'd loved since the moment she'd first heard their heartbeats. The third? Well, the intensity of her feelings for Cade should scare her. And they did.

But the more time she spent with him, the more she realized that he sparked something inside her. Something that burned brighter and more intensely than her fear of getting hurt. Something that made her want more, want everything with him. Companionship, intimacy, love . . . All of it. Her heart squeezed. She was falling so hard for this man. She was going to hold on to him. To them. For as long as he'd let her. Hopefully, that would be forever.

She glanced at her boys and smiled. The four of them would get through this craziness and find a way to make things work. Together.

"So, does Gavin only hire military guys?" Carter asked, pulling her from her revelation.

Cade finished chewing and swallowed before answering. "I'm pretty sure Bean didn't serve, but aside from her, I think everyone else is either former military or former alphabet agency."

"I'm sorry, what?" she asked, popping another gummy frog.

"Alphabet agency, Mom," Dylan replied. "You know . . . the FBI, CIA, ATF, NSA . . . That kind of thing."

She frowned. "Wait. How do *you* know that?"

"Movies, mostly. And they had a couple recruiters from the FBI and DHS on campus a few weeks ago."

"If you guys are interested in working with Hudson Security, you should just ask Gavin what skills he's looking for."

"You think we could?" Carter asked.

Poppy chuckled at the hero worship in Carter's eyes. "Yes, but be prepared. Gavin's a bit . . . intense. Wouldn't you say so, Cade?"

Cade smirked. "That's one way to put it."

"Uh, Mom, I think the word you're looking for is *badass,*" Dylan said past a mouthful of chicken.

She glared at him. "Seriously? Manners?"

"Sorry, Mom," he mumbled, eyes twinkling as he swallowed his food.

"D's got a point, though. Did you see how his entire crew just, like, took charge?" Carter asked, waving his drumstick at her. "It was like straight out of a movie."

"Well, thank god," Dylan said, waving his own drumstick. "Because everything that happened was fucking crazy!"

"Oh my god," Poppy muttered, pinching the bridge of her nose. "Language, please."

"Shit. Sorry, Mom." Dylan cringed, then laughed. "Sorry."

"But it *was* crazy, Mom. One second, me and D are working out with Jason Rokovich—*Jason Rokovich*, Mom!—and the next second, there's fu—er, um, tons of glass and fire raining down everywhere."

Poppy's stomach rolled, and what little she'd had for

dinner threatened to come back up. But when she spied Cade in her peripheral vision, doing the shut-the-hell-up slashing motion at Carter, her fear let up a little.

"Uh, but there's nothing to worry about," her son rushed on. "The fire sprinklers went off, and Cade and Jason and TJ sprayed the whole damn place with their fire extinguishers, so it's all good."

Good god. The boys, Cade . . . They'd come so close to getting hurt. Someone had *firebombed* them. If it hadn't been for the gym's safety mechanisms and the quick thinking of Cade and his coaches, today could have gone horribly different. She fought a shiver.

No, dammit! No what-ifs! The boys were safe. Cade was safe. That's what mattered. That's what she needed to focus on.

After a few more minutes of the boys going on and on about Gavin, Jason, and all the other "badasses" they'd met today, Carter slapped his brother on the chest and stood.

"I think D and I are gonna call it a night."

Dylan nodded, rising. "Yeah. If it's okay with you guys, I think we're gonna check out the Xbox upstairs for a little bit and then crash."

"There are games in the drawer to the right of the console," Cade said.

"Before you go, clean up, please," Poppy chimed in.

The boys groaned as expected, but they cleared all the plates and loaded the dishwasher. At the same time, she put the leftovers away and Cade wiped down the table and counters. Watching everyone move around the kitchen, a smile touched her lips. This domesticity was . . . nice. Normal. Natural. And it felt one thousand percent right.

CHAPTER THIRTY

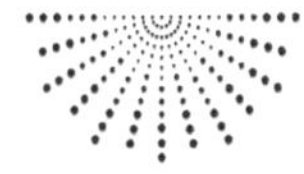

Holy shit, what a day.

Cade closed his bedroom door and sighed, dropping his chin to his chest. For a moment, he stayed like that, absorbing the depth of his gratitude. He was so damn thankful no one had been seriously hurt. So damn thankful those two teenage boys were sprawled out in one of his guest rooms, mindlessly playing *Madden*. So damn thankful their beautiful mother was in his bathroom getting ready for bed. With him.

After joining Poppy at the sink and brushing his teeth, he settled into his king-sized bed and pulled her close. He loved how she fit so perfectly against him, how her head nestled into his chest, how his arms wrapped around her so naturally. He wanted this. Her. For the rest of his life. He'd never been more certain of anything. Smiling, he tightened his embrace and kissed the top of her head.

"You okay?" she asked, tracing circles over his heart.

"I am now."

"I'm sure Gavin and his team will find something."

Cade pursed his lips. He sure as hell hoped so. Because he

had no clue who could be behind this. But the more he thought about it, the more his mind kept circling back to the lawsuit and that guy's connection to his former brother-in-law. How was—

He startled when Poppy traced a finger between his eyebrows.

"What's going on in that head of yours?" she asked.

He hadn't realized he'd been frowning.

"It just doesn't make sense," he said. No matter which way he turned it over in his mind, the dots wouldn't connect.

"What, babe?"

Despite his inner turmoil, he smiled. "I like it when you call me babe, babe."

"Right back at ya," Poppy said, turning and placing a kiss on his pec. "Now, what doesn't make sense?"

"All of it. I find it hard to believe that my former brother-in-law and Joshua Justin could be behind this."

"Why?"

"Alister is a deadbeat and a narcissist. Even Alana doesn't like him. At least, she didn't when we were married. And I sure as hell didn't, either. He was a hanger-on at best. And that other guy? Barely a blip in my memory. The lawsuit itself is ridiculous and . . . I don't know. What could they possibly gain? It just doesn't make sense."

"Cade. I hate to sound crass, but you have a lot of money. If these guys really are in debt to the mafia, then you look like an easy way out."

"That's what Gavin thinks, too, but I can't wrap my head around it. Why would they bomb the Seattle gym and throw Molotov cocktails at the Hudson gym if they're after my money?" He shook his head. "It's not like they've sent a note that says, 'Send us two million dollars or else.' The whole idea just seems far-fetched. And besides, the Alister I knew was lazy. I'm not exaggerating when I say he's an absolute deadbeat."

"How many years has it been since your divorce, though?"

Cade thought about that for a moment. On one hand, his accident, divorce, downward spiral, and climb back to the top felt like yesterday. But on the other, it felt like a lifetime ago. He'd come so far since that dark, dark time, and the knowledge filled him with pride and a resolve to do a little better each day. "Almost eight."

"A lot can change in eight years," Poppy said softly. "Besides, people do crazy things for money. Especially people who owe that money to the mafia. The whole pay-me-back-or-get-tortured-and-murdered thing would make anyone desperate."

She had some compelling points. "Doesn't that seem too simplistic, though?"

"Sometimes it *is* simple, Cade. If these guys need money, then who better to shake down than you?"

Yeah, but . . . "That still leaves the question of why there haven't been any demands for money. They're just destroying our gyms."

"Maybe they're trying to scare you first? I mean, yeah, it seems like a stupid plan to us, but desperate people do desperate things. Rarely do they make sense."

He nodded. "Fair point."

"Take Eli, for example," she continued. "He planted listening devices in my apartment. The only thing outstanding with our divorce is splitting the proceeds from the house sale. So, I can only imagine he did it to find some sort of dirt on me, something to either blackmail me with or ruin my reputation."

Eli was a piece of shit. Thankfully, a dumb piece of shit who'd left plenty of evidence behind. Likely because he was arrogant enough to think he wouldn't get caught. Cade frowned at the thought and ran a hand down Poppy's back. "Well, I'm glad that fiasco has been figured out, at least. Hopefully, Quinn will get everything squared away and hold that fucker accountable."

"I'm sure Quinn has everything under control. Including the stuff with the gym. Between him and the feds and Gavin's team, it will all get figured out."

He was sure Poppy was right, but that didn't stop him from worrying.

"You can talk to me, you know," she murmured, running a hand over his chest.

He remained silent for a few moments, then blew out his breath. "Today was . . . fucking awful."

"I can't imagine the fear you must have felt," she said, snuggling deeper into his side.

"I was terrified the boys were hurt."

She grabbed one of his hands and squeezed. "They weren't, Cade."

"I know." He nodded. "Some of the guys that were there . . . A few of them served, and I know it must have brought up some bad memories for them." He ran a hand over his face. "I hate that what happened today could have triggered something for them . . ."

"Hey," she said, straddling his lap and pulling him up into a hug. Leaning back, she traced a thumb between his eyebrows. "Don't beat yourself up. You'll call your guys tomorrow and check on them, make sure they're okay. I know you're worried about your people. It's one of the things that makes you so wonderful. You care. You take care of others." She pressed a soft kiss to his lips. "Will you let me take care of you?"

His chest clenched, and he could only stare at the marvelous woman in wonder. His heart was hers. Completely.

Tugging her close, bringing them nearly chest to chest, he cradled her face in his hands. A soft smile spread across his face as he ran a thumb over her plump lower lip. She was so damn perfect. "You don't have to say anything back," he whispered, "but, Poppy, babe, I'm absolutely falling in love with you."

He could see the surprise in her hazel eyes. Slowly, they went soft and misty. He kissed her, pouring every ounce of his feelings for her into their kiss. He wasn't certain if she was on the same page. Hell, he didn't expect her to be since he'd rushed to the end of the damn book. But he would wait. He would be patient. Because this woman was everything. Her warmth, her empathy, her strength . . . her beauty, her fire, her intoxicating taste . . . He would never get enough.

She trailed her hand down his chest to his abs, and all his blood surged south. He groaned against her lips. This woman lit him on fire. Their tongues tangled, and when her hand traveled even lower, he stilled.

"Uh, Poppy, babe—" He sucked in a breath as she slid her hand beneath his boxers and gripped his diamond-hard cock. "What are you doing?"

"Well, Mr. De la Rosa, I think it's quite apparent." Poppy smirked, stroking him from base to tip. She pressed a kiss to his chest, and he groaned when her tongue darted out to flick his nipple. "I think you've had a stressful day, and I want to help you relax. Not to mention you just gifted me with the sweetest words I've ever heard."

"Babe," he said, burying his hands in her hair. "You don't have to do this."

"Let me take care of you." She met his gaze as her hand continued to work him. "Please, Cade."

How the hell could he refuse her?

He couldn't.

At his slight nod, she released him and straightened. Cade

nearly swallowed his tongue when she made quick work of her tank top. He bent down and locked his lips around one of her perfect breasts, earning a sexy moan, then molded her other breast with his hand, pinching and twisting her hard nipple.

"Cade," she groaned before pushing him away. She framed his face in her hands and gave him the most devastating kiss. When he tightened his arms around her, she pulled away. "No distractions, mister." She playfully pushed his chest. "Now lie back."

Cade complied, watching as she stood over him and pulled down her pajama pants and panties in one swoop. His mouth watered. He reached for her but froze when she wagged a finger at him.

"Uh-uh-uh. I'm in charge right now."

His cock jerked. This woman was magnificent.

Poppy kneeled between his legs, and he went impossibly hard. Goosebumps rose on his skin as she teased her fingers down his chest and over his abs, then pulled off his boxers. When she gripped his straining cock and stroked, he moaned. "Holy fuck, Poppy."

"You're so hard for me," she murmured, her hot breath ghosting over the length of him.

Cade's arms trembled, and he gripped the sheets. Seeing her mouth so close drove him insane. "Fuck, babe. Suck me. Please."

She flashed him the sexiest grin. Then her tongue shot out and circled his tip. Her eyes locked with his as she took him deep in her mouth, lowering her head until he hit the back of her throat. His hands tangled in her hair, and he almost came right then.

"Poppy, babe," he groaned.

His skin turned electric as she worked him. Up and down she bobbed, sucking him like her life depended on it. Again and again, she took him deep in her throat. The sight made him let out a low curse. Her cheeks hollowed, and she hummed her pleasure around his cock. His spine tingled, and he gripped her hair harder.

"Poppy, I'm gonna come."

Instead of pulling off him, she took his cock deeper. Stars exploded as he jerked, coming hard down her throat while she swallowed. When he heaved out a breath, she released him, then licked around his spent cock like it was a fucking lollipop. He pulled her up his body and fused his mouth to hers, flipping them so she was on her back and he was on top.

"That was amazing," he said against her lips.

She grinned at him. *"You're* amazing."

Cade kissed her again, loving how their tongues danced, and slid a hand down her body. Dipping two fingers into her center, a groan left him at the moisture that coated his fingers. "Fuck, babe. Did sucking my cock get you this wet?"

"Yes," she moaned, arching into his touch.

He growled in satisfaction, pumping his fingers in and out of her pussy as he nibbled his way down her body. "I think it's my turn to take care of you."

As he settled between Poppy's luscious thighs, happiness filled him. He could wait for her to reciprocate his words because he knew she felt something for him, something beyond this wild lust they shared. In the meantime, he would do everything in his power to show her just how precious she was to him.

Starting with *this*.

CHAPTER THIRTY-ONE

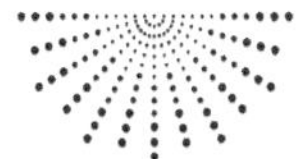

Poppy woke to the smell of bacon. With Cade still wrapped around her, she assumed it was the boys. She nudged him awake, and after some kisses that had her body humming, they rose from bed. With a long sigh, she searched for her clothes in the pile on the floor. If only they could linger in bed for the rest of the day. Continue what they'd started last night. Because it had been wonderful.

They'd worshiped each other's bodies, yes, but beyond that, the words Cade had spoken . . . about falling in love . . . They warmed everything in her. She'd desperately wanted to return them, but fear had closed her throat. Not because she didn't feel the same way. There was no doubt in her mind that she was absolutely falling for him. But because she feared he would eventually change his mind.

Finding her pajama pants and tank, she pulled them on, along with a bra, of course, while Cade dressed in sweatpants and a T-shirt. As she opened the bedroom door, he placed his hand against her lower back. She turned to him and wrapped her arms around his waist. A deep breath of his woodsy scent soothed her nerves. He tilted her chin up with his finger and gave her a kiss.

"You ready to face the boys?" he asked against her lips.

She winced. "Well, it smells like they made bacon, so it can't be *that* awkward, right?"

His eyebrows wagged. "Fingers crossed, babe. Fingers crossed."

They made their way downstairs with his arm slung over her shoulders and hers around his waist.

"Hope you don't mind that we kinda helped ourselves," Carter said, placing a platter of bacon in the center of the dining table. He took a seat while Dylan brought over platters of pancakes and scrambled eggs.

"Holy shit, guys," Cade muttered, his tone laced with wonder.

Poppy smiled. She'd made sure to teach her boys the basics before they'd moved out: cooking, cleaning, and laundry. Half the time, she wasn't sure they remembered a single thing she'd shown them. But this spread? Actual food and not just an assortment of Pop-Tarts? Well, it was safe to say that it made her mama-heart proud.

Carter filled his plate with bacon, eggs, and two giant pancakes. "What's on everyone's agenda for the day?"

Poppy poured herself a mug of coffee and took a sip. "Are you guys still planning on heading out tomorrow? Or are you going to take off tonight instead?"

Dylan shook his head, adding a nauseating amount of syrup to his pancakes. "No, we'll still head back tomorrow, but later in the day, so we don't hit Monday morning traffic."

"Well, since we should all stay on property today, do you guys want to come with me to the gym?" Cade asked, piling food on his own plate. "Dante and I are meeting with the insurance agent, and then I was going to meet with TJ and some of the other coaches. We need to figure out how to modify the upcoming training camps."

"Who are you training?" Dylan asked.

"Anton Patterson arrives next weekend for an eight-week training camp, and then a couple weeks later, we'll have Royce Oliveras for a six-week camp."

The boys' jaws dropped.

"Uh, yeah, we'll definitely go with you," Carter said in a rush.

"Holy crap, that's amazing!" Dylan exclaimed.

Cade grinned. "Just so I'm clear, Anton and Royce *aren't* actually going to be there today. It's just me, TJ, Dante, and some of our other coaches."

"Whatever, man. Count us in!"

Poppy laughed at her sons' enthusiasm.

"What about you?" Cade asked, facing her. "What are your plans for the day? Want to come with?"

"I took the weekend off, but . . ." She gestured to her phone. "It looks like I need to head to the boutique this afternoon. Bethany was scheduled to work all day, but she has to leave by two. Something about her mother-in-law making a surprise visit. I got her panicked text early this morning."

"Okay," Cade said. "I can have Dante handle the insurance agent and—"

"No, Cade." She shook her head. "You do what you need to do, and I'll—"

"It's not safe right now, Poppy."

"I know that," she snapped. Pressing her lips together, she sucked in a breath through her nose, then slowly released it.

"Oh, shit, dude," Carter mumbled. "You just got The Sigh."

"Yeah, you're in trouble." Dylan chuckled, shoveling a giant bite of pancake into his mouth.

She glared at her sons, who wisely turned their attention

to their plates. But not before they graced her with angelic little smiles.

Rolling her eyes, she said, "I know it's not safe, Cade. That's why—before you interrupted me—I was going to suggest seeing if Gavin had someone who could hang out at the shop with me today."

"Sorry, Poppy," he said, looking properly chastised. Well, if she discounted the smile he was clearly biting back.

His phone dinged with an incoming text, and he glanced at the message. Rising from the table, he murmured, "Speak of the devil."

"Eat," she said to her snickering boys.

Cade disappeared down the hall. She heard the front door open and shut, then the soft murmur of voices. Moments later, Cade walked back into the kitchen, followed by Gavin and Bean.

"Good morning," Poppy said, suddenly self-conscious that her crew were clad in loungewear while Gavin and Bean were in slacks and business tops. Granted, they were rumpled-and-wrinkled slacks and business tops, but still. "Can I get either of you coffee? Or a plate? There's plenty."

"No, thanks, Poppy. I'm good," Gavin said. Nodding to the boys, he added, "Gentlemen."

Her sons sat taller, preening as they returned Gavin's greeting.

A bittersweet feeling surged through her. It made her happy to see the boys thought so highly of Gavin. But knowing their admiration was, in part, due to the lack of positive male role models throughout their lives . . . Well, frankly, it was a bit of a sock to the gut. Yes, they'd had Four —who they all loved fiercely—but no one else. God knew Eli had shown them nothing positive.

That was going to change, though.

Poppy glanced between Cade and Gavin. Not only did the

boys still have Four, but now—if everything worked out the way she hoped—they would also have these strong men to emulate.

Pulling out the two extra chairs at the dining table, Gavin and Bean took a seat.

"There were some developments after you guys left our office yesterday." Gavin gestured to Bean, who was munching on a piece of bacon.

She wiped her fingers on a napkin, then pulled a laptop out of her bag. "So yesterday, I ran my facial recognition software on the Hudson Island ferry cameras going back a few days." Her palm shot up, halting the questions she must have sensed coming from the twins, and shook her head at them. "The less you guys know, the better. Trust me."

Carter and Dylan snapped their mouths shut, and looks of awe crossed their young faces. Poppy cleared her throat to hide a chuckle. It seemed like they had just developed a new respect for the Hudson Security IT specialist.

"Anyway, we got a couple pings." Bean spun her laptop around. Displayed onscreen was a grainy photo of two men on the ferry. Next to it were their driver's license photos. Both men were burly, with closely cropped hair and no necks. "These are Ivan Gurin and Lev Baranov. They're known muscle-for-hire with low-level ties to the Russian mafia."

"They're not exactly subtle-looking, are they?" Poppy mused, frowning at the photos. The guys looked like they'd come straight out of a James Bond movie. If you threw leather jackets and aviators on them, they'd make the perfect villains.

"The security photo is from them arriving on the two o'clock ferry on Friday," Gavin said. "There's no record of them staying at any of the hotels on Hudson, but they might have used aliases."

"Or they might have stayed somewhere else." Bean nodded at her laptop. "I have another program digging into rental property information for that timeframe now."

"Are they still here?" Cade asked, crossing his arms over his chest.

"No." Bean pulled up a second security photo of the men. This time, the shot was much clearer. "Their faces pinged on the ferry cameras early this morning. They were on the first ferry out of Hudson."

Gavin nodded. "We let the appropriate authorities know, and both men were apprehended when they reached the Whidbey Island ferry terminal."

The air whooshed from Poppy's lungs as she swung her gaze to Cade. Relief, hope, and wariness battled on his handsome face. She moved to stand behind his chair, draping her arms over his shoulders. He grabbed her hands and held them tight to his chest.

Universe, for Cade's sake, please let this be over.

"One of our operatives was in on the takedown and initial interrogation. Again, don't ask." Bean glanced at the boys and winked. "We received confirmation that Baranov had a similar Cuban M-16–type weapon in his duffel bag. Our operative also told us both men were quick to rat out who paid them."

"Who?" Cade tensed, gripping her hands.

"Joshua Justin," Gavin replied.

Cade's jaw flexed, and she heard his teeth grinding. "The fucker who's trying to sue me?"

"The very same," Gavin said. "Gurin and Baranov individually claimed that Justin hired them to bomb your Seattle gym."

"To what end?" Cade asked, disbelief tinging his words.

"Money," Bean said. "Apparently, they sent a note saying if you didn't pay up, the attacks would escalate."

Cade's head was shaking before Bean finished speaking. "But we didn't get any kind of note."

"Sorry." Bean shrugged. "That's just what they said."

"They also admitted they were the muscle hired to kidnap Jackie," Gavin continued.

"Holy shit," Cade growled. The anger in his voice was palpable. "*Kidnap?*"

Poppy moved her hands to his shoulders and began kneading.

"Yes. They said they paid the homeless addict to attack Jackie. That way, they could 'rescue' her so if there were witnesses, no one would question them taking her away." Gavin paused to nod at Carter and Dylan. "But that was stopped because of you two. Once they had Jackie, Gurin and Baranov were supposed to hold her, and Justin was going to demand ransom. They'd been paid half up front, but since Jackie got away, they didn't get the rest. So then, again according to them, Justin upped the ante and had them target your operation here."

"Has Justin been picked up?" Cade asked.

"Yes," Bean answered. "An hour and a half ago, he was picked up by the feds in Seattle. He claimed innocence, lawyered up, and isn't speaking."

"Wow." Poppy was stunned. There was so much to process. "So it's over?"

"I think it's too early to say that," Gavin admitted. "However, we definitely have a better idea of what's going on now."

She frowned. "I'm sorry, but I'm a bit confused. The two men who bombed the gyms have been arrested, along with the man who paid them. How is it not over?"

"Gurin and Baranov only implicated Justin, but that doesn't mean Alister Keys"—Bean glanced at Cade—"is innocent. The guy has been MIA for the last week, so that doesn't look good for him."

"Exactly," Gavin said. "So, even though we have a lot of the players identified and in custody, still stay sharp. Be on the lookout."

The hope that had been percolating in Poppy's chest fizzled out. There were still so many questions. "Will I still need security when I go off property? I need to head into work for a few hours this afternoon."

"I'd rather you have someone with you," Cade said, turning to look at her. "Just in case."

Gavin nodded. "I think it's smart to keep security high for at least the next week."

The worry line between Cade's eyebrows popped. "I agree, but any particular reason for that timeline?"

Gavin shrugged. The casual gesture was at odds with his serious expression. "Something still feels off."

"Shit," Dylan muttered. "Coming from you, that's terrifying."

The corners of Gavin's lips twitched. "True. But it's important to trust your gut." He met Poppy's gaze. "Since Dante's back and sticking to Rebecca like glue, I can have Xander accompany you to work today. Just let me know what time."

Poppy sighed. Yup, that tingle of hope was officially gone. "Thanks, Gavin."

"You can take my car, babe," Cade murmured.

"Ooh, your Range Rover SV Carmel Edition?" Carter wagged his eyebrows, adding much-needed levity to the room. "I'm sure that won't be a hardship, Mom. And I can act as your driver if you need. Definitely wouldn't be a hardship for me."

"Nope. I've heard about how you drive, dude," Cade said.

He pointed at Dylan. "Your brother is the only one of you two knuckleheads who can drive my Rover."

Once the boys' guffaws died down, Gavin said, "On a different note, Poppy, Quinn let me know that the arrest warrant was authorized last night. Eli was taken into custody this morning."

"Holy crap," she said, eyes wide. "While we were sleeping in and having a pancake breakfast, you guys were sure busy."

"It's always best to catch the bad guys unaware," Bean said, reaching for another piece of bacon.

"Eli will be charged with invasion of privacy and breaking and entering," Gavin said. "Unfortunately, the invasion of privacy is a misdemeanor at best. He should be convicted of both, and hopefully, the B and E will carry more weight. In the meantime, I think it would be wise for you and the boys to get a restraining order against him."

She glanced at Carter and Dylan, who both nodded at her. "Okay. I'll call my lawyer tomorrow."

The conversation continued for another ten minutes. Logistics, schedules, and security assignments were discussed, but Poppy had a hard time concentrating. All she registered was that Hudson Security had called in the majority of their team members, so by the end of the day, there would be more badasses prowling the De la Rosa property than she could imagine.

The news should have made her feel better. And it did. To a point. It was comforting to know her boys were safe at Cade's and would continue to be safe when they went back to school. But in truth, the only thing that could fully calm her nerves was life returning to normal. Until then, she'd just have to take things one step at a time.

A hand squeezed Poppy's, startling her.

"We'll get through this, babe," Cade whispered, pressing a

kiss to her palm. Then he nodded to the boys. "Let's get this cleaned up."

By noon, they'd all moved over to Cade's gym. An hour later, Xander arrived to pick her up.

"Cade said we could take his car," Poppy told the PSO.

"I rode my bike here, so that works out well." Xander pointed at one of the intact front windows. On the other side was a gleaming black motorcycle. "But I'll drive if that's okay with you. I like to be behind the wheel."

"Fine by me," she said, handing him Cade's keys. "I'll meet you out there in a few minutes."

"Great." Xander left her to say goodbye.

Poppy hugged each of her boys tight and only stopped messing with their hair after they both groaned out an exacerbated, "*Mommm!* We're fine!"

She turned to Cade and gave him a quick kiss and said, "Before you ask, I'll text you when I get to the shop, and I'll text you again when we're on our way back."

When she tried to step away, Cade hauled her back to him for another kiss. A couple of catcalls echoed through the gym, along with a couple of gagging sounds—from her boys, no doubt. Maybe Dante as well. She laughed and slapped him on the chest until he released her.

"I'll see you later." Without looking back, she walked through the gym's front doors and made her way over to his Range Rover.

Climbing into the passenger seat of Cade's car, she quickly buckled up. "Sorry you're stuck babysitting me, Xander."

He gave her a warm smile as he pulled out of the parking lot. "It's not a problem; it's what I'm here for. Besides, I've been with Rebecca this week, and it's been fine. But I'm not gonna lie. I'm really looking forward to how quiet your shop is going to be." He grimaced. "Don't get me wrong—the kids are great and all, but Rebecca's day care can get *loud*."

She chuckled. "I'll bet. When my boys were little, the decibel level was ridiculous. Still kind of is sometimes, and there are only two of them. How many does Rebecca take care of?"

"Five." He shuddered, turning onto the main road. "They're sweet kids, but they're freaking deafening. And, no joke, they all cry at the same damn time."

"I don't even want to imagine." She laughed, looking over at Xander. "I remember when the boys—"

Before she could blink, before she could even scream that there was a car coming straight at them, everything exploded.

The windows shattered, and Poppy was thrown against her door, then jerked painfully back. Screeches of metal on metal deafened her ears. Her eyes watered from the acrid smoke from the airbags, and the scents of burning rubber and pungent gasoline filled her nose. The coppery tang of blood coated her tongue.

When everything stilled, she turned her head and whimpered. The pounding in her skull had tears sliding down her face. Xander was slumped over the steering wheel and blood poured from his forehead. She could see the slight rise and fall of his chest, but it did little to curb her panic.

"Xander," she whispered, voice breaking as pain tore through her chest.

A deep, throaty laugh chilled her blood.

She whipped her head to the right, searching for the laugh's owner. The sharp movement intensified the pounding in her head. Bile surged up her throat, and vomit spewed from her mouth, covering her chin, and slithered down her neck.

"Shit, bitch. That's disgusting."

Her vision wavered, but the menace in the man's eyes was impossible to miss. She didn't recognize him. Not at all. But she knew she was in trouble.

"Fucking A, this is even better," he cackled, rubbing his hands together. "I thought I got the fucker, but nope." He bent down to peer through her blown-out window. "That fucker's not him. However, you're much, much better."

Poppy flinched as the man reached for her. However, she couldn't do more than that. Her arms felt like lead, and she couldn't prevent him from undoing her seat belt. She cried out when he grabbed her by the arms and yanked her out of the crushed vehicle. Her vision grayed when he threw her over his shoulder in a fireman's carry. The motion had her entire body throbbing in pain. More bile surged, and she puked again, spraying vomit down the man's back and legs. She immediately started choking, since she was hanging upside down.

"Fuck! You nasty bitch! You fucking puked on me!"

He let go, and Poppy slammed down on the ground like a rag doll. She hardly felt the impact. Vision fading, she looked up at the dark SUV she'd been dumped next to. Its grill was a crumpled mess, twisted around Cade's vehicle.

Holy crap, this man had T-boned them. Her eyes flicked toward Xander, though she couldn't see him from her current vantage point. *Please let him be okay.*

White-hot agony erupted in Poppy's side, and she groaned. The man had kicked her in the ribs. She tried to curl into a small ball but couldn't move fast enough. His boot came flying again, and she braced. Then everything went blessedly dark.

CHAPTER THIRTY-TWO

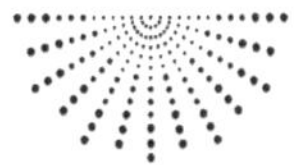

"We appreciate you coming out so fast," Cade said, shaking hands with the insurance agent.

The kind, middle-aged man in the drab beige suit—Cade had already forgotten his name—nodded and turned to shake Dante's hand. "Of course. I'm so sorry this happened. We'll expedite this claim, and I'll check in with the sheriff's department on my way out."

"Thank you," Dante said. "Have a safe trip home."

As the insurance agent departed, Cade let out a breath and scanned the destruction for the millionth time. The fans they'd placed throughout the facility hummed with constant white noise, and the scent of melted plastic still lingered in the air. The shattered windows were boarded up, but the charred mats remained untouched on the ground. Worst of all, much of the expensive gym equipment was now water-damaged and worthless.

"It's just stuff," he said to himself, watching Carter and Dylan search for items to salvage. He was thankful that they hadn't been hurt. That *no one* had been hurt.

"That's right, bro." Dante slapped him on the back. "We'll rebuild here just like we'll rebuild in Seattle. It'll be better than ever."

Cade nodded. Gesturing to the ruined mats, he called out, "Jason, TJ, let's roll this shit up and get it out of here." He moved to the edge of one and kneeled, yanking up the corner.

"Uh, Cade?"

He glanced at TJ, who gestured to the front door with his head. "Jason and I've got this. You probably need to deal with him."

Turning, Cade stood and spied Gavin storming into the gym. A sour rock formed in his gut as he noticed the grim, hard lines set in the man's face.

"What's going on?" he asked, hustling toward Gavin.

"Someone ambushed Xander and Poppy."

The blood drained from his head, leaving him dizzy. There's no way in hell he'd heard that right. "The fuck you say?"

Gavin met Cade's gaze, and the barely leashed fury in his friend's eyes had Cade bracing. "Tash and Wilson were driving back when they spotted your Rover off the side of the road. It got T-boned by a Suburban. Xander was still in the car, unconscious, but whoever did it took Poppy."

No. Fuck, no!

Cade's breath locked in his chest, and his skin vibrated with fear, anger, and disbelief.

"Tash is with Xander now. She said the EMTs just arrived. Wilson found some tracks he thinks belong to whoever took Poppy, so he's following them."

Holy fuck. His stomach twisted. This could not be happening.

"Brother, look at me," Gavin said.

Cade complied, and the steely determination staring back at him had the tight coil in his gut unfurling. Slightly.

"Wilson is one of the best there is at tracking. He knows these forests like the back of his fucking hand, and he *will* find Poppy."

But what if she was hurt? Would Wilson find her in time?

Gavin continued, "I'm going to head out and meet up with Tash—"

"I'm going with you."

Gavin slapped a hand to Cade's chest, stopping him. "No, man. You stay here. We've got this." He looked at Dante, who'd been listening a few feet away. "You guys head over to Bean's office. She put a drone up and will have comms on all of us."

"Will do," Dante said.

Gavin nodded, eyed Cade one more time, and then left.

Cade's heart hammered in his chest, and his blood roared in his ears. He scrubbed his tingling hands over his face, then fisted them in his hair, welcoming the sting. Seeing red, he stalked to the nearest heavy bag and released a guttural shout of rage as he began punching. It did nothing to ease the tightness in his chest. His fists hammered into the bag over and over and over again. Spots of blood appeared on the bag but he didn't give a fuck. Someone had taken his girl. And there wasn't a fucking thing he could do.

Why the fuck had he let her out of his sight? Why the fuck had he thought cleaning up the gym and meeting the fucking insurance agent were important? Fuck that! He should've been with her. They should have never left his house today. What the fuck had he been thinking?

A large body crashed into Cade, pinning his arms to his sides. For a moment, he fought back. Until he realized it was Dante, and his big brother's words penetrated his brain.

"Calm the fuck down, Cade!" Dante hissed.

"Calm down?" His chest heaved as he glared at his brother. The guy had to be fucking joking. "If it was Rebecca, you sure as fuck—"

"Those boys are freaking the fuck out right now, so wrangle your shit in."

Dante's words had Cade stilling. His gaze flew to the other side of the room. To Carter and Dylan. Who were staring at him, slack-jawed, their hazel eyes wide. Both deathly pale. *Fuck.*

Dante's grip moved up to Cade's shoulders, and he pressed their foreheads together. It was a familiar gesture from their childhood, one Dante had used when he'd needed Cade to calm down and really listen. "I know you're losing your mind right now, brother, but you've got to pull it together for them. Their mom is missing, and you need to tell them what's going on. Lock down your shit, because you've got to be fucking strong for them."

"Okay," Cade said, throat raw with emotion. He straightened. His chest was painfully tight, and tears stung the backs of his eyes. "She's the best thing that's ever happened to me. She's my fucking anchor. I can't lose her, D."

His brother hauled him into a bone-crushing hug. "Shut the fuck up right now. You don't put that shit out there, you hear me?" With a couple of hard slaps to Cade's back, he pulled away. "Now man the fuck up, little brother, and be strong for those boys. They're gonna need you. You say Poppy's your anchor? Well, you need to be that anchor for her boys right the fuck now. They'll be looking to you. Hear me?"

Cade took a deep breath and nodded. "Thanks, D."

Dante lifted his chin. "Always, little bro."

He waved at Carter and Dylan. Worry was etched on their faces as they hurried over.

"What's wrong?" they asked in unison.

"Come on," Cade said, guiding them out of the gym. "We need to head over to Bean's office. I'll tell you everything I know on the way."

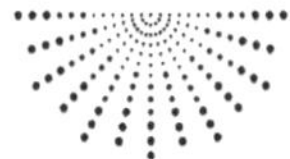

CHAPTER THIRTY-THREE

A jarring motion had Poppy's eyes flying open, and the arms locked around her chest had her wishing for oblivion. Someone was dragging her backward. Her head, which felt like it weighed a thousand pounds, throbbed in protest as it bounced with each drag across the uneven forest floor. Fire consumed her torso, and she couldn't stop a moan from escaping her lips.

"Wake the fuck up," her abductor hissed, dropping her.

Her head hit the dirt, and stars dotted her vision.

"Christ, who'd have thought you'd be so fucking heavy? You're tiny. That fucker better pay up now."

It took a couple of seconds to focus her eyes on the man standing over her, typing on his phone. "Who are you?" The effort to speak brought tears to her eyes. "What do you have against Cade?"

The man glared at her, face twisting in disgust. "That asshole ruined everything for me! Now he owes me."

The guy was nuts. There was no other way about it. She shifted onto her elbows, and everything tilted. Dry heaves tore through her body. She leaned to the side, waiting for her empty stomach to stop cramping.

"Jesus Christ, you're disgusting."

Returning to her elbows, she sucked in a breath and tried to ignore the pain piercing her lungs with each inhale. Gavin's people had to be looking for her by now. When Xander didn't check in . . .

Oh my god. Xander. Please be okay.

Poppy closed her eyes and fought to calm her racing heart. She was almost certain Gavin's people knew something was wrong. Eventually, they would come for her. But right at this moment? She needed to help herself. So, she examined the man, searching for any sign of weakness.

His skin was pasty white with bright-pink splotches of exertion, and his close-cropped hair was more red than blond. He wasn't quite as large or as fit as Cade, but he was also no slouch, unfortunately. She wouldn't be outrunning him anytime soon, especially in her current condition. The guy's Timberland boots and baggy jeans were splattered with mud and puke, but aside from that, they looked new. Like they were more fashion than function. His unbuttoned jacket was designer, and he had three gold chains of various sizes around his neck.

Hope sprouted deep in her gut. He was *not* an outdoorsy man. If she could somehow get a solid head start, there was no way he'd be able to track her. But she needed more time to gain strength before she could make a break for it. She had to stall. Besides, the longer she stayed in one spot, the more likely Gavin's people were to find her. *You can do this. You have to do this.*

"Cade will pay you whatever you want," she croaked, her throat impossibly raw.

"Damn straight he will. Cade and I are basically family, you know, and that fucker owes me."

Poppy's eyes narrowed. Holy shit, this guy had to be Cade's former brother-in-law. The infamous narcissist deadbeat. *Keep calm. Keep him talking.* "Alister?"

The grin that broke out over his face was one of pure satisfaction. "I knew that fucker still talked about me."

Her heart tripped with terror. But she had to make it home to Carter and Dylan. She had to make it home to Cade. This asshole wasn't going to stop her from seeing her boys grow up, dammit. And he sure as hell wasn't stopping her from seeing where her relationship with Cade went. Because even though she'd chickened out of saying it last night, she was falling in love with him.

So fuck this guy! Poppy needed to keep her wits about her if she wanted to survive this. Luckily, she knew narcissistic men. Knew how to keep them happy and talking. Knew to keep the conversation all about them. Aiming for a sympathetic tone, she asked, "What did Cade do to you?"

Alister's eyes gleamed as he spat on the ground. "Fucking divorced my bitch of a sister and didn't pay up."

Poppy nodded in agreement, though she knew it was the other way around; this guy's sister was the one who'd left Cade. But she sure as hell wasn't going to correct him. "Cade shortchanged her on the divorce?"

"Fuck yeah he did!" Alister was getting himself worked up. He began pacing like an agitated bear, and she prayed all the noise he was making would draw some sort of attention to them. "Then the dumb bitch refused to help me out of a jam. Said she didn't have the fucking money. Bullshit! So you know what? I took matters into my own fucking hands."

Poppy froze when he reached behind him and pulled a gun from his waistband.

"Picture time, bitch," he said, waving the gun at her.

She held perfectly still as Alister approached. He propped her up into a seated position, and her head swam.

"Hold this." He tossed his phone on her lap, then stepped behind her and dropped to his knees, yanking her into a tight headlock. "You're gonna take a selfie of us. Got it?" His arm constricted around her neck, and she whimpered as he jabbed the muzzle of the gun into her temple. "Take the selfie now, bitch."

The camera app was already open. With trembling arms, she raised the phone and looked at the screen. She gasped. Her face was streaked with dirt and vomit and blood, and her eyes were bulging with fear. The matte-black gun was pressed so hard against her head that it tore her skin. Hovering over her shoulder was Alister, a sadistic grin splitting his lips.

Holy shit. The man wasn't nuts; he was fucking crazy.

"Do it!" he screamed, putting all his strength into the grip around her throat.

Unable to breathe, Poppy took the photo. He released her in an instant, shoving her forward. She hit the ground, gasping for air.

Alister stood and tucked the gun into the front of his jeans. "Now we send this lovely shot to Cade," he said, collecting his phone from her hands. His thumbs flew over the screen for a few seconds before he paused and glanced down at her. "I'm thinking a cool five mil sounds about right. Cash." He resumed typing, and when he finally stashed his phone in his pocket, that sadistic smile was on his face again.

"We really should get going, but you know what . . ."

"Go where?" she croaked. *Keep stalling!*

"The Suburban's fucked, but I have a second car stashed at the trailhead."

Her eyes widened.

"Yeah, that's right. I have a backup plan," he said, chuckling. The laughter died on his lips as he leered at her. "But now that you can walk, I'm thinking we've got time. I mean, you've gotta be some kind of fun to have bagged the big, bad Cade de la Rosa."

Her stomach rolled.

He stalked forward, and she watched his every move, however minor, with intense focus. Which was how she spotted a slight rustle in the bushes behind him. Before she could wonder if it was an animal or if someone had finally found her, a giant man pounced.

Alister's shocked cry cut off as the person tackled him. He was easily outmatched, and the sound of a fist smacking flesh rang out in the otherwise quiet forest. The sound of bones crunching came next, followed by Alister's deep moan. The latter was one of the most satisfying things Poppy had ever heard.

Hands settled onto her shoulders. She yelped, and her heart nearly flew out of her chest.

"You're okay. We've got you," a familiar voice soothed.

Poppy glanced up and found Gavin looking down at her. After a moment, his usual stern expression softened, and she promptly burst into tears.

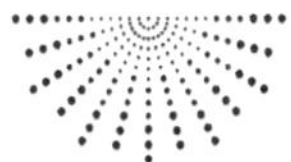

CHAPTER THIRTY-FOUR

The throbbing in Poppy's head was at an all-time high, and the flashing lights of a nearby Hudson Island Sheriff's Department cruiser weren't helping matters. Seated in the open cargo area of Gavin's armored SUV, her legs dangled over the edge and a crinkly silver Mylar blanket covered her trembling shoulders. "Shock," one of the emergency responders had murmured when he'd attended to her earlier.

The ambulance had left with Xander moments ago—it had taken a considerable amount of time to pull him from the mangled Range Rover—and the firefighters were now making all sorts of noise as they put equipment back in their truck. Images of them using the Jaws of Life to pry Xander from the wreckage flashed through her mind. Thank god he'd regained consciousness and was alert while the firefighters worked to free him. He'd been pinned by the steering wheel, but as Xander was being loaded onto a stretcher, he'd claimed it looked worse than it was. Poppy prayed he'd been telling the truth.

The SUV dipped as Gavin sat next to her. "How are you holding up, Pop?"

Keeping her head as still as possible, she stared at the road the ambulance had raced down. "Is Xander going to be okay?"

"The EMTs think so. Besides, the guy's stubborn as fuck. I'm sure he'll make a speedy recovery just to prove a point."

"Good," she whispered. A shiver racked her frame, and her head began to swim. "Gavin?"

"Yeah, Poppy?"

Her mouth grew thick. "I don't feel so good."

Gavin put an arm over her shoulders, and she leaned into him. "I know you don't. You have a nasty concussion, honey, and we're just waiting for the chopper to get here. Just lean on me for a little bit longer."

"Chopper?" Had she heard that correctly?

"That's right. The ambulance took Xander, but we need to get you to a hospital, too."

She exhaled. The burning in her head had somehow lessened, but now everything was hazy. Fuzzy. "Are my boys all right? Is Cade?"

"Yeah, honey. The boys are okay. Cade's okay. They're all gonna be on that chopper with you. So hang on just a little longer. Can you do that?"

Poppy thought she nodded, but she wasn't quite sure. She was so tired.

A thunderous thwup-thwup-thwup came from the sky, and she cringed, clutching her head in renewed agony. Gavin pulled her fully into his chest, shielding her from the sudden wind. Then she was being laid on a stretcher in a slightly inclined position. A man put a strap across her chest, and she winced when it tightened.

"Sorry about that," he muttered, tossing a second strap to a man on her opposite side.

Gavin gave her foot a squeeze, and then the two men wheeled her toward the horribly loud thwuping noise. Her hair flew wildly around her face, and she felt each jostle of the stretcher like a hit to her temples. A door slammed, and the deafening noise was muffled. She winced again when someone placed something over her ears.

"Mom!"

Her gaze drifted to the right, and she realized Carter and Dylan occupied two seats along the side of the helicopter. Wearing large headphones, they leaned forward and grabbed her hand. The relief on their faces had tears spilling down her cheeks.

"I'm okay, boys," she reassured them, squeezing their hands. "No need to worry, all right?"

They nodded stoically, and she wanted to scoop them up.

"We're going with you to the hospital," Carter said. "We're not leaving your side."

"We're going to help you when you get home, too," Dylan added. "We texted our professors, and they gave the okay. You're gonna be fine, Mom."

The clamp on her heart released. Her boys were okay. Thank god.

"Hey, babe."

The familiar murmur brought more tears to her eyes. A moment later, Cade filled her vision as he sat on the stretcher. Taking her left hand, he brushed his lips over the backs of her knuckles. She met his gaze, and a sob ripped from her throat.

"I'm so damn sorry this happened, Pop." There was turmoil in his dark-brown eyes, and it hurt her heart.

"No, Cade," she said, gripping his fingers hard. "This is not your fault."

He nodded, but she saw the hesitation in his eyes.

Tugging on his hand, she brought him closer. "Babe, it's not your fault. It's really not."

"Okay," he said, tucking a strand of hair behind her ear. Some of the darkness faded from his eyes.

Despite her exhaustion and vertigo, she strove for a firm, decisive tone as she added, "We are *not* wasting time thinking about Alister and his greed. Because you know what?"

"There's my strong, sassy girl," he said, pressing a kiss to her forehead. "What's that, babe?"

"Remember how you said you were falling in love with me?"

He grinned, and his eyes twinkled. "Yeah, babe. I do."

"Good. Because I'm falling in love with you, too, Cade de la Rosa."

"I love you, Poppy," he murmured, lowering his lips to hers. Their kiss was gentle and sweet before he pulled away. The medic waved at him, and Cade nodded. "Rest now. Your boys and I are here. And we love you more than anything."

EPILOGUE

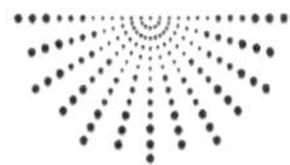

Poppy had been airlifted to Jefferson Healthcare in Port Townsend and kept overnight for observation. Cade and the twins had never left her side. She'd suffered multiple bruised ribs and a severe concussion, but thankfully, her CT scans had come back clear. After two weeks of complete rest —during which Carter, Dylan, and Cade had been at her beck and call, despite her numerous protests—her doctors had finally permitted her to resume all regular activity.

The boys had gone back to school, and she'd prepared to go back to work. However, Cade had insisted she take one extra week off. Just to be safe. She'd humored him because his intent had been sweet. And luckily, her staff at Rainy Day Boutique had been more than happy to pick up the extra hours. But being the busybody she was, Poppy hadn't been able to sit still for seven more days.

So, she'd utilized the time to talk with James Rokovich— Jason's older brother and an architect in Seattle—about redoing her apartment. She had decided to follow Cade's suggestion of combining her existing apartment with the storage space across the landing. Taking input from him and the boys, she and James had drawn up new plans. And when they'd all agreed on one, she'd pulled the trigger with the proceeds from her divorce.

Now, two months later, the renovation appeared about a month or so away from finishing up.

Poppy grinned as she stepped onto the new landing and looked around. The space was enormous. The layout on the left was still the same, except the kitchen had been built out to include a little breakfast nook and the living area had been extended. On the right, two additional bedrooms and another bathroom were framed out. With James' magic, the apartment had gone from five hundred fifty square feet to nearly fourteen hundred. She'd had no clue the area she'd been using for storage was so large!

"Looks great, don't you think?" she called out, moving around the beams.

Cade only grunted.

She looked over at him in question. "Everything all right, babe?"

Rocking back on his heels, he shoved his hands into his jeans pockets and asked, "Can I be honest with you, Poppy?"

"You know you can always be honest with me," she said, worry turning her stomach.

He opened and closed his mouth a couple of times. Then he blurted, "This place would make a great rental property."

She was pretty sure her eyebrows hit her hairline. "What?"

"Shit," he muttered, scrubbing his hands over his face. "I'm not doing this right."

"Doing what right, Cade?"

Hands laced atop his head, he heaved a great sigh. "Poppy, I don't want you to move out."

Her jaw dropped.

Cade crossed the short distance between them and pulled

her into an embrace. "Pop, I love living with you. I love falling asleep with you in my arms. I love having your face be the first one I see in the morning and the last one I see at night."

The worry vanished, and she melted. If Cade hadn't been holding her up, she would have turned into a puddle of goo right at his feet.

"Remember when we first started dating?" he asked. "How we talked about getting to know each other better?"

A smile lifted the corners of her lips. "Yeah."

"Well, Pop, I still don't know everything about you." He shot her that half smirk she loved and pulled her even closer, leaving zero space between them. "I need more time."

She looped her arms around his neck. "Oh yeah?"

"Yeah." He nodded. "I have to warn you, though. It might take months, years . . . *decades* even. I want to know everything about you."

Her heart soared, and she pulled him down for a kiss. God, this amazing man . . .

Once they came up for air, he asked, "What do you say, babe?"

Her eyes narrowed, but she kept her tone playful. "What exactly is it you're asking me?"

"Move in with me permanently? Let me be an everyday part of your life? Allow me to be an official stepdad to your boys?"

She gasped, and again, her jaw dropped.

Cade chuckled. "To clarify, I'm not proposing. Not right now." He pressed his lips to hers. "But I will, babe. I sure as hell will. Another day. When we're not in jeans and don't have more errands to run."

Blinking back happy tears, she smiled. "I don't need fancy, Cade."

"I know. But I want to give you fancy. I want to give you every damn thing."

Warmth filled her heart, her soul. "I just need you."

His answering grin was blinding. "You have me, babe. You've had me from the very start. I love you, Poppy."

Butterflies took flight in her belly. She would never, ever get tired of hearing those words. "I love you, too, Cade de la Rosa."

His lips met hers once more, and everything else melted away.

ENJOY THIS BOOK?

Reviews & ratings encourage other readers to try out a book & I would love your help in spreading the word! If you could take a quick moment to rate or leave a review on your favorite book site, I would be forever grateful! You can do that on Amazon, Goodreads and/or Bookbub. Thank you!

ABOUT THE AUTHOR

Christina Sol is an award-winning author who writes what she loves to read—romance books filled with heart, heat, and suspense.

An avid reader from the get-go, Christina was obsessed with The Babysitters Club, Sweet Valley Twins, Sweet Valley High, Christopher Pike, and all things V. C. Andrews. Her love for romance started with the Sunfire books, a YA historical romance series. Caroline by Willo Davis Roberts was her favorite of the series, and a copy of the 1984 novel is one of her most treasured possessions. Then she discovered Danielle Steele and Nora Roberts. And never looked back. She's still a voracious reader and enjoys all genres of romance but leans toward romantic suspense and dark romance.

She lives in the inland Pacific Northwest with her husband and two kids. When she's not writing, reading, or knitting, she's watching football or fueling her planner, sticker, and washi-tape obsession.

To find out more, visit: www.christinasol.com

ACKNOWLEDGMENTS

My wonderful readers: thank you! I am forever grateful to you for choosing to spend your valuable time reading Cade & Poppy's story. Life is hectic and busy, and I truly appreciate you giving this story your precious time.

Heather G: critique partner extraordinaire! Thank you, thank you, thank you!!!

Jen C. & Danielle R: I value you both so freaking much! Your comments, feedback, honesty, and the support you've given me means so, so, SO much! Thank you!

Megan S: Thank you for all your comments, suggestions & edits. And for catching all the repetitive phrases! lol

Shelli S: Thank you for always lending an ear, giving sage advice, and for your help on the dreaded blurb!

Joel T: Thank you for letting me pick your brain on all things MMA. From fighting and coaching to gym ownership . . . your insight was invaluable!

LJ at Mayhem Cover Creations: your covers are stunning—thank you!

My family & friends: from the depths of my heart—thank

you! Your enthusiasm and support have truly meant the world to me.